MADE & UNMADE

A DETROIT MOBSTER'S STORY

J.G.COPE

ALKIRA
PUBLISHING

DEDICATION

For the one I made a promise to a lifetime ago in that vacant field in Livonia, Michigan. Sorry it took so long.

Chapter 1

It's odd the things you remember about your first time. I mean the stupid, insignificant shit. There was this pretty little toenail moon. You know, when just that very outer edge is lit up, like a glowing arc up in the sky. Just sitting up there above the houses. Every so often just the faintest wisp of a cloud would drift by it. Sometimes when I can't sleep at night I just close my eyes and picture that. So calm and peaceful.

I was scrunched up tight, sitting on the ground with my back against the cinder block wall of a garage, tucked up behind an arborvitae, just a few feet outside the farthest reach of the back porch light. All in black. Black overcoat, black pants, black hat, black gloves, even a face mask, but that was camouflage, like the turkey hunters use. No one knew where I was. All alone. Temporarily non-existent. Just me and that pretty little toenail moon. So peaceful.

I locked up dead still when the car pulled into the driveway. I waited until it drove into the garage before I eased the old Winchester pump up into position, butt tight on my right shoulder, stock firm in my left arm on top of my left knee to steady the aim, safety clicked off, you know, just like the turkey hunters do. I waited until the mark got to the back door and put in his key. I was invisible, he was clear as day under that back porch light. I put the bead on his neck and slammed a load of double aught into his head, neck, and upper back.

On the surface, this seems like an idiotic thing to do. I mean, setting off a big boom like that in the middle of a suburban neighborhood. But, once you think about it, it isn't so crazy. To begin with, it was late enough that most people were already in bed. No doubt, quite a few people heard it, but so what? I mean, think about it, you hear a big boom, maybe even think it is a gunshot, but you're not really sure and can't really tell where, exactly, it even came from. That's the key to a deal like this: shoot only once. I hadn't even bothered to bring an extra shell. No doubt someone would call the police to report a "loud noise" or "possible gunshot," but not having much on details, the police are only going to take it so far. They would send a car to cruise around the neighborhood, but with no further reports and nothing to see, that would be it.

I left the shotgun on the ground as I stood up. I had been assured it was a clean gun. Probably bought at a garage sale for like fifty bucks. I walked around the corner of the garage, through the backyard to the four-foot chain-link fence, pulling off the face mask along the way and stuffing it in the pocket of my overcoat. A quick hop over the fence put me on a thin strip of lawn between the back neighbor's driveway and a tall hedge, which led out to the sidewalk of a cul-de-sac. I pulled the brim of my ball cap down to obscure my face, lowered my head, put my hands in my coat pockets, and calmly walked away. Why in the movies and on TV do the bad guys always run away? That's just dumb, like you're trying to draw attention to yourself.

It was just a couple of blocks to where I had left the car parked on the street. Exactly halfway between two streetlights. In the hazy zone between the two rings of light. I already had the keys in my hand when I got to the back of the car and popped open the trunk. In went the overcoat and gloves, out came a clean pair of leather driving gloves. This is basic tradecraft. Should the police stop me, anything in a locked trunk requires a search warrant to get at. No point in taking chances with clothes containing gunshot residue left "in plain view."

Then I just casually drove away. No speeding. No screeching tires. No reason for anyone to notice me or remember any details. It was a long but peaceful drive to the used car lot I had gotten the car from. I left the keys under the seat where I had found them, and drove home in my own car. On the off chance someone had taken down the plate number, the lot owner at least had plausible deniability.

I had no idea who the mark was. I had no idea why he got hit. I didn't know who ordered the hit. I didn't know who did the recon work to figure the time and place for the job. I didn't care. The less I knew, the better. My boss said do the job, I did it. When I saw him next I would let him know it was done. That was it. Beyond that, it never happened. I wasn't there. I would never talk about it with anybody. Even if a member of my own crew brought it up, I would admit to nothing. That is how it has to be. That is ironclad. As soon as it's done, it never happened.

I wish I could jazz it up some, but most of these deals go about like that. There is no special skill set or advanced training. It really just comes down to a willingness to do what most men won't, without hesitation, without remorse. You can't over think it. Sure, all kinds of things could go wrong. I could have been caught. Someone involved could shoot his mouth off or get pinched on something else and play "let's make a deal." The guy I hit was likely a fellow thug and if his guys were looking to even the score, they may come after me as an easier target than the guy higher up who actually ordered the hit. It's like a soldier in a war zone: Sure, at any given moment you could have a bomb land on you, or get your ass shot off, but you don't dwell on it. You follow orders and do your fucking job. That's just how it goes.

The way I figured it, once it was decided this guy had to go, he was as good as dead. It didn't matter if it was me, or someone else. It could just as easily have been the other way around. The path I was on could ultimately lead only to death or imprisonment. Not that I was thinking about that at the time. Not that I had figured any of it out yet.

In all of Earth's existence I doubt there has ever been a stupider animal than a young man.

CHAPTER 2

But, I'm starting the story in the middle. I guess I should go back to the beginning. Actually, I'm not sure where, exactly, the beginning was. There really is no good reason for someone like me to have ended up this way. I grew up in the most average, vanilla, white-bread, mind-numbingly boring, middle-class Detroit suburb you have ever seen. You know, rows of neat little houses, trim lawns set off with an endless grid of chain-link fences, sidewalks, kids on bikes, ice cream trucks, the smell of burning charcoal in the air every summer weekend, and all that shit. Purgatory on Earth. Nothing particularly bad about it, but nothing particularly good about it either. A mix of upper blue-collar and lower white-collar. Mostly descendants from that turn-of-the-century immigration wave. Lots of Italian, some Irish, lots of Polish, and other eastern Europeans. Strongly Catholic. Just about everyone either worked for one of the "Big Three" automakers, or one of their vendors.

My dad worked as a crane operator for Ford at their

Rouge River plant. He was killed when I was ten. I never got the whole story, but somehow his crane tipped over. It was a real tragedy, Mom was devastated, and all that usual shit. I can't truly say it messed me up much, though. I didn't really ever have much of a relationship with him anyway. He was what I guess you would call a "functioning alcoholic." He was always on time for work and put in a full, cold sober, professional day's work, then all evening it was one beer after another in the recliner watching TV. Same thing all weekend, then cold sober and back to work. He was a good provider. Not at all violent or abusive. A living Purgatory. Nothing particularly bad, but nothing particularly good. He managed to simultaneously exist and not exist.

I never got the whole story, but I guess the union took care of things. We never wanted for money. Mom took a part-time job as a secretary at a big doctor's office. She arranged things so she was always there to see me off to school in the morning. Brown paper bag. Peanut butter and jelly sandwich (always). Some kind of fruit. Maybe a few cookies, or one of those little cans of pudding that came in a six-pack with two vanilla, two chocolate, and two tapioca. I didn't like the goddamn tapioca—that shit is nasty—but I took it anyway and either choked it down or traded it off to one of the other kids. I didn't want to cause Mom any trouble over little shit like that. She was a good mom and a real trooper, but she never really got over losing Dad.

She did her best to get me into all kinds of extracurricular activities like sports teams, swimming lessons, martial arts, Boy Scouts, and shit like that. I never stuck with any of it longer than a few months. None of it held my interest. Well, except the Boy Scouts, kind of. I did that for three years and liked it well enough. I learned some cool stuff. I still know some of the basic knots. Like the taut-line hitch, for example. That's actually a damn useful knot. All the coaches, teachers, and Scout leaders I dealt with were fine people. I was never mistreated in any way, so no excuses there either.

In high school I was a loner. I was the guy who was on a friendly basis with just about everyone, but had no real friends. I mostly just wanted to be left the fuck alone. I viewed it like a four-year prison sentence: Keep your head down, do what needs to be done to get by, and do your time. Let's face it, all teenagers are absolute morons and most are also flat-out assholes. People who look back glowingly on their high school days make no sense to me. If ten years after graduation you're looking forward to your high school reunion to remember your glory days, you have seriously screwed up along the way. Please put on your big boy pants and grow the fuck up.

I did my best to avoid the three stupids: Don't go to stupid places with stupid people to do stupid things. I didn't shy away, though, when trouble came to me. Like I said, I was looking to just do my time clean and get through it, but wasn't going to put up with taking shit I didn't deserve. The way I look at it, life is hard enough all by itself, there's no need to help it along by acting like an asshole.

For example: junior in high school. Second half of the day on a fall Friday and it's an attendance-required pep rally for homecoming. I gave serious thought to skipping it, but they really looked out for that and it was an automatic one-day suspension. Really, though, it meant the only way to get home would be a three-mile hike, so I chose the lesser evil. I hated that rah-rah, sis-boom-bah nonsense. School spirit? What the fuck is that? I had no choice whether to be there and had no choice in which school I got sent to, so how does that invoke any type of pride or loyalty? I mean, it would be like a bunch of inmates getting together, "Hip-hip-hooray! Cellblock nine all the way!" Makes no fucking sense.

Anyway, I plunked down in the middle of an open section of bleachers, content to muddle through. Out of nowhere two random dudes show up who I never saw before in my life or had any dealings with, and they sit down on either side of me. One pops off, "Right nut!" the other "Left nut!" then together, "Who's the dick in the middle?" Oh, hell no. I mean, if I at least kind of knew one of them well enough to joke around a little, or if I had messed with them at some earlier point, maybe. But to just randomly fuck with me like that? Oh. Hell. No.

I didn't say a word. I stood up, slammed a straight right into the face of the guy to my left, turned, and caught the chin of the guy on my right with a nice left hook. Brief mayhem. Other students, then faculty, piled in to break things up. Bundled off to the principal's office. "Lost your temper?" No, I was calm, rational, and matter-of-the-fact about it. The way I looked at it, it was the equivalent of two guys walking up to me at random, poking me in the chest, and challenging me to a fight. What else was I going to do? The principal acted like he wasn't buying it, but at that time and school, fighting was an automatic three-day suspension, and I only got one, so maybe he did see my side of it.

While there were a few other incidents in my junior and senior years, I never got into any serious trouble over them. My philosophy has always been that while, generally speaking, violence is no way to do things, it is, however, extraordinarily effective, and as such, sometimes has to be considered. Let's face it, humans at our core are animals, and all animals understand fear and pain. I guess I got a reputation as a violent guy. Not that I ever went looking for it. I wasn't trying to show off by being some kind of badass. I most certainly wasn't a bully. Just the opposite: For reasons I don't understand, bullies really set me off.

Like this one time: Jennifer Something-Or-Other (I swear one out of every ten girls at my high school was Jennifer Something-Or-Other) comes strolling down the hall absolutely rocking her skintight denim mini skirt with her white blouse unbuttoned just enough at the top. Some asshole guy starts making lewd remarks. Naturally, she flips him off. So as she goes by he grabs her ass. No, not a little pinch or tap, I mean a hard grab, possibly leave-a-bruise type of thing. I just reacted. His hand was off her all of three-tenths of a second before I slammed into him full bore and sent him ten lockers down the hall. Standing over him with a look that could kill. "Man! What the fuck is wrong with you!?" I just walked away.

Jennifer was appreciative. Very appreciative. Several times over the next few weeks after school before her parents came home from work. This feels like the first time I got rewarded for being violent, but I can't be sure. Maybe that's where I got messed up in the head.

I've never been to one but I bet a shrink would find me fascinating. No doubt he would find at least a dozen things wrong with me. He would probably have me on at least five different medications and in talk therapy twice a week. "Interesting, veeeery interesting," while he contemplatively stroked his chin and scribbled vigorously in his notebook. No doubt I would be diagnosed a psychopath, or sociopath, or some other word ending in -path. No doubt he would glom on to my dad dying when I was young, or my non-relationship with him, or something along those lines. I mean, what else is there? There has to be a cause. Those guys need an illness to name and treat.

The problem is, being nuts is the basic human condition. We're all fucked up in our own special ways. It's innate. No doubt, for some it's worse than others, and for some so bad as to need professional help, but for most it's a matter of figuring out how to cope with their own personal brand of lunacy. A shrink would say I have "a propensity for violence." I would say I have "an acceptance for violence." There is a subtle but important difference. In the first, violence is the master; in the second, it is the servant.

So, I get through high school and have no fucking idea what to do next. Mom wanted me to go to college. She assured me money had already been set aside. I did okay in school. I'm a smart enough guy and can learn just about anything if I'm interested in it and have a teacher that's worth a damn. But I didn't really like school much, and the idea of four more years of that shit was dreadful.

The fairy tale that gets crammed down the throats of every teenager is that you follow your passion, go to college to get a degree in that field, find a job doing what you love, and live happily ever after. College is a great opportunity, though, to get drunk and fornicate as much as possible while delaying the realities of adulthood for at least a few more years, so that was tempting. Meanwhile you're either spending a shitload of someone else's money or taking on a shitload of student loan debt. My main hang-up on it was I wasn't passionate about anything and had no idea what degree to pursue. Of course, what they tell you then is to just do it anyway, spend two years getting your general ed credits, and figure out your major later. So, basically, spend an obscene amount of time and money to learn crap you don't care about with the hope that somewhere along the way you kiss the right frog and it turns into Prince Charming.

Why is so much time in high school spent teaching crap you will never in your life need to know while so little time is spent teaching what you actually need to function as an adult? At least a third of senior year should be devoted to "life skills." You have a high school diploma. You're eighteen and legally an adult. You know trig functions and can use algebra to solve for X, but have no basis in doing the cost/benefit analysis of taking on X amount of expense to gain the earning potential of college degree Y. You can read Shakespeare and Hemingway but have no basis in understanding a lease or any other basic contract. You can write a well-structured essay to compare and contrast—pick any two random things—but don't even know how to write a check. It's like teaching a kid every arcane detail of shipbuilding and maritime history, then dumping him overboard in the middle of the lake and expecting him to swim ashore. Makes no fucking sense.

For about two seconds I considered the military. At least with that Uncle Sam is paying you to learn a profession while you're out there in the middle of the lake floundering around trying to figure out which way to swim. It can be a good deal for the right person. I figured, though, that wasn't me. I was too much of a loner and an individual. I imagine I would have made it—at best—a week into basic training before I punched out the drill instructor and ended up in the stockade. Well, probably worse than that since I doubt eighteen-year-old me could have taken the average drill instructor, so I would have ended up in the base hospital, *then* the stockade.

Of course, I could always just find a job and go straight into the workforce. That's what my dad's generation did. Get in at the ground floor with one of the Big Three, or something like that, spend forty years doing some shit job you hate but pays okay with good union benefits, then retire to Florida and have a few good years before you kick the bucket. Every generation wants something more for the next generation. The son of a blue-collar guy needs to get a college degree and do better. It's a great concept on paper, but if you take two steps back and look at it, how is that possible generation after generation? It's like Icarus soaring higher and higher toward the sun. It's that fine line between the American Dream and the American Fantasy. Reality sucks.

So, I didn't have a plan. Hell, I didn't even have a plan to figure out a plan. I decided to find a summer job, anything really, then maybe take some classes at the community college in the fall to pacify Mom. So, basically, to tread water and hope a ship came by. The problem with a deal like that, though, is that then any ship coming by looks good. I didn't intend to end up a murdering piece of shit thug on a pirate ship, but that's more or less what ended up happening.

Chapter 3

It started simply enough. It was just after graduation. This guy I was kind of friends with, Russell Malic, asked me to go shoot pool one Friday night. Not like at a bar with a few pool tables, at this place that had dozens of tables and you could rent one by the hour and just hang out and shoot pool and bullshit. I hung out there regularly. I was a decent pool player. My problem was, though, while I learned to make the individual shots, I never figured out how to plan ahead and leave the ball positioned for the next shot. Russell was about my equal on shooting, but better at strategy, so he mostly won. I still enjoyed it, though. It was a way to be in a crowd and be inside your own little world at the same time.

At the table next to us was this couple that looked to be in their mid-twenties. He was short, but well-muscled. He was what, at the time, I thought of as your typical greaser Italian. Hair slicked back. Lots of gold jewelry. Nose a little too big. He was shooting pool with this flat-out gorgeous brunette. She had on those Jordache jeans, you remember, dark blue denim with white stitching highlighting the back pockets. Form-fitting. Very distracting every time she leaned over the table for a shot.

I was trying not to stare and be a complete dick. The guys at the next table over from them weren't. Shit. Everyone knows the type. Wearing high school letter jackets. Yes, they left them on in June while shooting pool. I mean, without them how could everyone know what superstar studs they were? You know when you see a guy wearing a letter jacket like that he's going to be somewhere on the spectrum from mildly annoying jerk to complete asshole.

These two were complete assholes. Every time the girl took a shot they stopped to stare, whistled, made comments they thought were funny, and shit like that. Very fucking annoying.

I could see the guy she was with was getting annoyed too. Slow burn. Just about chain-smoking through a pack of Camels. I took a Marlboro Light out of my pack and made like I lost my lighter, calling him over for a light, "Just as soon as you've taken enough shit from those pricks, ask them outside. Me and my buddy will back you."

"Really?"

"Sure. Annoying little shits! The only reason I haven't gone over there and shoved this pool stick up their asses is I'm afraid they'd like it too much."

He laughed, "You sure? Not fucking with me?"

"Absolutely. I mean, c'mon, they're begging for it."

He just smiled and nodded.

I clued Russell in on some possible trouble. He just shrugged, said, "Whatever," and lined up his next shot.

It didn't take much longer. The guy reached his shit quotient, threw his pool stick down on their table with a clatter, and barked, "Outside! Now!" They both smiled like kids on Halloween that get a full-sized Snickers bar, instead of a lame fun size. A chance to show what big swinging dicks they were. Two on one and both of them towering over him and at least twenty pounds heavier. Fucking pricks.

I followed about ten feet back. Close enough to rush in when needed, far enough to not be noticed. When they got out to the parking lot the guy turned to face them. I bull-rushed Prick One and Prick Two from behind. One got shoved straight to my new friend. I don't know if he had some boxing experience, or worked out regularly on a heavy bag, or what, but lightning-fast he worked the guy's midsection over with a series of vicious body blows. I swear I heard ribs cracking. The guy just crumpled in a heap at his feet. The other guy turned back toward me, but was already off balance, so when I slammed my fist into his face, he was knocked flat on his ass.

Before they could recover my new friend barked, calm but ominous, "Stay down. If you get up you're going to the hospital, and we're going to jail. Not a good deal for anyone." That was all it took. No big deal. I intended to go back inside and shoot more pool. But the guy trotted over and stopped me, "By now someone definitely called the cops. We need to get the fuck out of here. Tell you what. There's a place a couple of miles down on the left, Salducci's." And he pointed north along the road we were next to. "Let me buy you guys a pizza."

So we met him at Salducci's for some damn fine pizza. I introduced myself, "Joe Rose, and this is my friend Russell Malic."

"Vince DeLuca and this is Gina Sabatini."

That was the one and only time I met Gina. I don't usually remember names but that girl was so gorgeous her name stuck in my head. If she didn't go on to become some kind of supermodel earning a million dollars a year for making men drool, there is no justice in this world.

Anyway, we got to talking. I mentioned how I was just out of high school and looking for a job to at least get me through the summer. Vince set down his slice and said, "Hey, yeah, maybe could help ya out there."

"Oh yeah?"

"Yeah, maybe. My uncle, Tony Mano, owns a construction company, Mano Construction. Just got going on a contract to put in a small subdivision, over in Novi. I just happen to be the foreman on that project. Always looking for help."

"That sounds great, but, don't have any…well, um…construction-type experience."

Vince waved the objection away, "Course not. Who does at your age? Dependable and hardworking, that's all I need."

"Okay, but I'm telling ya, can't even build a fucking birdhouse!"

Vince laughed and waved away that objection too, "Everyone focuses on the specific skills to do something. Fuck that. Any moron with half a brain can learn what to do. Show up on time. Work hard. Give half a fuck about doing it right. Then just keep doing that every day. Those are the real skills. A guy like that will always have a job."

I nodded, "Okay, yeah, sure. I mean, thanks, yeah, I'd like to give it a try."

"Good, good." Vince took out a little notebook and pen. He wrote down directions to the construction site. He handed it to me, "Monday, seven a.m., sharp. I'll be in an office in the trailer onsite."

I just nodded and put the paper in my pocket.

Vince turned to Russell, "How about you? You looking?"

Russell shook his head, "Naw, just gotta help my old man. He's a plumber."

"Oh, a plumber," Vince said. "That's good. That's good honest work. If a guy can't make a decent living doing plumbing—but hey, if it don't work out—I mean, working with family can be tough, you know. If it don't work out, you find me, okay?"

Russell nodded while chewing a big bite of pepperoni and Italian sausage pizza.

The whole time Gina just sat, looking hotter than a pizza right out of the oven. I couldn't help but wonder how a guy like Vince got a girl like that.

So, that's what I did, I showed up at the construction site on Monday morning and found Vince in the trailer. I was made a mason's assistant. I found out later this was considered to be the worst job on the crew. It involved spending all day hauling bricks, bags of mortar, loads of sand, and other such heavy, dirty stuff. I loved it, though. At the time I was into working out and lifting weights and basically the job was to do that all day. I also liked being outside. If I ever had a job that kept me cooped up at a desk all day, I would end up with either a whiskey bottle or a gun in my mouth after a day and a half.

I got along fine with the other guys on the crew. Blue-collar guys have an interesting way of interacting. They are constantly ragging on each other. At times it looks like it's getting really heated with every cuss word you've ever heard in every combination you've ever heard, plus a few new ones. Then, in the snap of a finger the same two guys are talking about the game that was on last night, or some little thing like that, and next it's, "I'm having a cookout this Sunday, you should come by. Oh, and have your wife make that sour cream chip dip she's famous for."

I mostly helped out one of the senior masons. He was a real craftsman, coming from a long line of masons in the old country. He was born in Italy, moving to the States when he was nineteen, so he still had a heavy Italian accent. Sergio—I can't remember his last name. Started with a C and ended with an I, and really long, like five syllables. Everyone just called him Serge. A real gentleman, that guy. A class act. To me class has nothing to do with money, status, or where you come from. It has to do with how you treat other people. I was just this peon, know-nothing-kid, but he was always respectful. He didn't bark orders, he asked me to do things. When I screwed up he didn't get pissy or cuss me out, he just told me what I did wrong.

He would actually compliment me sometimes. Blue-collar guys always seem damn reluctant to do this. I guess it's considered a sign of weakness, and unmanly. I learned pretty quick how to mix the mortar just like he liked it. He would take a big scoop with his trowel and plop it back into the trough to test it. "Ooh, like-a-butta!" with a big smile. He taught me some how to lay brick. Sometimes toward the end of the day when his age started to show, he let me do the straight, easy runs, then followed along behind to pretty up the joints. Other than my mom he was one of the few genuinely good people I've ever known.

About from the beginning I heard all kinds of rumors and innuendo about the big boss, Tony Mano, being mafia. I didn't put much stock in it. I had heard that kind of shit my whole life. Just about every Italian was either "mobbed up," or, more commonly, had a close relative who was. Any man of Italian descent who owned a business or had any level of financial success had to have mob connections, or so it was claimed. Likewise all Pollacks were morons, all Irish were short-tempered drunks, and the list goes on.

Why do people get all hung up and angsty on that shit? Every little thing gets labeled some kind of ism, anti-this, or hate-that.

Human beings are inherently xenophobic. We spent the vast majority of our evolution living in small tribes. The guys in the other tribe were different and, therefore, inferior. How else could you justify killing them and taking their stuff? But the bigger problem is that human groups, by their nature, are hierarchical. Abraham Lincoln said, "You can't make a weak man strong by making a strong man weak." I hate to break it ole Honest Abe, but while he's right in the ideal sense, he's wrong in the practical sense. Any kid who spent a January recess in Michigan playing King of the Mountain on the snow heap plowed up at the edge of the school parking lot knows this. But for most people it's more mundane than that. Whatever is wrong in your life you can make yourself feel better about by blaming someone else, or dragging them down to your level. I mean, god fucking forbid you deal with the realities of life. Reality sucks, avoid it as much as possible.

I couldn't help but notice, though, that there was an unusual amount of what looked like non-construction-type activity around the office in the trailer at the site. Nicer cars than you would expect. Always men. Not in typical blue-collar, construction guy-type clothes. Some would stay a few minutes, some a few hours. I figured it was none of my business.

Every couple of days or so Vince would walk around the site to check on things. He always stopped by to ask how I was doing. Me, always, simply, "Fine." Then, "Serge, the kid doing okay?" and Serge would give him a thumbs up. That's how I expected the whole summer to go. I would have been happy if that's all there was to it. Well, not happy, because I'm not actually capable of that, but content. Vince had other ideas.

Friday, the end of my second full week on the job. Lunch break. Most guys brought lunch in a small cooler and gathered at a makeshift break spot on site. Benches made with two five-gallon buckets spanned with scrap lumber in the shade of one of the few big trees left when the site was bulldozed. Naturally, being the new guy, and worse yet, a kid, the guys had to razz me, "Hey Joe! Mommy pack you a nice lunch?"

Then another guy joins in, "Yeah, I bet it's a yummy PB & J!"

Like I said before, this kind of thing isn't like some asshole fucking with you to be a dick about it, it's just messing around, so I played along. I pulled out my sandwich and held it aloft, "Behold! The world's perfect lunch! Peanut butter and jelly on Wonder Bread! But…" and just enough hesitation for that perfect comic timing, "…you know what makes it so damn good?" and another perfect pause, "It's chock full of mama love! Don't you all be jealous now!" and I took a big bite while everyone roared with laughter. It was actually ham and cheese on wheat, but no point in letting the facts get in the way of a good story.

Anyway, no sooner did I get done eating when Vince comes along and pulls me aside. "I have this little project I could use some help with tomorrow. Easy shit. Only take a couple hours. How about I pick you up around noon?" Vince had this real skill for what a salesman would call the "assumptive close." He didn't so much ask you as tell you, and just assume you would go along with it. He was always very sparing with the details. I hadn't learned yet to not ask for information he didn't think I needed.

"Doing what?" I asked.

"Oh, easy shit. I gotta go see a guy about a horse. Only take a couple hours. Noon tomorrow."

I didn't know what to do but nod. He slapped me on the shoulder with a smile and just walked away.

So, right at noon the next day he picks me up. I noticed he wasn't driving his usual car. I had always seen him in the past in a primo, cobalt blue Ford Mustang. That day he was driving an older but decent, white Ford LTD. A massive hunk of Detroit steel. You could fit four dead bodies in the trunk. A backseat like a sofa. Never mind enough room to bang your girlfriend, you could invite a few more and have a damn orgy back there. I didn't ask why he changed cars, although I figured it out later.

We drove to a horse racing track in…shit, I can't remember exactly. The problem with the Detroit Metro area is that way-back-when, the area was surveyed using the township method. A township is a square six miles by six miles, so thirty-six square miles. As the area grew the more populous townships became cities. So, as you drive through the area, every six miles you cross into another city or township. Actually it's even more complicated than that since some of the townships got further cut up into various towns, villages, cities, or whatever. I have met many people over the years who said they were from the Detroit area, then I ask them where, and they toss out a name I swear I have never, in my life, heard of. I don't remember the name of the track either. Ladbrook, I think, or maybe Ladybrook, or something along those lines. It just kind of sat there looking out of place in the middle of an endless sea of suburban houses and strip malls.

Anyway, we got there and the place was much bigger

than I expected. The parking lot was huge. I guess it was the only place for miles around where the gambling junkies could get a fix. Vince pulled in at one corner of the lot and started cruising up and down every aisle. At first I thought he was looking for a parking spot with enough room to get that LTD into, but after he passed by a handful of wide open spots, I figured out he was looking for something. We were about two-thirds of the way through the lot before he found what he was looking for, "Ah, here we go." I don't remember what kind of car it was. Some old piece of shit, kind of a golden brown.

Vince turned the LTD like he was going into the parking spot right on top of the other car, then stopped just before the right corner of his bumper made contact with the parked car. He hopped out, pulled a little notebook and pen from his pocket, and jotted down the license plate number. He motioned to me to come out and join him. When I did, he tore the page out of the notebook and handed it to me, telling me, "This guy's been dodging me 'cause he owes me a pile of money. I need to talk to him about that. Take this inside to the office and tell them you dinged this car while trying to park and you need them to page the owner over the loudspeaker to come out and meet you. Then come right back out and wait in front of our car for him. I'll take it from there."

So I did. When I came back to the car I could see Vince had moved two cars up, toward the building, and was crouched down between the cars where someone coming from the racetrack wouldn't see him. I just leaned against the hood of the LTD, crossed my arms, and waited.

It only took about five minutes. I knew it was the right guy by how he walked. Brisk pace. Agitated. Making a beeline for me. Kind of a big guy, but flabby. Maybe forty, with thinning dirty blond hair slicked back, polyester pants too high in the waist, and a button-down polyester shirt with a too busy, swirly type print. The height of late '70s fashion, except this was in the late '80s. When he reached me it looked like he was getting ready to cuss me out. Never got the chance.

Vince slipped up from behind and hooked a punch up into the guy's lower abdomen, just right to crack one of the floating ribs. As he doubled over, Vince grabbed him and threw him down on the pavement between the parked cars. In the blink of an eye, Vince was hunched over him raining down punches, kicks, and stomps, with a barrage of colorful comments mixed in, "Fucking piece of shit—making me chase you down like this—goddamn degenerate. You have money to bet the ponies, but can't fucking pay what you owe?" Then he stopped the beating and with a calmer tone, went, "Give me whatever money you have. Every. Fucking. Penny."

The guy dug around in his pockets and came up with a wad of crinkled bills. Vince snatched them out of his hand, then with a light kick to the gut, "Wallet too, asshole." The guy dug out his wallet and handed it to Vince, who took out the cash and dropped the wallet back on the guy's chest. Fanning the money out in his hand, Vince boiled over again. "Shit! This isn't even close to what you owe!" Then getting more intense yet, "Goddamn it, Bill, I'm sick of this shit. I'm just—fuck you!—I'm at the end of my fucking rope with you. One week," holding his right index finger to make the number one and leaning over to put it in Bill's face. "*One fucking week!* If you aren't paid off by then—"

Then in a snap he went from Mr. Hyde to Doctor Jekyll. With a calm, friendly tone, he called me over, "Joey, come get a look at this guy."

(Joey? Fucking Italians, always have to put a goddamn vowel on the end of everyone's name.)

Turning back to Bill, Vince threw up his arms in frustration, "This is the guy they send when all hope is lost and it's time to write off a bad debt." Then back to me, "Have a good look at this guy so you remember his face. Let him know what you're gonna do if he isn't square in one week."

I had no idea what to say. I leaned over poor, battered, scared shitless Bill with my hands on my hips and just glared into his eyes for thirty long seconds. While I stared at him I pictured his face as a big bowl of disgusting tapioca pudding I would have to choke down. Then I gave him a big smile, stood upright, turned to Vince with, "He knows," and walked away.

That was it. We just got back in the car and drove away. Vince didn't say a word about it. It was like it never even happened. The whole way back to my place it was "Any plans this weekend? Seen any good movies lately? How 'bout this weather?" and shit like that. I took the hint. The next Monday back at the job when Serge asked if I did anything over the weekend I told him, "No, not a damn thing." Then I started mixing the mortar. Like-a-butta.

It was the following Thursday when Vince came by and asked me to stop by the office and see him before I left for the day. When I got to his office Vince opened his top desk drawer and took out a plain white envelope, unsealed. He slid it across the desk to me. I picked it up and looked inside. Seven twenty-dollar bills, and one ten. "What's this?" I asked.

"Your cut."

"Of what?"

Vince got a big smile on his face, "I guess that look you gave ole Bill put the fear of God into him. He paid, the whole thing. Three grand. The collection fee is ten percent, that's your half."

Now, I know what most people would be thinking, "Hundred and fifty bucks, big fucking deal," but at the time I was working my ass off for eight bucks an hour, so this was like half a week's pay for doing almost nothing. Vince only gave me a few seconds for that to sink in, and before I could say anything, he hit me with, "So, I have a similar-type deal cooking for tomorrow night I need help with. Pick you up around nine?"

I just shrugged. "Sure."

So, he picked me up the next evening around nine. Again, not driving his Mustang. Or the LTD. He had some I-can't-remember-exactly-what, run-of-the-mill, average-type, gray sedan. He took me to a strip club. No, I don't remember the name of the place. No, I don't remember which city in the hundred or so places that make up the endless sea of boring suburbs around Detroit it was in. I expressed some concern, telling him, "I'm not old enough to get in."

Vince was nonchalant. "Don't worry about it, just walk in like it's nothing and no one's gonna ask."

Sure enough, we strolled in like we owned the place, and sat down at an open table. When the waitress came over Vince ordered two beers. She didn't ask for ID. I never really have cared much for beer, and have never been much of a drinker, so I just nursed mine to blend in.

Just often enough to keep the men from leaving, a girl would come out and do her routine. On TV and in the movies they always have these scenes at a strip club, loaded with all these smoking hot women. Your average stripper at any of a gajillion little nudie bars strewn about the land ain't that. They're more along the lines of the girl who, when you're out with the guys drinking, or whatever, you hook up with if she's willing, but then afterward your buddies aren't exactly high-fiving you but they're not ragging on you either. Young(ish). At least somewhat attractive. Able to learn the moves. Willing to show it all off. That's the basic resume.

Anyway, this tall brunette comes onstage to do her thing. This one I liked, much more attractive than any so far, but I may have been biased. I have always had a thing for well-built brunettes. She had just enough flab to give her soft curves, and a little too big in the butt, but very pretty and wonderful body. Vince noticed my interest. "Like that one?"

"Best I've seen so far."

Vince chuckled, "She's the girl we're here to see. When she finishes we'll go backstage for a chat."

For a chat? I was concerned. The last time he said he needed to "talk" to someone he beat the shit out of the guy. I wasn't about to hurt a woman.

Vince seemed to pick up on it, "No, I mean really, just need to talk to her."

So I just sat back and enjoyed the show. Beautiful eyes. Wonderful tits.

When she finished and headed offstage Vince got up to follow, with me in tow. Very casual. Very cool, like he owned the place. No one tried to stop us from following this almost-naked girl backstage. Seemed odd.

When we got to the small dressing room behind the stage where the girls changed their clothes, she was in there with her back to the door, putting on a robe. Vince got her attention, "Amber, sweetheart, how ya been?"

She turned to face him. I could tell by the look on her face she was not happy, at all, to see him. She said, "Shit, Vince—what do you want?" She was trying to sound annoyed but couldn't hide the fear in her voice.

Vince's annoyance was genuine and clear, "You *know* why I'm here. I need to find him. Now. Tonight. I *know* you know what hole he's crawled into." She started to object but Vince cut her off with a wave of his hand, "Don't fuck with me, Amber. I like you. I don't want to see you get hurt. I just need to talk with him, Amber, but," and using his left thumb to point toward me, "look at this animal they sent with me…" and he let the thought just trail off and sink in for a few seconds. Vince was standing next to a crappy little plywood table with a mirror on it where the girls sat to do their makeup. He rapped on it twice, like someone knocking on a door, "C'mon, now, out with it." He took that little notebook and pen out of his pocket. When she didn't respond, he knocked on the table two more times, louder, "Longer this goes on, the worse it gets for him. Now, Amber!"

Amber sat down at the table with a dejected plop, head down, starting to cry.

Vince gave her a few seconds, used a gentle tone, "Now."

She spat out the name of some fleabag motel and a room number.

"See how easy that was?" Vince asked. He leaned down beside her ear, and in a loud whisper, "I *know* you have a key to the room." He snapped his fingers twice in front of her face and held out his hand.

She hesitated only a moment before reaching under the table and pulling out her purse. She rooted around in it a bit and pulled out a motel room key, then with a trembling hand, gave it to Vince. By now she was flat-out sobbing. "Oh Vince, oh Vince, please—oh, oh please don't hurt him."

Vince got down on one knee in front of her and stroked her arm, "I'll try not to. I mean I *really* will try not to."

It was a twenty-minute or so drive to the motel. Someplace

on Telegraph Road. Only a couple dozen rooms, all side by side in a single row in the style common back in the '50s and '60s for a roadside motel. We found the room. The drapes were closed, but the light was on, and there was a flickering against the thin drapes that showed the TV was on.

Vince unlocked the door, flung it open, and rushed in in one fluid motion. He snatched the room's occupant out of a chair in front of the TV and threw him on the floor next to the bed. Before the guy could react, Vince boomed, "Stay down! If you get off that floor we're gonna have to kick your ass." Then after a deep breath, "I promised Amber I would try not to have to hurt you. For the life of me I will never understand why, but that girl really loves you. Don't make me break my promise to her." Changing to his calmer, down-to-business tone, "You know why I'm here. And *I* know if you're stashed in this roach motel it means you don't got the money. We *both* know there's only one way this can go." He let that sink in a few seconds before continuing, "Give me your car keys."

The guy started to stammer, like he was trying to object. Vince stepped toward him and drew his right foot back to tee up a massive kick. The guy winced and curled his body into a protective position. But Vince held back the kick, replacing it with, "Goddammit, Andy! Why are you gonna make me hurt you?"

That was enough. Andy dug his key ring out of his pants pocket and after fumbling around for a while with shaky hands, managed to remove his car keys and hand them to Vince. Then I guess he decided to try a last-minute appeal, "C'mon, Vince, you know that car is worth way more than I owe."

Vince clenched his fists and his eyes widened, "You damn

well better hope so! You think I'm gonna put a fucking ad in the Free Press? No! I'm gonna dump it wholesale for whatever I can get. Besides, you gotta figure in a…aggravation fee. Look here," he said, gesturing toward me, "I had to bring an extra man. Look at this young stud. It's Friday night for shit's sake! He should be out partying with the boys. What time is it?" He looked at his watch. "A little after eleven! By now he woulda been banging some hot piece of ass, but noooo, instead he's stuck in some shithole motel room helping me deal with your sorry ass. Yeah, you damn well better hope that car is worth more than you owe! A lot more!" He started to storm out of the room, but then wheeled back around, "Oh, and don't even *think* about reporting this car stolen." When there was no immediate response he stamped his foot, "You hear me, Andy?"

"Yeah, yeah, I know."

It was a nice car. Burgundy Cadillac. Looked fairly new. Vince gave me the keys to the gray sedan so I could follow him. He did warn me it was going to be "kind of a long drive." It was. We ended up out in Wixom, what would be considered "out in the country," to the west of Detroit. It looked to be a combination used car lot, junkyard, and auto shop. The sign above the office was green letters in a fancy, flowing cursive, "Shillelagh's Auto," with a shamrock to dot the "I," and two big green shamrocks on each side of the name. It was a place I would end up knowing well.

Vince parked the caddy behind a large, three-bay garage, out of sight from the road, and left the car keys under the driver's seat. I gave Vince back the keys to the car I had driven because I had no idea where the fuck we were or how to get home. It was about a week later that Vince handed me another plain, white, unsealed envelope with 250 in cash.

I guess that's how I got sucked into the thug life. Judas sold his soul for thirty pieces of silver. I sold mine for four hundred bucks. It came in handy. I put it with another lump I had managed to save and used it for a security deposit and first month's rent on a decent but tiny one-bedroom in Westbury Apartments, over there in Westland. Mom gave me a little grief over it. I finally sold her on it by pointing out how close it was to Schoolcraft College, where (at the time) I intended to take at least a class or two in the fall. Of course, I couldn't tell her the main reason: Twice now, I had had—well, whatever the fuck Vince Deluca was—come and pick me up *at my mom's house*, to go off and do…well, whatever the fuck it was we were doing.

I never have quite figured out why Vince took me along on those collections. No doubt I was kind of a big, muscular guy, and Vince knew I could handle myself and back him up in a pinch, but I wonder if it wasn't intended as some kind of test, or feeling-out process, to see how I would react. I guess at this point a shrink would ask, "How did it make you *feel?*" I don't know. It didn't make me feel good, but it didn't make me feel bad either.

I guess I rationalized it. It's like when you're a kid on the playground and some bully takes your ball, or whatever, and won't give it back, so you punch him in the head and take it back. What's wrong with that? Besides, it's not like guys like Bill and Andy didn't know what they were getting into. Even without knowing the specifics, I knew they had agreed to make some kind of deal with some kind of devil and couldn't very well bitch when a couple demons showed up to knock them down and tap dance on their heads when they didn't keep up their ends of the bargain.

Fucking thieves. I mean, basically that's what these guys

were, fucking thieves. I don't get it. If you walk into the 7-Eleven and walk out with a six-pack and a handful of Slim Jims without paying, the cops jump on you and haul your ass to jail. But if you hire a plumber, or somebody like that, to fix your house, then stiff him on the bill, or take out a loan from the bank and don't pay it back, that's not "criminal," it's "a civil matter." What? Taking a store for ten bucks worth of crap is a "crime," but ripping off a plumber for two hundred bucks in repairs or the bank for two grand in an unpaid loan is "civil?" Makes no fucking sense. Is it wrong to steal from a thief? Is it wrong to force a thief to give back what he's stolen? I guess that's how I rationalized it.

People are funny. We are supposed to be highly intelligent and use our big, logical brains to decide on the right actions, but really we are these emotional animals that use our big brains to find "logical" reasons to justify doing what even the average child knows is wrong.

Chapter 4

The rest of the summer went about like that. A few times a week I would "help" Vince with some "little thing" or another. There were a handful of other collections-type deals. A couple times the guys we went to see wanted to make things difficult and I did have to do some ass-kicking. Nothing worth talking about.

Most of what I did was more like errand boy-type shit. Most of the time I had no idea what, exactly, I was even doing. I picked up and delivered all kinds of "packages" to and from all kinds of places. There were only two rules on those deals: One, never look inside the package. Two, always keep the package locked in the trunk while in transit. Quite a bit of this delivery boy crap centered around Shillelagh's Auto. Sometimes it was an actual package of some sort, coming in or going out. Other times I had to go pick up a car there and drop it off somewhere else, or pick up a car left parked somewhere and drive it back to Shillelagh's.

I got to know the owner of the place. Jim Mackelroy,

but everyone called him Mack. A proud Irish American. At the time I guess he was in his sixties. He looked like your stereotypical, blue-collar, hard-ass Irishman. He was a little on the short side but with broad shoulders and a bent nose, obviously broken at least twice. He was always gruff, in a perpetual state of grumpy old man, but once you got to know him and worked your way past that he was easy to get along with. He seemed to know just about everything there was to know about the history of organized crime in Detroit.

As a young man he had been a boxer, actually getting to the professional level, but not for very long. Like a lot of aspiring fighters at that time he made ends meet doing "leg breaker" work for local mobsters. That was his first step on the slippery slope. When he managed to save up enough money to open his own garage he morphed into the "mechanic of the mob." Whatever "tools" were needed, like hard-to-trace cars, "clean" guns, or other such stuff, he could supply it, then, if needed, make it disappear. So, like if the mob was an army, Mack was its quartermaster. Meanwhile, he bought and sold used cars, had several acres of old cars available for parts, and kept two full-time auto repair mechanics employed. Shillelagh's Auto was a fully functioning, legitimate business.

Some of what I did was more along the lines of what you might call reconnaissance, or stakeout, type shit. It was usually just a few hours of something mundane. Like once I was told to park a few doors down from this house and write down a description of any people who came to visit, along with a description of their cars. I have no idea why. Another time I had to sit in the parking lot of a bar and watch for a guy I had a general description of, driving a certain car. Then when he got there, I had to go to the pay phone outside the place and call a number I was given and tell whoever answered something like, "Come join us for a drink at the Mustang Bar." Then I just had to leave. No idea what came of it. Other times I just sat and watched some unremembered place for some vague person or car that never showed. There was another deal like this, though, that was more involved, and led to meeting another major player in the shitstorm I was stumbling my way into.

As usual, Vince asked me to stop by the office after work to see him. There was another guy already there. Vince introduced him just as "Big Ed" who was something along the lines of, "Tony's main guy." Just enough for me to understand how seriously I needed to regard the guy, but without really giving any details on exactly why.

It was later, in bits and pieces that I came to know the man well. Ed Kowalski, but everyone just called him Big Ed. Looked to be in his thirties. A mountain of a man. Not like a pumped-up, meat-head weightlifter type, just a naturally big, tall, muscular guy. A face like a gargoyle statue on top of a Gothic cathedral. He kept it somewhat hidden with a full, neatly trimmed, reddish-brown beard. Maybe a gnarly scar under it on his left check, but hard to tell for sure. He had these very pale blue, very intense, eyes. When you stared into them it was like this vast, vacant space, like staring deep into the abyss. If the mob was the Philistine army, this was their Goliath.

For the first time ever, I actually got clear, detailed instructions. First from Vince. "You're gonna be helping Big Ed for a couple weeks. Do whatever he says. If it interferes with coming in to work, try to call me, but don't sweat it. I'll cover it." Then he walked out and left me alone in his office with Big Ed. I came to learn this was a standard way these guys compartmentalized things. Each guy just needed to know his part. Like bulkheads in a ship, if there's a leak, it can't sink the whole ship.

Big Ed handed me a pen and a spiral-bound notebook, you know, like the kind you use to take notes in school. "This is gonna be detailed, kid. Gonna need to write some stuff down so you don't fuck it up."

You always see in the movies and on TV how the bad guys never write anything down. That's evidence! Gotta memorize everything! Bullshit. Not possible. The key is to write down just the bits and pieces you have to, then after it's no longer needed, light it up.

Big Ed laid out the job. "For the next two weeks or so—however long it takes—you're gonna go sit outside this apartment building in Dearborn, watch for a certain guy." Big Ed had me write down the address, then continued, "Okay, now, very fucking important. You *will* get there every night no later than 8 p.m. If the guy shows, you stay until he leaves, even if it's all fucking night. But, if he don't show up by 1 a.m., he ain't coming, go home. Got it?"

I nodded.

"Good, so he'll be driving a black Lincoln Town Car." And Big Ed had me write down the license plate number. He gave me a somewhat detailed description of the guy, but I didn't write that down, figuring it would be easy enough to remember. Big Ed continued the instructions. "Every time the guy shows up, you write down the exact time he gets there, and the exact time he leaves. You use your notebook, there, draw a diagram of the parking lot and the building, and note where he parks and even what route he takes to the building. Got it, kid?"

"Got it."

"Okay, so Vince tells me you done some work like this—

he tells me you can find your ass with both hands, ya know—but park someplace with a clear view of the building, but outta the way enough to not be noticed. Some nosey fuck comes poking around, you say you're waiting for a girl who lives in the building to come out. If things get any hotter than that, you just keep playing the dumb, confused, horny guy and find an excuse to get outta there. Have a girl's name ready in your head. Got it?"

"Got it." *Ooh, ooh, I know, Gina, Gina Sabatini. Oh, that's a nice thought.*

He gave me his phone number and a beeper number if I needed to get ahold of him, "But don't call unless there's some serious shit. I'll stop by the construction site every few days to check up on things." He tossed me a set of car keys. "Parked outside. Use it for the job. Bring that car to work each day. Keep that notebook locked in the trunk. That's it. We good?"

"Trust me." *Oops.*

Big Ed scoffed, "Look, kid, don't be telling me to trust you. I don't know you from fucking Adam. I trust Vince, and he seems to trust you. I'll trust you when you show me you're worth a fuck." He stood up and walked out the door, shaking his head, "Trust me, he says! Shit, like saying you're rich. If you gotta say it, you ain't."

So, that's what I did. It was a nice, higher-end-type apartment complex. The building I had to watch was at one end of the complex and all the way in the back. There was only one way into the parking lot, so that made things easy. There was one light above the front entryway to the building, and one light in the middle of the parking lot, but the lot was big enough there were plenty of shadowy places around the edges where I felt I could see well enough while not being noticed.

You know how in the movies and on TV when they show the police detectives, or whoever, doing a stakeout, and they always bitch about what a drag it is? That's dead-on accurate. Kids' piano recital-boring. I drank a lot of Mountain Dew. I ate a lot of junk food. My favorite was those mini powdered doughnuts that come in a sleeve of six. I smoked a lot of Marlboro Lights. I would keep them cupped in my hand, you know, like you do when having a smoke outside on a rainy day to keep the rain from putting out the cigarette, except I was doing it so no one would see the burning ember. I got very good at peeing into an empty Mountain Dew bottle while sitting in a car.

Most nights it was just five excruciating hours like that. The good nights were the few times the guy actually showed. He always got there around 9:30, and was gone by 11:30, at the latest, so I could leave early. Every few days Big Ed would stop by the construction site and check on me. Then he would have me drive all the way out to goddamn Wixon to Shillelagh's to swap out for a new car. Meanwhile, I didn't miss a minute of work on the construction site. It was exhausting. Definitely young men's work!

I was never told, and damn for sure wasn't going to ask, but it didn't take a rocket scientist to figure out what was going on. I mean, here's this middle-aged guy showing up twice a week in a little too nice of a car and dressed a little too nice to go spend an hour and a half in an apartment. Obviously he had some hot young thing stashed away there. Go in and fuck her, take about an hour to recover, fuck her again, go home to the wife and kids.

And, I was never told, and damn for sure wasn't going to ask, but it didn't take a rocket scientist to figure out why I was watching the guy. When a hunter wants to go after a trophy buck he does what's called "patterning the buck." For weeks before the hunting season he gets out there and watches that animal to learn its travel pattern. Then when hunting season starts he knows where and when to set up an ambush. I doubt that poor sap, whoever he was, survived more than two weeks after I gave Big Ed my final report. Not that it was any of my business.

I was never directly paid for work like this. I mean, other than on the collection deals where Vince would give me a pile of cash as "my cut," although I had no way of knowing what, if anything, had actually been collected. For all the other stuff there was never any mention of money, it was always presented as if I was being asked to do a favor for a friend. I did notice though, that the more "favors" I did, the more overtime would show up on my paychecks for hours I hadn't worked. Well, I mean, hadn't worked at the construction site. That first three months I ended up making about double my actual forty hours a week wage.

It's said if you want to cook a frog, you can't just toss him in a pot of boiling water because he'll just hop right back out. Instead, you put him in a pot of warm water and let him relax and swim around while you ease up the temperature. By the time he figures it out, it's too late and he's cooked. I guess that's kind of what happened to me.

The next bump up on the burner came at the end of August. Vince told me about how Tony Mano always had a big end-of-summer cookout for Labor Day and I was invited. I tried to weasel out of it. I'm not much for hanging out with a shitload of people I don't know. It's not that I actively dislike my fellow human beings, it's that I don't actively like them either. As I said before, I'm a loner. I think I would have made a good monk. A contemplative monk. Just sit around all day thinking about shit. Vow of silence? No problem, I don't really want to talk to anyone anyway. The no-sex thing would be a drag, though. What would work better would be every Sunday instead of going to mass you go to the local cat house. Yeah, that would be a sweet deal. Someone should get with the Pope and start working on that right away.

Anyway, Vince made it clear there was no weaseling out of it. Tony had asked that I be there, and that was it. Tony had a nice place. It was in Livonia near Six Mile and Middlebelt. It looked like it had started out as a typical suburban brick rancher, but had been added onto here and there to become a sprawling, H-shaped deal, about three times bigger.

The lot was huge, at least compared to most in the area. He had about two acres that gently sloped down to a little creek. The other side of the creek was floodplain, so it was all in woods, and the lot was big enough he was able to let woods grow up on each side. This gave him a private backyard. The kind of yard where you could just whip it out and take a piss whenever you needed to without having to worry the neighbors would see you. On the back of the house he had this super-show-off patio made from some fancy-looking stone. He had a swimming pool. This wasn't all that uncommon in that neighborhood, but most people had an above-ground pool. Tony had an inground pool, which for that time and place was considered a step above.

There were a few dozen people in attendance. Families mostly. Husbands, wives, kids of all ages running around the big backyard or splashing in the pool. It looked like your typical suburban crowd. I wondered how many of them were—well, I wasn't sure what to call them—guys like Vince, or Big Ed—or Mack?, or Tony Mano?, or me? Not that it really mattered, I didn't yet have the desire or ability to give up the bliss of ignorance.

I enjoy people-watching. Fascinating creatures. In a crowd like this there's always one who somehow just pops, just stands out. She looked to be about thirty. Blond hair, about shoulder-length, feathered, kind of like Farrah Fawcett, but not to that extreme. Big blue eyes. Pretty enough, but not beautiful. Her nose was a little too chicken beaky and her jaw a little too squared. But her body—holy, fucking, shit. Hand-crafted personally by God Almighty and cast upon this Earth to make men go insane. Cut-off shorts, just short enough and just tight enough to tempt without being tacky. A tight, thin, white tank top over a blue bikini top. She seemed to know everyone, flitting from one group to another, a butterfly dancing in and out of conversations. Everyone seemed happy to see her. None of the wives seemed to take offense when she hugged their husbands, or stroked an arm, or the men stole a long glance at her pert little heart-shaped ass as she walked away.

It didn't take long for Vince to find me. "C'mon, I'll introduce you to Tony." I already knew what Tony looked like, having seen him a few times at the construction site and being told by Serge, "That's the boss, Mr. Mano." Tall and lanky. About forty. Jet-black hair, thinning. A small, round face with lips a little too big, and big, white teeth to match, almost like a horse's mouth. Dark skin showing he was both southern Italian and had spent plenty of time outside over the summer. Wire-rim glasses. The kind of guy who looked more like an accountant or a middle manager than a mafioso.

Vince introduced me as "Joey Rose," so I guess that fucking "Joey" moniker was going to stick, then excused himself. We exchanged the usual handshake and pleasantries, then Tony led me to an empty table away from everyone else for a private chat. He started off with, "I wanted to meet you because I've heard a lot of good things about you. Vince tells me you've been doing a very good job for him."

My mom taught me when someone compliments you and you're not sure what to say, the proper response is simply, "Thank you," so that's what I said.

Tony seemed fixated on my family background, "Rose, what kind of name is that? You do look like you could be Italian."

"Croatian, actually. Over there the name was Ruzo, R-u-z-o, but I'm not sure how exactly it was pronounced. Anyway, it means rose, so that's what my great-grandfather changed it to when he came over."

"Oh, very good! We're next-door neighbors then. Geographically, I mean. You know what the Croatians are known for?"

"Um…no."

"For being tough people. Good fighters. Good soldiers. Other countries in Europe used to hire them as mercenaries. Their whole existence they've been under the thumb of one superpower or another, but they've held their own, kept their culture, their language, stayed Catholic—"

The history lesson was cut short when the social butterfly flitted in. Coming up behind Tony she wrapped her arms around his shoulders and gave him a quick kiss on his left cheek. He didn't even need to look to know who it was, "Barbara, honey!" Then gesturing toward me, "This is a friend of mine, Joey Rose."

We exchanged hellos.

Barbara seemed to know she was interrupting, so standing back upright she patted Tony on the shoulder, "Getcha a beer?"

"Sure."

Then turning to me, she asked, "How 'bout you, sweety?"

"No thanks."

And off she flitted. I made it a point not to check out her ass as she went.

Tony started back up, "Oh, you don't drink?"

Shit. I was only eighteen but had already learned that with most men this was kind of a loaded question. Real men were expected to drink, so someone who didn't was perceived as suspicious. The truth was I just didn't much care for alcohol. Most of it tasted like crap to me. I didn't like the loss of control. I didn't like feeling like shit the next day. The concept of drinking to forget your problems never worked for me. I always found that the problems were just waiting for me on the other side, with reinforcements. Ultimately, I learned the best way to enjoy alcohol was to let other people drink it, then watch the stupid things they did. But rather than trying to explain all that, I had found a foolproof way to deal with this, "I drink some, but not much." Then the kicker that always got me off the hook. "My dad was an alcoholic. He died when I was ten." That's all it took. No matter how drunk the other guy was, or how much of an asshole he was, it was always, "Sorry to hear that," "I understand," and a dead stop on the peer pressure.

That segued the conversation into typical chit-chatty type shit about where I grew up, what school I went to, which church I went to, what family I had in the area, and all that usual feeling-out type stuff. I don't remember the exact details, and they aren't important anyway. The interesting part of the conversation came at the end. Tony asked something along the lines of, "How are things with the work you're doing? I mean, the job going okay for you?"

I will admit there was a moment of panic. I wasn't sure what, exactly, he was asking about. I decided the best approach would be to push things a little and see where the edge of the envelope was. "Which work, the stuff on the construction site, or the other stuff?"

Tony rocked back in his seat. For a moment I thought maybe I had screwed up. But he got a big smile on his face. "Very good! That's how men are supposed to talk to one another. Straightforward. No bullshitting. I mean the after-hours stuff. You got any problems with that?"

I wasn't really sure how to respond to that. What kind of response was he looking for? I decided to not overthink it and that it was one of those occasions where simplicity is best. Looking him square in the eye, I said, "No."

He hesitated a few seconds like he expected more, but then gave a satisfied nod. Then, I guess, he decided to push things and look for the edge of my envelope. "You have any questions for me?"

I gave him a wry smile and said, "None I would expect you to actually answer," and a bit of a chuckle.

Tony gave me that big, toothy smile again. "That's good. Vince told me you were a smart kid. What you need to know, you'll be told, what you don't need to know, you'll be better off not knowing."

"I understand."

Tony reached across the table to give me a firm handshake. "Okay, Joey, I think we'll get along just fine."

I guess that was sort of like a job interview, and I guess I did okay. About a week later Vince sent me over to Shillelagh's for a pick-up, like I had done a few dozen times before. This time, though, Mack gave me a gray Ford Taurus with 61,000 miles on it and told me it was a gift from Tony, "Consider it a performance bonus, kid. Tony told me to make sure it was a Ford, you know, 'cause your dad was a Ford guy. I had my guys go over it top to bottom, it's in good shape." Then with a kick to the front tire, he added, "And brand-new tires." At the time I was driving a terrible Pontiac 6000 that leaked oil into the air filter, among other things. Mack took it off my hands for six hundred, cash.

Well, shit, ain't no such thing as a free lunch, and it didn't take too much longer to find out what Tony had in mind.

Chapter 5

Louis Lafata, but everyone called him Little Louie. (He had me just call him Louie, though). I never did figure out where the "little" part of the name came from. It could have been because he was anything but little. While it's true he wasn't much over five feet tall, he was just about as wide. Not really fat, though, more cube-shaped. No neck. Stubby arms and legs. Like an Angus bull, bulky but surprisingly fast and nimble when he needed to be.

Or it could have been because he was actually Louis Lafata Junior. His father had been a somewhat high-up and a well-respected Detroit mobster. Before that his grandfather ran a crew that drove trucks across the frozen Detroit River, at night, with no headlights, to smuggle booze out of Canada during Prohibition. So I guess he was sort of a third-generation thug.

Or it could be because he was famous for always carrying around a small Louisville Slugger, like the kind used by little kids for tee ball. His was the classic style, with the barrel that natural yellowish-white of the ash wood, and the handle painted black. Its small size allowed him to use it with one hand.

His main job was to be a "tax collector." This was sort of like the old-timey "protection racket," but targeted only at illegal business enterprises. Within the mob-controlled neighborhoods, other criminals were sort of given a "license" to operate and then had to pay a small percentage of their ill-gotten gains to the mob as a "tax." Louie was one of several guys who went around on a regular schedule to collect. His route was in the city of Detroit itself, sort of the southwestern part, roughly between I-75 and I-96.

My involvement with him came directly as a "request" from Tony. He sold it as sort of like an apprenticeship, a chance for an experienced guy to teach the new guy the basics. It was later I figured out this wasn't all there was to it. If I had been more experienced at the time I would have known right away something wasn't adding up. As a rule, guys from different crews don't get paired up like this. For the most part, each crew is a semi-autonomous unit; if there's going to be any apprenticeship-type thing, it's going to be done in-house, within the crew. I don't know how Tony sold it to Louie. I guess he just appealed to his ego. I did end up learning a lot in the brief time I spent with Louie, though. Some came from direct lessons and instructions, much more trickled in by keeping my mouth mostly shut and my ears mostly open.

He had all these "rules" he wanted to make sure got drummed into my head. There were four that were paramount. "If you want to stay alive, kid, there are four things you never do. If you do, you're gonna find yourself in hot water fast!" First, no stealing (from the mob). This was the underworld equivalent of tax evasion. Every ill-gotten gain had to be accounted for to the penny, and the appropriate cut "kicked upstairs." In the case of this street tax collection type of thing, that meant no skimming, but it also meant no charging a little extra tax and pocketing it, or charging a little less in exchange for some favor. All of that was considered stealing and, with a clap of his hands for emphasis, "You're whacked."

Second, he told me, "No drug dealing. Everyone has a major hard-on right now over this war on drugs bullshit. Local cops, state cops, the feds, everyone and his fucking brother. Guys are getting more time in the can for nickel-and-dime drug deals than for manslaughter, for shit's sake! There's a shitload of what looks like easy money in it, but don't be tempted. You *will* get caught, and when you do, it *will* be a major problem." He went on to explain how the enforcement was so aggressive and the penalties so steep that the temptation to "turn rat" was so high you become too much of a risk, and, with another dramatic clap of the hands, said, "You're whacked." He also recommended against even the recreational use of any illegal drugs, saying, "Same issue. The cops just *love* busting drug users. Not worth taking a chance on, kid."

Third was similar, but less ironclad. It had to do with carrying weapons. Specifically, handguns. "Kind of the same thing as the drug problem. Very strict laws. An unregistered gun, or any concealed handgun and, bang!, federal offense, kid. Zero tolerance from any cop. If you need a gun for a job, keep it locked in the trunk, take it out only for the job, then lock it back up. If the shit hits the fan and a war breaks out, or something, and the higher-ups tell you to carry a gun, fine, but don't make a habit of it. Besides," he added, tapping his trusty tee ball bat, "There's all kinds of better tools anyway. I've actually been stopped several times by cops that wanted to give me shit over little Louie here. I always just flat-out tell 'em, 'Yeah, it's a tough neighborhood and I want some protection,' then they give me a little more shit over it and let me go. They got bigger shit to worry about." Then after a little reflection he felt obliged to add, "Well, I'm talking about city cops, not those guys out in the burbs. Those fuckers would probably string you up for carrying a Boy Scout pocketknife!"

Louie did want me armed in some way, though, "in case you need to back me up," so he gave me this nifty head-knocker he made himself. What he did was take one of those hollow steel tubes about eighteen inches long that come in a weightlifting set to make a dumbbell out of, then attached the two clamps that hold the weights onto one end of the tube. Kind of like a mace those medieval knights would use. He did warn me to use it only if absolutely necessary, "You can seriously fuck a guy up easier than you think with this thing." At the time I was in the habit of always wearing this long, black overcoat and I found the homemade mace-club-thingy fit well in the left, inside pocket of my coat. I must admit it made me feel better when going into some of the shithole neighborhoods we had to visit. I always carried it when running the route with him, then kept it locked in my car trunk the rest of the time.

The fourth rule was the most important, but also the one I had already pretty well figured out, the need for strict secrecy. "Don't talk about this shit with anyone. Don't tell your best friend, your girlfriend, your dog, your fucking teddy bear, no one! Don't get to bragging about doing 'this' or doing 'that,' even with other guys like us."

What was more helpful was his specific instructions on dealing with the law. "Sling whatever bullshit you think you need to to wriggle out of an encounter, but, if it gets serious, like if you get taken in, then it's time to shut the fuck up and it's nothing but 'name, rank, and serial number.' Give them whatever info they need to identify you, like name, date of birth, where you live, that shit, but from there it's only two things: 'I did nothing,' or 'I know nothing,' and 'I want a lawyer.' That's it! Don't play their fucking game. They are very fucking good at what they do. It's like stepping into the ring with a professional boxer, you may think you're tough and you've got some moves, but you're gonna get your ass kicked. They have all kinds of subtle tricks. They're allowed to flat-out lie to you. Prisons are full of guys who thought they were smarter than the cops. Even if it's some deal you had nothing to do with, tell it to your lawyer and let him tell it to the cops. Meanwhile, shit in a stainless-steel bowl, eat some crappy food, and take a lot of naps; jail ain't no big deal, kid."

It was fortunate and educational for me that Louie wasn't strict about practicing as he preached. He was a chatty guy and it didn't take much to nudge him a bit this way or that to find things out. It came in bits and pieces over many semi-coherent, somewhat addled conversations as I drove him from stop to stop over the course of the next six weeks.

What I pieced together was a much clearer picture of what, exactly, I had managed to stumble my way into. The crew I was part of was what the other crews somewhat jokingly called the "Cowboy Crew." Part of this was because it controlled the westernmost suburbs of Detroit, roughly the area west of Telegraph Road, although at no point did I ever find out where, exactly, the boundaries were. The other reason for the name was because this crew was largely made up of cowboy types. What in the vernacular have been called things like enforcers, hitmen, or, simply, muscle. Tony Mano had been working for years to turn his crew into the muscular right arm of the Detroit mob.

It had always been a well-established practice nationwide that individual crews have their own muscle, and more importantly, flex that muscle within their own designated territories. At the same time, though, it had always been seen as advantageous to bring in "outside muscle," at least to handle particularly delicate work. The highest-risk, most difficult, and most unpleasant work was murder. The Detroit Family had always been very strict in not allowing any outside muscle within their territory. If a mob hit was going to be done in Detroit, their guys were going to do it. Tony set up a situation where his crew could provide the benefits of outside muscle that was still under the control of the Family. He made it known to all the Captains and higher-ups that his guys were ready, willing, and able to go anyplace within the Detroit Family territory to do whatever work needed to be done. So, it was like in a company where all the managers know that if they need to discipline or fire an employee, they can call up the human resources division and have them do the dirty work. Slow but steady, more and more of this type of work was being relegated to Tony Mano.

This makes it sound like Tony was the Captain (i.e., "Capo," although I never heard that term actually used) of the Cowboy Crew. He wasn't. Within the official hierarchy of the Family, the Captain was Mike Picano. He had started as the Captain of a crew in Toledo, but as he got older, decided he wanted to slow down. The Cowboy Crew was the smallest and least significant of the crews within the Family, so he was given control of it. Wanting to remain semi-retired, he turned day-to-day control over to Tony Mano. So it's like an absentee landlord who has a property manager.

Normally, this isn't done, but as Louie pointed out, "You

have to understand, up to a few decades ago, that whole area was just farmland. Even now there's not a whole hell of a lot of money to be made there. As long as some cash is coming in and everything's running smooth, the big guys don't care." He went on to explain how the power center was and always had been Detroit itself, along with Windsor and Toledo. All the top guys were clustered in the posh neighborhoods along Lake St. Claire (the eastern edge of Detroit), in places like Grosse Pointe. As far as they were concerned the Cowboy Crew was a far-flung, minor holding. Besides, in recent years they had been enjoying the benefits of having Tony's guys come into their core areas to handle "problems," then retreat back to the relative obscurity of the outer suburbs.

The job with Louie was just four days a week, from about two or three in the afternoon until nine or ten at night. I started by driving to Louie's place. He had a bizarre living arrangement. He lived in what had been an insurance agency office smack dab in the middle of a strip mall just outside Detroit in Melvindale. He ended up there something along the lines of "After my second wife kicked my ass to the curb and took the house." He used what had been the break room as his kitchen, then one back office as a bedroom and a second back office beside it as his living room. He had sheets of plywood put up to cover the front windows, making it look from the front to just be a vacant, boarded-up space. He parked behind the building and only used the back door.

The basic procedure was I would get there exactly on time, then spend thirty minutes to an hour trying to wrangle Louie into actually getting going. I always drove, but we always used his car, a late-model, high-end, ivory-colored Crown Victoria with a brick-red leather interior. The first stop always had to be Mamma Leone's, this cute corner store that was part ethnic

Italian grocery store and part quaint Italian cafe. This wasn't part of the collection route, Louie just always needed to go there for an espresso and a cannoli, so that wasted another thirty minutes minimum, although I do admit they made the best cannolis I ever had.

The first two weeks went smoothly enough. My main headache was trying to learn how to navigate around Detroit. It was kind of fucked up, and not what I was used to. Out in the suburbs the main roads mostly followed the old township-based surveying lines, so a neat and orderly grid with main roads one mile apart running east and west, intersecting with roads a mile apart running north and south. Detroit wasn't like that. It was a more jumbled mish-mash of roads. I found it damn confusing. Even after six weeks I felt at least half lost at least half of the time.

Louie was okay to work with, and I learned a lot fast. Then the honeymoon ended and I started to figure out the ulterior motives behind putting me with Louie. Louie couldn't hide his true colors much past those first two weeks. Not that he was a bad guy. He was just an absolute mess. If nothing else, he needed me as a designated driver. In the entire time I spent with him I don't believe there was a single minute when he wasn't impaired in one way or another.

Booze? Yes. Always hard liquor, anything available in a half-gallon bottle, but mostly Johnny Walker Red. But that wasn't the worst of it. I honestly believe that you could have given him any kind of drug, in any kind of form, and he would take it without even asking what it was. He was a major pill-head. Various prescription pill bottles strewn about. All kinds of assorted shapes and colors of tablets of god-knows-what in little plastic bags. It was a major headache just getting him going every time I came to pick him up. Once he got going, he wasn't too bad, but it was apparent I was there as a babysitter and cat herder.

From what I was told, he wasn't always like this. He had spent decades as a rock-solid soldier. Something had changed in the past year. Tony said he was, "going through his mid-life crisis." It was only later in life from my own experience and in what I observed in other men that I came to understand this. I don't know about women, but for men this does appear to be a real thing. It can be one of the most dangerous times in a man's life. His body betrays him. He loses that physical prowess that is so deeply attached to the male ego. The demons in his mind pepper him with a constant barrage of woulda-coulda-shoulda. The dreams of his youth are far away on one horizon while the promised bliss of retirement is far away on the opposite horizon. Stuck on the train tracks in the middle of a long, dark tunnel. For most it is just diets, workouts, hair dyes, and sports cars, with no real damage done. For too many it's crumpling up a perfectly good twenty-year marriage and throwing it in the trash can to chase women half his age, or throwing away a perfectly good twenty-year career to chase his "true passion," or "get paid what he's worth," or whatever bullshit the hobgoblins in his mind dream up as a false salvation. For Louis Lafata, Jr. it was seeking pleasure, or at least relief, in booze, drugs, prostitutes, gambling—anything that he could bring in from the outside to compensate for how dead he felt inside. His life had become one of total debauchery.

Tony would have me come see him once a week to quiz me on how things were going with Louie. It became apparent I wasn't just intended as a babysitter but also as a spy. I felt uneasy about this. I didn't know where the lines were. Between a rock and a hard place. Loyal soldier to Tony equaled rat to Louie? After some pussy-footing around by both of us, Tony laid it out. "For some time the higher-ups have been concerned about him. I'm just trying to get at how bad the situation really is."

Still, I tried to straddle the fence. I liked Louie. I mean, he was a complete degenerate, but behind that you could see this smart, funny, likable guy. I wouldn't say I admired him. I wouldn't say I pitied him. I guess it was a weird mix of both. I guess at that point Tony decided to table the issue and see how things developed. It didn't take long to find out. Louie's life had become a car speeding through a snowstorm, it wasn't a matter of if he would wreck, it was a matter of when and how bad.

CHAPTER 6

It was a Tuesday afternoon in early November. That sad, brown, and gray time, after the fall color show but before the soft edges of the winter snow cover. I drove over to Louie's place, parked behind the building, and knocked on the rust-flecked steel back door, as usual. No answer. This had been becoming more and more common in recent weeks. It got to the point where two weeks before, while out on the route, I stopped at a neighborhood hardware store and had a copy of Louie's key made so I could just let myself in, wake him up, and drag his sorry ass to work. So, I let myself in.

I found Louie slumped over on his couch in a ratty terry cloth bathrobe and his tighty-whities. It took some doing to wake him up. I couldn't get him on his feet. He would mumble incoherently and slump back down on the couch. At one point I heard a noise in his bedroom and peeked in just long enough to see a lumpy blob of naked female flesh roll over on the bed and pass back out. I figured Louie and one of his hooker friends must have gotten into some especially potent god-knows-what the night before. I tried for nearly an hour. He just simply couldn't stay on his feet. Finally he managed to mumble, "You know the route, kid, go without me."

I briefly considered calling Tony. He had given me his home phone number, a beeper number, and another number for his car phone. Car phones were still cutting edge at that time and very few people had one, but Tony was always a high-tech guy. If things had gone differently for him, he probably would have ended up a computer wiz at some Fortune 500 company. I decided to not call him. I still didn't want to get Louie into any trouble. And I figured real men are supposed to take the initiative and get the job done, so I decided to just run the route myself. It was an easy enough job and we had never run into any serious trouble in the time I spent following Louie around.

I did decide to make one small change. We usually went to Mamma Leone's, then started with the stop furthest from Louie's place, working our way back. I decided to do it backward, which put my last stop near I-96, which I could then hop on and zip home. It's funny in life how sometimes there's some tiny, seemingly insignificant decision that ends up being the pivot point for a life-changing event. I guess that's what ended up happening.

Everything went just fine, until it didn't. Last stop, but like I said before, what was usually the first stop on this route. Fairly typical of what this type of racket deals with. Most were legitimate businesses of one sort or another that had some kind of illicit side hustle going. This place was what we called in Michigan a liquor store, a little neighborhood convenience store that also sold booze. The kind of place you pop into for a bag of Doritos, a scratch-off lotto ticket, or a pint of peach schnapps, you know, to loosen up the head cheerleader so you can get a little sis-boom-bah in the backseat. *Go team!* It was run by a family of Pakistanis who were also importing knock-offs from Asia and selling them out the back door. It was always a simple pick-up: Park in the alley behind the store, enter the unlocked back door, down a narrow hallway to an office on the right, and pick up a small brown bag from the little geeky guy who worked in the office behind the actual store. Simple.

In the past the pick-up had always been around three o'clock, but that night I didn't get there until a little after eight. I figured that since the place was open until two in the morning anyway, it wouldn't make any difference. I parked behind the store and went in the back door, as usual. That's when all hell broke loose.

As soon as I swung the door open three big Pakistani dudes came storming down the hall toward me making wild gestures and yelling in some language I didn't understand. For almost everyone when something like this happens the body instinctively reacts with shock, the world speeds up, and everything becomes a blur. For a select few the opposite happens. The world goes into slow motion. The senses become heightened, to the point of super awareness. The mind and body sync perfectly.

The hallway was narrow enough that they had to come at me one on one. That was my edge. I drew that club out of my inside coat pocket and cracked the first guy square on top of his head. As he crumpled at my feet I walked right over top of him and cracked the next guy, then the next. Pop, pop, pop, just like that, then rushed down the hall into the office. One look at me brandishing that bloody weapon and the little geeky guy dove under the desk to hide.

I was surprised by what I saw. In the middle of the small

office was one of those six-foot-long folding wooden tables, you know, like they set up in the church basement for bingo night. It was almost completely covered with stacks of cash. I seemed to automatically know what to do. Beside the desk was a box of printer paper. I dumped it out on the floor, then shoveled all the cash into the box using my arms so my hands never touched the table. It barely all fit. I had to put the lid on the box, then keep it compressed between my left arm and ribs to keep the loot from falling out.

I returned to the hallway, club raised at the ready, expecting to have to fight my way out. One of the guys wasn't moving at all. The other two were writhing around a little and groaning, but seemed pretty out of it. There was blood everywhere. Pooling on the floor. Splattered all over the walls on both sides of the hallway. Holy shit. I had never seen so much blood in my life.

I marched right over top of the busted-up guys. On the way out the door I somehow just knew that the only hard surface I had touched was the doorknob, so I stopped for a second to wipe it off with my coat sleeve. My car was parked about thirty feet down the alley. It had rained the night before and I made it a point to zig-zag down the alley, sloshing through every puddle to try to get any blood on my shoes washed off. I opened the trunk and put in the box of money and my bloody overcoat, with the club wrapped up inside. Then I just drove away, calm and casual.

I hopped on 96, just like I had planned, and headed west. It was after a few miles that the panic started to seep in. I had to figure out what to do. After about ten miles I knew I was in over my head and needed to call Tony, so I took the next exit and stopped at the closest gas station to use the pay phone.

I don't remember what I told Tony but I managed to

get across enough for him to understand there was serious trouble. He stopped me before I went into detail, telling me, "Hold on there. Give me two minutes and call me back on my car phone." I suppose, with good reason, guys like Tony were always super paranoid about what was said over the phone. I guess he figured the car phone was safer. I don't know if that was true, but, like I said before, they were still a new thing back then, so, I suppose, harder to tap.

When I called him back he let me go into more detail about what had happened. Twice he asked, "So, Louie wasn't with you?" He seemed pissed off at that. He told me to continue on toward home, then find another pay phone in about ten minutes and call him on his car phone again for instructions on where to go, but, "Don't go home."

When I called him back he had me write down an address and gave me directions for a house out in Canton Township, which at that time was still quite rural. "See the woman there. She's a friend of ours. Do whatever she tells you."

So that's what I did. It was a cute little bungalow, set back a ways off a washboard-rutted dirt road and surrounded by scrubby fields and small woods. There was a screened porch on the side of the house. The light was on in there, with someone sitting at a small, round table in the middle of the porch.

It turned out to be Barbara, the social butterfly from Tony's cookout with the masterpiece body. She stopped me on the porch, saying, "Now, sweetie, I need you to do exactly what I tell ya, okay?"

"Um, yeah, sure."

"This ain't my first rodeo so you need to trust me."

"Sure."

"I need your clothes. All of them. Strip naked and leave

them in a pile here. If you're shy, I'll go outside. Then go through that door," she said, and pointed, "through the kitchen, turn left, and straight ahead is a bathroom. Take a shower. A long shower. Lotsa soap. Scrub down everything."

As I started to disrobe she asked, "Anything in the car we need to deal with?"

"An overcoat. In the trunk. And what's inside it, but not the cardboard box," and I handed her my car keys before she asked for them. While she went to my car for the coat I finished stripping and found the bathroom. I took a ten-minute shower, soaping and rubbing down every square inch of my skin at least three times.

It was only when I got out that it occurred to me I had no clothes. I wrapped a towel around my waist and went out to find Barbara sitting at the kitchen table, smoking one of my Marlboro Lights. She had placed my lighter, cigarettes, wallet, and car keys in the middle of the table, but my clothes were nowhere to be seen. I sat down across from her and lit a cigarette myself before asking, "What about my clothes?'

"Burned 'em"

What the hell? "All of them?"

"Look, Joey," reaching across the table to pat my hand, "you do understand if there's even a drop of blood on your clothes and the cops find it, you're cooked."

I just nodded.

She continued, "Okay, this shit—whatever it is that happened—when was that?"

"A little after eight."

"Okay then, here's the deal. We met at Tony's party. We hit it off. I invited you over. You got here at seven and spent the night."

"Oh, shit, I wish! I mean, isn't that kinda hard to believe?"

She gave a sly smile, a wink, and with a dash of sugar and spice in her voice, "Oh, I don't know. Don't sell yourself short, Joey, you look pretty damn good in that towel."

I laughed it off.

She asked me if I wanted a drink.

"No."

"Getcha something to eat?"

I hadn't eaten since lunch and my stomach was empty, but I just had no appetite, "No, I just need to relax and decompress a bit." She led me out to her living room, sat me down on the couch, and turned on the TV, then excused herself. I don't remember what was on. Something stupid and annoying, but I guess that describes 99 percent of TV shows. As soon as I sat on the couch the adrenaline rush I had been on crashed. I could feel the energy just seep right out of my body into the couch cushions. I went into a deep, coma-like sleep.

It was around two in the morning that I snapped out of the coma. The TV was still on, but the house was otherwise dark. I stumbled into the kitchen and rooted around for my cigarettes, trying to just use that little bit of light coming from the TV in the next room. I found them and went back into the living room.

I guess my bumping around woke up Barbara. She was standing in front of the TV in a lacy, pale-yellow nightie. Very short. Very tight and low cut around the top. Lord. Have. Mercy. Held on by two thin shoulder straps any man alive would sell his soul to the devil to slip down her arms. Women think men can control this, while, in reality, we have no control over it at all. I guess I just couldn't help it. Maybe it was just that time of night when it just naturally happens by itself anyway. I turned that towel I was wearing into a teepee. Barbara didn't say a word, just bit her lower lip, a wild flash in her eyes. The first time was hard and fast on the couch. After that I calmed down a bit, relaxed with a smoke, and spent the rest of the night in her bed.

The next morning Barbara suddenly remembered she had a sweatshirt and a pair of sweatpants that would fit me. She also came up with a pair of socks, but no shoes. She gave me my next set of instructions: I was to go home to change clothes, then drive my car over to Shillelagh's, but was to call Tony beforehand so he could meet me there. Then she gripped my hands, gave a tight squeeze, and leaned into my ear, "Best to not tell anyone about what we did last night."

After that I became her regular Tuesday night thing. Tuesday night only. There by eight, gone by midnight. That was it. It became apparent Barbara simply used men. Mostly older, richer men. She clearly lived above her means. She worked at a florist shop for this gay guy named Paul, but had a nice house, high-end clothes, all kinds of fancy jewelry, and a completely free-and-clear little red corvette. No, really, just like in the Prince song. I don't doubt Prince wrote that song about some woman he knew who was very much like Barbara. I don't doubt that some rich old dude gave that car to Barbara after hearing that song and thinking, "Hey, that makes me think of Barbara!"

This isn't to say Barbara was some kind of slut or gold digger. She simply recognized that she had been blessed with certain assets and talents, and made the most of them. Let's face it, throughout all of human existence, to one extent or another women have always been selling it, and, to one extent or another, men have always been buying it. I did ask her once why she kept letting me come around, when, "You're clearly out of my league."

She just shrugged, got that sly smile, and wild flash in her eyes, "Sometimes a woman just wants to find a young stud and get her brains fucked out." Worked for me.

So, I did like I was told. As soon as I pulled up in front of the office at Shillelagh's, Mack came out to see me. He directed me to go through the garage to a breakroom on the back where Tony was already waiting. I decided I had better get that box out of the trunk and take it with me. While I was doing that Mack asked, deadpan, "Hypothetically, if there was any blood in this car, where would it be?"

I didn't even need to think about it, "Driver-side floor, and trunk." He had me leave him my car keys.

I found Tony sitting at a table in the middle of the break room. The building seemed otherwise empty. I don't know if Mack had given his mechanics the day off, or if they were out running an errand or something. I came to learn that this type of arrangement was the mainstay whenever Tony needed to discuss anything in detail. He always found some place that was private and out of the way. He never talked details inside any space that could be easily associated with him, like inside his house or any office space he regularly used. He seldom used the same place twice. This was basic survival paranoia for guys like this. You can't put in a bug and listen in if you don't know where to bug. It was an odd skill these guys developed. On the one hand, they led these high-risk, high-reward lifestyles, while on the other hand, they needed to be ultra-careful. Like a NASCAR driver expertly working the gas pedal with one foot and the brake with the other while hurtling around and around the track at two hundred miles per hour, the whole time mere inches away from complete disaster.

I walked into the breakroom, set the box in the middle of

the table, and sat down across from Tony. Gesturing toward the box, he asked, "What's this?"

"The money I mentioned."

He stood up, took the lid off the box, and let out a long, low whistle, "Holy shit! How much is in here?"

"Don't know, didn't count it."

He grilled me for a good twenty minutes, having me go back and forth over every detail of the events of the previous evening. Then, once he was satisfied he had the whole picture, laid it out plain. "Okay, I don't know what to make of this, but I'm gonna find out. Meanwhile, you go home and stay there. Don't talk to no one about this. Whatever you do, don't talk to Little Louie, I'll handle him. In fact, don't answer your phone at all. It'll take a day or so, but once I get it sorted out, I'll beep you." Before I left he stressed again, "Really, Joey, don't talk about this shit, *with anybody*."

When I went back out to my car, Mack already had the carpeting in the trunk and driver-side floor torn out and was working the bare metal over with a rag and what smelled like bleach water, "Leave your car with me, I may need a few days to find new carpeting." Meanwhile he loaned me a white Ford Escort to use.

So I went home and waited. Longest twenty-four hours of my life, at least up to that point, anyway. I paced back and forth in that tiny apartment so many times I worried I was going to wear a rut in the carpeting and not get my security deposit back. It's odd in life how the ball bounces. It seems, so often, the same action can just as easily make a guy a hero as make him a villain. I didn't know with this deal which side of the line the ball was going to land on. I had no fucking idea what I was doing. I guess all of adult life is like that. All of us are just making it up as we go along and hoping it's good enough. No one knows what the fuck to do, but everyone has to do something, so we muddle through the best we can. So much of life is like stumbling around a dark room looking for a black cat that may, or may not, actually be there.

It did only take a day for Tony to contact me. He gave me directions to meet him at a nearly finished spec house he was building nearby. When I got there, I could see his car (a black Cadillac, I mean, what the fuck else could a guy like this drive?) parked outside, but no one else was around. I went inside. In retrospect, I'm glad I was so naive at the time and didn't know to be scared shitless. Set-ups like this are one of the common ways guys get set up to be whacked.

As soon as I walked in, Tony was on me. He grabbed my right hand, pulled me in, and clapped me on the back, "Joey! Joey! This is some crazy shit. Come in, come in. Shoulda got ya a chair. This is some crazy shit."

Ah, okay. What? I half expected—

"Okay, so, I talked to the guy in charge of that area," Tony continued, "And…" He shook his head.

"Yeah, yeah, I get it. Some crazy shit. You're killing me here, man. How much trouble am I in?"

Tony laughed, "Trouble? Oh, hell no, Joey. You're a fucking hero, kid! They're gonna put your picture on the fucking recruiting poster."

The wave of relief almost knocked me off my feet. Yeah, a chair would have been nice.

"So, here's the deal, Joey: Turns out, that liquor store you had trouble at wasn't just importing knock-off watches and handbags, and shit like that from Asia. Know what else gets imported from Asia?"

Deer in headlights

"Heroin. Yeah. That back office was being used as the

trap house for a decent-sized heroin distribution network, if ya don't mind a little cop lingo. Little Louie, who's supposed to know this shit, didn't have a clue. Not a fucking clue! Can you believe that bullshit? So anyway, they'd pay him taxes on the knock-off trade every Tuesday around three, then were free to start bringing in the cash on their real enterprise." Tony shook his head, "See why we were concerned about Louie? Now, brace yourself, Joey, I'm about to get to the good part."

I had already put a hand on the wall to lean against it.

Tony got his usual horse-mouth grin, "So, while maybe it was just dumb luck you stumbled onto it, the higher-ups were able to play it like…like they knew about it. Like, then we sent you in to bust those guys up and take the money as a warning, and a penalty fee." Tony laughed and patted me on the shoulder, "Fuck it, Joey, it's like they always say, better to be lucky than be good!" Then he got more serious. "So, I talked to the guy in charge of that area. And I—I kinda fucked with the guy, 'cause, you know. So, anyway, yeah, seriously, he's just embarrassed as fuck. I mean, this shit happened on his watch, you know. As far as he's concerned he has no claim on the cash, it stays with our crew." Tony let that sink in a few moments before continuing, "So, look, Joey, the rules on a deal like this are clear. You took it, so that money belongs to you."

I hadn't even noticed but there was a paper grocery bag on the floor against the wall behind him. Tony reached for it and handed it to me with, "I took the liberty of taking out the taxes. Your end comes to fifty-eight grand, and change. Be careful with it! Don't go splashing around a bunch of cash and drawing attention."

Stunned. *What do I say?*

Then he suddenly changed the subject. "Oh, I've been meaning to ask, what'd you think of Barbara?" He was trying to play it cool, but I could tell he was fishing for something.

I just shrugged, "She seemed just fine. By the time I got there I was wiped out. Basically just crashed on the couch."

He seemed satisfied with that and just nodded. I'm guessing this was at least part of the reason Barbara insisted on me keeping quiet about how things with her had played out. Tony Mano seemed like exactly the kind of jockey the little red corvette would have in her stable. I wonder which night he got assigned?

I never saw Louie or even spoke to him after that. No one ever mentioned him again, as if he had never existed. It didn't take any hard math to figure how he ended up, though. The first clue was when Big Ed asked me to give him the key I had to Louie's place. The hardest part about taking a guy out is always finding some way to get at him at a time and a place where you have some hope of both success and secrecy. The combination of a key to walk right in at any time, the private set-up of his living arrangement, and his constant drug-addled state made Louie a sitting duck that even the average twelve-year-old kid could whack and get away with it.

The second clue came that Friday. I was still doing some part-time work at the construction site. Vince asked me to stay after work to help Big Ed with "a little project." After everyone else had gone for the day Big Ed took me to where there was a basement dug out for one of the houses yet to be built. He put a ladder down into the pit and by the light of one of those propane lanterns you use for camping, we dug a big hole down in there. The ground was this compacted clay, hard as fuck. We had to wail away it with picks to bust up a few inches, then scoop that out with shovels. We dug out a block about six feet long by five feet wide. It looked like a grave, but extra wide. It took two hours to go down three feet, at which point Big Ed declared it "good enough" and sent me home.

I couldn't help but notice when I got to the construction site the next Monday morning that there was already a cement truck there, pouring that basement. That did seem a little odd, it was rather late in the year for cement work. Not that it was any of my business, but I have little doubt Louie was under that basement.

Some years later, just out of curiosity, you know, I did drive around that neighborhood and try to figure out which house it was. Enough had changed by then that I wasn't sure which one it was. I pictured the setup like the basement in the house I grew up in. We had a TV and one of those big, fluffy couches down there. When I was a little kid I would always go down early every Saturday morning to watch cartoons. When I got older, I would sneak girls down there whenever I got the chance. I got my first blowjob on that couch. I hoped Big Ed had buried Louie face up so he could enjoy the show. Watch some Bugs Bunny. Cheer on a pair of teeny-boppers getting hot and heavy. "There you go kid, safe on second base! Steal third!, slide, kid, slide! Atta boy!" Poor Little Louie. Oh well. I hope at least Big Ed buried him with his tee ball bat.

Meanwhile, I had no idea what to do with the money. You have to understand, back then fifty-eight grand was the annual salary of a guy with a comfortable middle-class, or maybe more like upper-middle-class, income. Here I was, just turning nineteen and I had what for me was like two years pay all at once. I decided to just rent a safe deposit box at the local bank and plunk it down in there. It would end up being the start of a nest egg that would later prove essential.

I wish it hadn't taken me as long as it did to figure things out. Hindsight is always twenty-twenty. Everyone wishes, "If I could go back when, knowing what I know now..." Of course, life doesn't work that way. But if I was allowed just one trip back in a time machine, I would go back to that moment and tell my dumbass nineteen-year-old self, "Take the money and run, son, run!"

There was one other little thing that happened after that, which wasn't all that interesting but ended up sort of coming into play later, so I will mention it. Tony invited me to go along with him and some of the other guys on a deer hunting trip. At that time deer were scarce in the southern part of Michigan, so to hunt deer guys would "go up north." The season was always just two weeks long, from November 15 to November 30. The season bag limit was just one buck deer. During those two weeks each year any two men meeting at any place in the northern half of the state didn't greet one another with "Hi," or "How ya doing?" It was "Got yer buck yet?"

No surprise, Tony had access to a swanky deer camp up near Gladwin with a spacious, well-outfitted cabin, and stout hunting stands with comfortable seats and roofs to keep the weather off you, strategically positioned at age-old deer hotspots spread out over several hundred acres of private hunting ground. Mack loaned me an old lever action 30-30 with iron sights. He assured me the sights were "spot on" but recommended I try to keep my shots inside sixty yards or so. To that end, I was set up in a mini log cabin-type blind with one wall low enough to shoot over and a tin roof. It was stuck into a steep hillside overlooking a small wooded valley with a trickle of a stream running through the bottom of it about fifty yards out. They assured me that's where the deer liked to travel through.

On the surface, deer hunting is about the stupidest thing imaginable. You get up ungodly early, stumble out into the woods in pitch blackness, then spend the next few hours freezing your ass off to mostly just watch empty woods. I suppose any hobby or pastime could be rationally deconstructed as equally ludicrous. But, with some surprise, I really enjoyed it. I mean, I *did* freeze my ass off. No amount of what seemed like over-dressing at the cabin was capable of compensating for what happens to the body when you just sit on your ass for hours on end out in the cold. Still, there's such a beautiful, simple peace that comes from being alone in the tranquility of nature. If nothing else it's a few hours when the rest of the world may be going to hell in a handbasket, but you neither know, nor care. I found it oddly spiritual, a chance to relax and contemplate in God's original cathedral. I never saw a single deer and, again with some surprise, that didn't detract from the experience one bit.

I did end up making a kill, though. It was just before ten on my third, and last, morning there. It was getting to be about the time the hunters packed it in to go back to the cabin, warm up, have lunch, and catch a nap to get ready to go back out around two or three for the evening hunt. A little movement caught my eye, on the hillside upslope on the other side of the little stream, maybe seventy-five or eighty yards out. It wasn't a deer. It was one of those snowshoe hares common "up north." Just hop, hop, hop, stop for a nibble, repeat.

I thought, *What the hell, why not try?* I knew with the deer rifle that if I shot the little guy in the body it would blow a big enough hole in him there wouldn't be anything left, so I decided the thing to do was to try to shoot him in the head.

The next time he stopped for a nibble I lined up those old iron sights on his eye and squeezed off the shot. Miracle of miracles, it worked. His head exploded. When I went to pick him up, all that was left of it was two long, thin flaps of skin with his ears attached at the ends.

I strutted back into deer camp triumphant. "Got one! But, hey, you guys didn't tell me the deer were so damn small around here." Everyone thought it was hilarious.

Tony joked, "Where's the antlers?! You know you can only shoot bucks!"

"Blew the damn thing's right off his head!" And everyone laughed their asses off.

Mack inspected the trophy and declared it, "A fine fat hare. I'll make a proper Irish rabbit stew for dinner."

I spent the rest of the winter as a full-time employee of Mano Construction Company, although there wasn't much to actually do and I was seldom actually there. I did a lot more recon work. I got to the point where I actually enjoyed it. It was kind of peaceful, like sitting in that deer blind in the quiet woods. I helped Vince and Big Ed on various collection-type deals. To make extra money I went along a few times to help on shakedowns, or at times, flat-out rip-offs, of drug dealers. We considered drug dealers to be the scum of the earth, so preyed on them whenever possible.

Meanwhile, I never did end up taking any classes at Schoolcraft College, or anywhere else. Why bother? Oh, except for Mom. Yeah, shit. She didn't deserve a son like me. I lied to her. I tried to convince her I was doing well at Mano Construction, had been given a raise, was learning a trade, found my passion, and all that bullshit. I don't know. She acted okay with it but…but, shit, I think I kind of broke her heart. The bridge wasn't burned, but it damn for sure was singed.

That was the first of many relationships I would fuck up as I stumbled my way deeper into scumbag land. I really just don't want to talk about it. She was a good mom and deserved better. That's all I'm going to say about it.

So, anyway, that winter I was out there earning and hustling and doing whatever "after-hours" shit Tony, or Vince, or Big Ed asked me to do. You would think that kind of work would have been good enough, but Tony had other ideas. Let's face it, that deal at the liquor store I pulled off wasn't just dumb luck. Damn few guys would have had the cool to not panic and get run off. Tony was smart enough to see the potential of a guy like that.

The mob runs on money. That money comes from control. Control comes from fear. Fear comes from violence. The ultimate fear is fear of death. The ultimate violence is murder. Ergo, he who controls the murders makes the money possible. In *The Prince* Machiavelli wrote about whether it was better for a prince to be loved, or feared. He concluded that while a prince should try to be both, of the two, feared was more powerful. Tony Mano was Machiavellian to the hilt. He had pathological ambition. Adding just one more hardcore hitman to his crew would be the equivalent of Julius Caesar adding a full legion to his army. Tony needed to find out if I was that kind of soldier.

So, it was that spring that I did the hit I described in the beginning, under that pretty little toenail moon. I was intentionally kept out of doing the recon work. All I did was drive through the neighborhood the day before to get the lay of the land. I "stole" the car I used that night from Shillelagh's. The shotgun was already in the trunk. A few days before, Mack took me out behind his shop to make sure I knew how to use a pump action shotgun. He showed me how to take the barrel off, "like to clean it," without needing to mention that would also be how I would take it apart to smuggle it in under my overcoat. He gave me instructions on what to do, but not as, "do this." He always had this slick way of giving detailed instructions. He would tell it like it was a story, "Back in the old days this guy got hit and this is how it was done…"

It was just another job. I was just the shooter. It was not a pleasant experience. I mean, in the moment there's an adrenaline rush. There's a level of satisfaction in pulling off a hard job most guys can't do. There's a thrill in knowing you got away with doing that which no one is supposed to be able to get away with. But it isn't the thrill of a roller coaster ride or the pleasure of hot, banging sex, or the satisfaction of winning the championship game. It is something that, once done, you have no desire to do again, while at the same time there is a deep…well, I don't really know how to describe it…comfort?…in knowing you are *capable* of it, and *can* do it again.

And therein lies the barb on the hook. Once that line is crossed, there is no going back. The toothpaste is out of the tube. Now I was a murderer, and that was what I would always be. In that moment I pulled the trigger I became both an extremely valuable asset and the most dangerous of liabilities. There is no statute of limitations on murder. First-degree murder carries a life sentence. Anyone involved in the conspiracy is on the hook for it for the rest of their lives.

At the same time, even within a hardcore criminal enterprise like the mob, rock-solid hitmen are few and far between. A great many mob associates, and even soldiers, go through their entire criminal careers without ever having to kill anyone. And, while it may be claimed that to become an official member, a "made man," one has to "make his bones," what that really means is that he has to satisfy a contract for a hit, that is, make it happen, not be the actual killer. More often than not, the actual killing gets subcontracted out to those few, rare, reliably capable men who can kill without hesitation, then carry on as if nothing happened. Those whose minds and bodies can be made to overcome what is an innately abhorrent act, then can pack their feelings in a box inside the psyche, wall it off, and walk away.

Vince kept me closer than usual for a week or so afterward. I could tell he was trying to see how I would react to it. The most dangerous position a guy can end up in with a deal like this is to be perceived as being the weak link in the chain of the conspiracy. No doubt, by that time Vince and I had become good friends. But, no doubt, if he got the idea in his head I might crack under the guilt, or fear, or whatever, he wouldn't hesitate to take me out. I wouldn't be surprised if he already had the hole dug. The saddest part, the really shameful, disgusting part is, what I felt at the time was...well, simply, nothing. No guilt. No remorse. No fear. What the fuck was wrong with me?

It is the natural human tendency to seek power. It is the natural human tendency to seek as much control as possible over the chaotic shitstorm that is life upon this earth. We pursue wealth, influence, and fame, piling them up as stones in a fortress wall, believing they will keep out the woes of the world. Perhaps that is why murder is considered the most deplorable of crimes. The ultimate control is the control over life and death. It trumps all. Whatever wealth, influence, or fame the guy may have had was stolen in a second when I pulled the trigger. All it took was a fifty-dollar gun, a fifty-cent shotgun shell, and a nineteen-year-old psychopath.

Going forward, whatever else I did for "the mob," or "the Cowboy Crew," or Tony Mano, or whoever the fuck was the puppeteer behind the curtain pulling the strings, my main function was to be a killer. The other, four-felonies-a-week typical mob associate shit was merely background noise. The next few years were...well, very bad.

Chapter 7

The Canelli brothers. Paul and Pete. Fraternal twins. Lifelong badasses, they figured out in kindergarten that if they stuck together, they made a formidable force. As teenagers they had a well-earned reputation as the toughest guys at their high school. An ideal Friday night meant find a store that didn't mind selling beer to underage buyers, which led to getting messed up enough to get into a fight, which duly impressed any fine young babes that were about, which then led to getting laid. They financed such ventures by smashing car windows to snatch fuzz busters, car stereos, or whatever else they could grab and run. They did also set up a small-scale loan sharking operation while still in high school. How, exactly, they ended up in the mob wasn't clear, but, at the same time, wasn't all that surprising. They were part of what we called the "Down River Crew," controlling the area south of Detroit (i.e., "down river"), along the west side of the Detroit River.

At the time, they had just turned twenty-eight and were

entering another of the dangerous, fucked-up times in a man's life. What I call the Icarus Phase. What pilots know as the two-hundred-hour rule. What country folk know as "getting too big for yer britches." It is that phase when a man has been in his chosen profession long enough to get good enough at it that his ego starts to run into overdrive, convincing him, without doubt, that he is smarter and more skilled than he really is. Like the follies-of-youth phase and the midlife crisis phase, his mind just gets turned upside down. He has no doubt he can fly right into the sun with wings of wax.

The Canelli brothers wanted to make lots of money. They wanted it now. In the underworld the rocket ship that could put you into the stratosphere of fat stacks was drugs. Of course, it was also the quickest, easiest way to end up dead or in prison. Oh, and there was that pesky prohibition against drug dealing that the Detroit Family insisted on clinging to. This didn't bother the Canellis at all. They were smart enough and tough enough to get away with it. The idea that the American Mafia had a prohibition on drug dealing was already well on its way to becoming a fairy tale by this time, anyway. Among others, the Gambinos in New York were getting fat and happy on heroin, and were looking for distributors. The Canelli brothers became one of their pipelines into the Detroit market.

This created an intolerable situation. To begin with, whatever the Boss of the Family ordered was ironclad law. He was like the general of an army. When he said "charge," you ran your ass up the hill. When he said "retreat," you ran your ass down the hill. There was no debate or wiggle room. As soldiers, "theirs was not to wonder why, theirs was but to do and die." Just as the army cannot tolerate flagrant insubordination, neither can the mob.

The connection to the Gambinos was another stone in the shoe. The Detroit Family had a long history of being ultra-territorial. They did not like outside influences. To have the most powerful of the New York Families assisting Detroit soldiers in a blatant defiance of the orders of the Detroit boss was an insult that could not be ignored.

The bigger problem, though, was one of "tax evasion." When they first started dabbling in drugs, the Canellis "kicked upstairs," or paid taxes, if you will, by claiming the drug income as income from other, permitted rackets. As they got more and more into it, though, they were making way more money than they could launder by claiming it came from other sources. So, they did what most criminals end up doing: They just didn't bother to pay their taxes, to either the IRS or the Family. This left the Boss with the liability of a drug bust royally fucking his criminal enterprise but without the benefit of being paid a cut. That shit don't fly.

Paul and Pete Canelli had to go. That was an etched-in-stone, non-negotiable deal. It fell to the Captain of the Downriver Crew to get it done, hard and fast. But, that was easier said than done. To begin with, the Canelli brothers were the main muscle of that crew. Jobs like this usually went to them. "Okay, boys, go whack yourselves" wasn't going to work.

Another problem was that once the Captain (whose name I never learned) started to try to get any of his other guys together to do the job, it would be oh too easy for word to leak to the Canellis. The hardest part about hitting a guy was finding an opportunity to actually pull the job off. In that sense, it's mostly an issue of logistics. What you want is a deal like that snowshoe hare I shot while hunting: He's just going about his usual business completely unaware, then bang, his head is blown off. If the Canellis knew there was a contract on them, it would make it damn near impossible to get at them. Worse yet, they could seek allies within their crew who were willing to join up with them, and, just like that, you have a civil war.

This was a perfect example of the kind of mess Tony Mano had set up the Cowboy Crew to deal with. As luck would have it, Vince already had a connection with the Canelli brothers. Vince, Big Ed, and, occasionally me, were in the business of ripping off drug dealers whenever an opportunity presented itself. Our primary targets were the "trap houses" where the cash from the street dealers got collected together and stashed, or sent on to a larger "bank." It goes without saying, such locations were prime targets for both the cops and other crooks, so they were well protected, mostly by being kept secret and moving locations often. The key to finding one was having some inside information.

The Canellis, being in the trade themselves, sometimes could develop such leads. They would pass them on to Vince for the double benefit of a finder's fee on the take and as a way to hurt their competition. It was a sweet deal for all involved. Well, except the poor saps that got raided, that is. But, they were mostly scumbag heroin dealers, so fuck them. Personally, I'm in favor of legalizing drugs. I mean, it's a dumb thing to do, to use drugs, but if someone wants to piss their money away and fuck up their life, what business is it of mine? The one exception I might make, though, would be on heroin. That's just nasty, nasty shit. Super addictive, and once a person is on it, about impossible to get back off. That's why we always considered heroin dealers to be the lowest of the low. It's also why it made so much money.

Anyway, Vince came up with a plan to set up Paul and

Pete for a hit, and, hopefully, make us some money along the way. He called up Paul, who was always more of the level-headed, down-to-business half of the partnership. He told Paul he needed help with a problem. This aspect is key. When dealing with a spiraling upward Icarus, always appeal to his ego. Vince claimed that we hit a trap house, but our intel must have been off, because instead of a pile of cash, all we found were two uncut kilos of heroin. In the heat of the moment, and not wanting the high-risk raid to be a wasted effort, we took the drugs. Now Vince was regretting that. He was scared shitless his uncle, or someone else, would find out, and he would get whacked.

He was hoping the Canellis would be willing to help him out and take the stuff off his hands. He acknowledged that he wasn't expecting full wholesale value, telling them, "I just need to dump this shit. Be as fair as you can with me." In exchange Vince insisted on three conditions. First, the deal needed to happen fast, the sooner the better. Second, he would only deal directly with Paul and Peter, if they felt like they needed to bring anyone else, fine, but they had to stay outside where they wouldn't see Vince. Third, it had to be done at a location Vince chose. Normally, this would be a major red flag on a deal like this. Vince sold it as he was so scared to even do the deal, it had to be "way out in the country, away from either crew's normal territory." Vince assured Paul he already had a safe, fairly convenient location scouted out.

They say timing is everything. If a deal like this had been offered to the Canelli brothers a few years earlier, they would have passed either because they couldn't raise that much dough right away, or it just seemed too much of a risk to deal with a guy they only sort of knew. If the deal had been offered a few years later, after the Icarus phase had waned and they were a bit older and wiser, they would have seen it as too good of a deal, and there must be a catch. As it was, they were having their egos stroked and their soaring greed and ambition stoked, so they went for it. Ambition is like medicine, too little or too much is a bad thing. Ambition is both the greatest producer and the greatest destroyer. In this case, it was the moment Paul and Peter Icarus decided to fly too high.

I don't know how Vince found the place he chose for the exchange. It was an abandoned farm out in Washtenaw County, kind of south of Ann Arbor. The old timer who had owned the place had passed away a few years before. His kids were squabbling over the inheritance. At least one of them was convinced that if they just held out a little longer, they could find a developer willing to pay big bucks to convert the land into a subdivision. The smart thing to do would have been to at least lease the land out for farming in the meantime, but they didn't bother. Meanwhile, every year that slipped by the land was costing them money in taxes, generating no income, the buildings were getting run down, and the land was losing value as farmland as the fields went increasingly wild and harder to reclaim. Like a pack of hyenas that find a dead elephant but then are so busy nipping at one another for a bigger chunk of the windfall that the carcass slowly rots away. Greedy dumbasses. They should have just found a real estate agent, taken the best offer, and be happy they got manna from heaven they had done nothing to earn.

Anyway, there was an old barn on the property, next to and kind of behind the old farmhouse. That's where the exchange was to go off. It would have been nice to go out there to map out the plan of attack, but Vince deemed it too risky. Even out in the sticks, he saw no point in taking the chance that the wrong busybody may happen by at the wrong time. Survival paranoia. I was still too green to have developed it, but had learned enough not to question it.

Vince held me back one evening at the construction site we were working at the time. As the last of the construction crew drove out, Big Ed drove in. I don't remember what kind of car he was driving. Big Ed seemed to have a different car about every two weeks. More of that survival paranoia—I guess.

Vince led us out into the construction site a ways, where there was some shade from one of the more complete houses being built, and where no one passing by could see us.

"Oh, planning it out cowboy style," Big Ed said, "I like it."

Vince gave a short laugh, "Yeah, all that's missing is a campfire and a big pot of beans."

Big Ed patted his stomach with both hands, "Yeah, I could eat."

"But beans?" Vince said.

"The key is to put some bacon in there while they cook," Big Ed said.

"Snacks would be lovely—maybe sandwiches…" I said.

Vince turned to me and smirked, "Good idea. Next time Joey brings sandwiches."

I gave a goofy smile and thumbs up.

Using a two-foot scrap piece of rebar, Vince scratched out a diagram in the dirt. Poking the ground with the end of the rebar, he explained, "Driveway. House. Barn." He then drew an arc from the driveway around to the back of the barn. "There's a dirt drive that goes behind the barn like this." Poking that spot on the diagram hard enough to leave pockmarks in the dirt. "That's our sweet spot. We park there. I'll tell the Canellis to park there too. That hides us from anyone driving by. Over here…" Tapping the left side of the barn, the side away from the house, he said, "there's a side door to the barn. That's where I'm gonna have the Canellis come in. You and me…" gesturing toward Big Ed, he went on, "we'll be waiting. As soon as they're all the way in, we pull .38 autos and start blasting. That should be the simple part." Vince paused to take a deep breath.

"Yeah. Simple is good," Big Ed said.

I was a statue.

"Okay, so the less simple part," Vince said, "I expect the Canellis are gonna have at least one other guy with them, maybe more…"

"Yeah, two would be what I would want," Big Ed said, "but maybe just one if I knew the guy enough to trust him. More than two and—"

Vince cut him off with a wave of his hand, "Back burner for now, I'll get back to that." He used the rebar pointer to give me a slight tap on the leg, "This is where you come in, ace sniper, slayer of bunnies. You're gonna be up in the loft of the barn with a deer rifle. From up there, you have complete control of the action behind the barn. As soon as you hear us pop off the first shot, you take out any guys waiting in the car. If there's more than one, get the driver first. Then—and really hear me on this—stay in position until me and Big Ed come out of the barn to signal you down. If something goes sideways, and one of the Canellis pops loose, you start chucking lead at 'em. You good?"

I just nodded.

"Okay, last part," Vince said, "worst-case scenario. Let's face it, these guys aren't dumb. If word somehow leaked to them, or if they just smell a rat, we may be in trouble. They may roll in with a small army and try to turn the tables on us." Tapping my leg again with the rod, "You're our alarm.

If they show up with a bunch of guys—well, only so many fit in one car—if they show up with more than one car, you start dumping rounds through the windshields before anyone even gets out. That will be the signal to me and Big Ed that the shit has hit the fan." He turned his attention to Big Ed. "We'll have shotguns stashed in the barn in case that happens. I figure the three of us inside a building with big guns can fight off a small army. Questions?"

I just shook my head.

Big Ed crossed his arms, looked up to the sky for two seconds, then lowered his head. "Get a semi-auto for Joey. If this thing goes OK Corral on us, I want him able to rain bullets."

Vince folded his arms and scuffed the ground with his shoe. "Yeah, good thought, good thought."

Vince set the meet for 10:30 Sunday morning when most of the good, salt-of-the-earth country folk would be in church and less likely to notice anything going on. We got there at 9:30 to set up ahead of time. The Canellis pulled in at exactly 10:30. Just one car. Good. Parked right behind the barn. Good. One driver, two guys in the backseat. Good. The two guys in the backseat got out and headed into the barn. I had never seen the Canelli brothers, but from Vince's description, it looked like them.

The driver stayed in the car. Engine running. I noticed he was wearing his seatbelt. That amused me. Remember good old Little Louie? Well, in addition to the major rules he taught me, he had all kinds of minor rules. One was about seatbelts. He was adamant that seatbelts should always be worn when driving around, but, as soon as you stop somewhere, you always take your seatbelt off. You never sit in a parked car with your seatbelt on, "Makes you a sitting duck," he insisted.

For the rest of my life, no matter where I was or what I was doing, I never sat in a parked vehicle with my seatbelt still on.

Anyway, I lined up the rifle sights of the thirty-aught six on the driver. It only took ten or fifteen seconds and shots started popping off in the barn. I slammed a bullet through the driver's side window. The driver slumped to the side and looked like he was done, but I ran another slug through him anyway.

It was only a few seconds more and Vince and Big Ed came out of the barn. Thirty-eight autos pointed at the car. Approaching the car with one on each side. Big Ed came up on the driver's side. I guess he was satisfied the driver was good and dead because he didn't put another round into him. Reaching in through the blown-out window he turned the ignition off and removed the keys. Moving to the back of the car he met up with Vince and they opened the trunk, took out a small black gym bag, and motioned for me to come down. The bag and our guns went into the trunk of our car. Me and Big Ed crouched down in the back seat. Vince put on a baseball cap and sunglasses and drove us out. That's all there was to it.

On a deal like this one of the tricky things is always what to do with the bodies. Ideally, it's nice if there's some way to just make them disappear. That's actually really hard to do. The risk of what evidence the cops will get from knowing there was a murder, along with how and where, has to be weighed against the risk of moving and trying to hide three big lumps of meat. Then there's also the matter of the car with a shot-out window and a huge bloodstain that would need to be moved and disposed of.

In this case, though, it didn't matter. The powers that be wanted the bodies found. They wanted it well known within the Family these guys got taken out. The next day Vince arranged for an anonymous tip to be called in to the Washtenaw County Sheriff's Office. He was going to wait longer, but this was in the middle of July, and as a matter of respect to the families of the recently departed, he didn't want the bodies too bloated and rotten and eaten on by vultures and shit. I always thought that was damn decent of him.

It was a good piece of work. Clinical. No Hollywood. I don't know how much money was in the bag, or how it got cut up. I was given fifteen grand as my cut. I couldn't help but wonder, though, who the poor sap I shot sitting in that car had been. I couldn't help but realize how easily that situation could have been turned around and it could have been me.

CHAPTER 8

Ripping off the drug dealers' trap houses tended to be an easy enough deal. Once we had a lead we would do just enough recon to confirm, and plan out how to hit the place. The actual raid was like a flashbang grenade, just bust in, yell some bullshit like, "Police! Search warrant! Everyone on the ground!" Then just cram the cash into bags and get the fuck out before they figured it out. One minute, tops. We always had guns, but never had to shoot anyone, just do a lot of threatening and a little shoving and kicking. We never talked to anyone about who, when, or where we had hit. That was paramount. The guys higher up the food chain in the drug ring always "put the word out on the street" they were willing to pay big for info on who hit them, and they never got so much as a hint. Tony didn't even know the details. Hell, afterward, we didn't even talk about it among ourselves. There was one deal like this, though, that was way, way more involved.

This was during what, at the time, was being hyped as "the crack cocaine epidemic." Huge amounts of money were being made with crack. This aspect of the drug trade belonged almost entirely to the black street gangs.

In a mere decade, they had come a long way. They started as just neighborhood groups of young men that would protect one another against other groups of young men, almost entirely just using their fists. As the drug trade came into play, and especially with the insane money crack brought in, those gangs became bigger, more organized, and an order of magnitude more violent. In the span of a decade they went from fists, to knives, to Saturday night specials, to the kind of military hardware the streets of Detroit hadn't seen since the Tommy gun days at the height of Prohibition. The gangbangers were all young, rash, and ultra-violent. We thought they were all insane, and they really just scared the shit out of us. Most of them seemed like they didn't care whether they lived or died. We didn't fuck with them.

Until we did. Maybe it was because there was so much money involved. Maybe it was because we had excellent intel and the set-up was ripe for a rip-off. What I really suspect, though, was that someone higher up wanted the place hit. Maybe the gangbangers pissed off the wrong guy. Maybe it was some kind of favor to someone in law enforcement. Maybe the old-timey Mafia just wanted to put the young up-and-coming thugs in their place. Don't know. Way above my pay grade. I was just a soldier. Charge!—and up the hill I go.

The gangbangers had found a sweet place to set up what I guess you would call either a high-volume trap house, or more like a bank, where the take from several trap houses was gathered together. They were set up in this old, two-story brick building, in…well, I remember exactly where, but based on how things turned out, even now, I don't want to say.

Anyway, the building had started out decades before as a

furniture warehouse. Some overly ambitious developer bought the abandoned warehouse and decided to convert it into three retail spaces below with office space above. Somewhere along the way he hit a snag and the project stalled. The gangbangers had moved into the middle space of the building. They had it set up as an absolute citadel.

First, they boarded up and barricaded the front doors. You would need a tank to get in from the front. This left the back door as the only entry. A narrow alley ran along the back, with the brick wall of the building on one side and a ten-foot chain-link fence on the other. On the other side of the fence was a large drainage ditch, almost more of a man-made creek, six feet wide and always with a couple feet of water in it. On each side of the drainage sat a hundred feet or so of open land, left to grow wild. The fence along the alley then turned and met up tight against the back corner of the building, then continued on straight back from the opposite corner, creating a shooting gallery for anybody trying to enter. The only way to get to that back door while the bank was operating would be to go through the back door.

But it got worse. The actual bank was on the second floor. A stairway led up there with a door at the top, but the gangbangers had barricaded it as well. The only access to the second floor was a freight elevator that had been used, originally, to move furniture between floors. The gangbangers had disabled the elevator controls on the first floor. While the bank was in operation, the elevator stayed up on the second floor and was only sent down to be loaded with cash when someone from downstairs called up to the people in the bank. At the end of the night the people working in the bank would ride down the elevator, leaving it on the first floor until the next time they needed to use the bank.

This did create the rather obvious problem of how to get back up to the second floor to get at the elevator controls the next time around. They came up with a creative solution. Someone had cut a one-square-foot access in the ceiling at just the right spot so a long extension pole could be poked up there and used to push the button to raise the elevator. While the bank was in operation, a large chunk of cement was slid over this hole from the floor above to block it off.

Now, it would appear there is yet one more problem: If the cops did get brave enough to run the gauntlet of crazy gunslinging gangbangers and get control of the first floor, the people on the second floor would be trapped and it would only be a matter of time before the cops found a way to dig them out. Ah, but not so fast, my friend! There was a small utility room toward the front of that middle portion of the building that served as the access to the warehouse's flat roof. There was a steel ladder and a hatch door that would allow the bank tellers to bundle up the money and escape up to the roof. Up on the roof they kept an aluminum extension ladder that could then be lowered down the far side of the building, into that fenced-in plot of overgrown land along the drainage ditch.

It really was a brilliant set-up. Well, that is, up to the point where someone figures out that what can work in one direction can just as easily work in the opposite direction. And, just like that, a system's greatest strength becomes its greatest weakness.

We had two things going for us straight away: One, the building was only used by the gangbangers on certain nights, and two, it was otherwise abandoned. This made it easy to get in and do some serious recon work. We started one fine Friday morning in mid-September. Me, Vince, and Big Ed drove an old pickup truck with a ladder rack on it up to the front corner of the building, next to the fence, and as far away from the back entrance as we could get. We put up an extension ladder and just climbed up there with buckets of tar, brushes, and a tool bag, like we were there to fix a leak in the roof. The tool bag was because we didn't know what the roof access hatch was going to be like and figured we were going to need to find some way to take it apart or jimmy it open from the roof side. In a stroke of luck, we found that the building was old enough that the roof access was just a sturdy wooden box with tar paper covering it, easily pushed aside from inside, or just lifted off from the roof.

Inside we found the layout was everything we had hoped for. The utility room didn't have a door, but its entrance was 180 degrees opposite the elevator, so someone could come down the ladder unseen, then spin around the corner and the elevator was about twelve feet away. From there it was another ten or twelve feet through an open doorway into the large room on the back of the building where the money was handled.

I worked the elevator controls to bring the elevator up, then Vince got in and I sent him down so he could check out the first floor. Meanwhile, Big Ed inspected every square inch of the second floor. He was pleased to see that while the original layout had included large archways in the brick walls to make the entire second floor, in essence, one space, the developer had gotten far enough in the project to brick over those openings, so that middle section really was only accessible by the elevator.

My job was to just stand next to the elevator and wait. When I heard Vince bang on the first-floor elevator door, I hit the button to bring him back up. As the elevator door opened, Big Ed was waiting. "Well?"

"About like you were told," Vince answered, "but not as much junk piled up on the stairs as I would like."

Big Ed pointed toward the heavy steel door that accessed the stairway. I hadn't even noticed, but it had been spanned by four evenly spaced two-by-fours, screwed down tight.

"Doesn't matter," Big Ed said, "The fucking SWAT team would take a while to get through."

"How does this end look?" asked Vince.

Big Ed ran his hand through his hair and let out a puff of air. "Well…and, shit, I hope I don't jinx it by saying—it looks…everything I could hope for." Putting his hand up in the halt position, "Stay there a sec." He walked back to the utility room, then came back around the corner with a mock long gun pointed at Vince. "Yeah…yeah, just like that. Depends how many guys are guarding…" He paused and looked up at the ceiling, then back at us. "I expect just one. Maybe two. Then three or four in the money room. With piles of cash, best to keep the smallest crew possible. At least one on the money will be packing." He paced back and forth a couple of times. "It's going to have to be hard and fast. No fucking around. No 'pretend we're cops' bullshit. Twelves and buckshot."

Vince touched his chin and nodded, "Yeah—really no choice there."

Back up on the roof Big Ed marched to the far edge of the roof. With hands on hips, he surveyed the brushy drainage area. Then he went to the back corner to make sure the blind alley created by the fence and building wall really was tight. He nodded. "Looks good." Rubbing his chin, he said, "The timing is tight, but I think we better hit this place fast. Tonight, if possible. God only knows how much longer they'll stick here. And those leaves," pointing toward the woods, he said, "going to be dropping soon. If they start spraying bullets, I want as much cover as possible." He folded his arms and stared at me and Vince. No need to ask. No objections.

It took some wrangling and cussing but we got our ladder set up on the other side of the fence, back into the brush enough that the casual observer wouldn't see it. From there we had to set up the other side of the entry and escape. Big Ed had already decided to enter the drainage from behind a strip mall on the other side of the ditch. He had brought a pair of cutters to make a hole in the fence on that side, but getting over there, found that someone had already cut an access. Crouching down to look through it, he saw no sign of recent use.

"Muskrat trappers," he said, more to himself than to us.

"Muskrat trappers?" I asked.

"It's fairly common for guys to sneak into places like this later in the fall to trap muskrats in the ditches," Big Ed said. "Someone that knows what he's doing can make an extra fifty bucks fairly easy with just a couple dozen traps and one weekend to run them."

The truck we used needed to be returned to Shillelagh's. When we got there Big Ed parked it back behind the buildings in the junk car lot. He dropped the tailgate and sat down. We had a quick planning session among the rust and weeds.

"Cowboy style, again, I see," I said.

"Hey that's right," Vince said with a playful smack to my arm, "Joey was supposed to bring sandwiches."

I just rolled my eyes.

"Hold on now, this is serious shit. How can we trust you to cover our asses on a deal like this if we can't even count on you for ham on rye?"

Fucking smartass. I held up my hands in surrender. "Tell ya what, if you agree to make the fire next time, I'll bring the steaks."

Big Ed broke in, "Now, now children. Plan your picnic later. Let's get down to it."

Big Ed's body went rigid and he gripped the edges of the tailgate so hard his knuckles turned white. "This is gonna be some serious shit, guys. Hard and fast—but smooth. I'm told there's a small army of bangers that guard the alley and first floor. Can't give 'em too much time. Don't know how well they're armed—"

"AKs?" Vince asked.

"Oh hell, hope not. That's some serious firepower. The bangers out west are using them regular, but I've not heard of the guys here getting them yet. Okay, so, you and me will handle the cash. I figure we have one minute, tops. Whatever we can grab in that amount of time; if there's more, leave it. Joey covers the elevator area. That much shooting, the cops are gonna roll. Bangers will keep 'em busy at first. I figure at least ten minutes for them to set up a wider perimeter, probably twenty, but I want us out on the road in less than ten. Any concerns?"

Vince shook his head.

I followed suit. I kept my concerns to myself: A pile of dough, shot full of holes, in jail, or some combination thereof? Only one way to find out.

Big Ed released his grip on the tailgate and set his hands on his knees, "Okay, good. But, there's one more issue. I've already kinda discussed this with Vince, so he's maybe prepared, but Joey—here's the deal: We can't slaughter—however many it's gonna take—and steal bags full of cash without some major fallout. The bangers are gonna be pissed, gonna do everything they can to try to find out who hit them. Cops will swarm. Local, probably state, and, hell, probably feds. Major heat. You and Vince need to get outta town. Right after. That night. Stay away a week minimum, maybe two. Now, I know this is fast, but—and no details, just yes or no—think you can handle that?"

"Yes."

"You sure? I mean, I get it, it's last minute."

"Yes."

"Okay, good. Don't tell anyone where you're going."

I nodded, "What about you?"

"I stay as our eyes and ears. I got all kinds of holes to hide in and all kinds of contacts to get info from. I'll let you and Vince know when the smoke clears."

We parked in the alley behind a closed store in the strip mall at 11:30 that night. In retrospect, we maybe should have cleared a pathway through the brush when we scouted the location that morning. It was rough going. We had to wade through the drainage ditch and deep, thick mud on both sides. There were these fucking blackberry bushes everywhere. Nasty, tearing thorns. We had flashlights but were trying not to use them, just turned them on and held our hands over the lenses to let out a tiny bit of light to try to avoid those ruthless thorns, or get untangled from them. We hadn't had a freeze yet either, so the mosquitos were vicious. By the time we made it to the ladder, between the bugs and the thorns we must have been down a pint of blood each.

Up the ladder and across the roof, slow and easy. As quiet as a mouse sneaking out from under the stove to steal kibble from the cat's bowl. I headed down the ladder and into the utility room first, then Vince, then Big Ed, who had to wait at the bottom of the ladder because there wasn't enough space in that little room for all of us. One deep breath. Game time.

I came out of the utility room and around the corner with the shotgun already on my shoulder. There was one guard controlling the elevator. I hammered him down with buckshot before he could even react. Vince and Big Ed rushed past me into the room used as the bank. A quick succession of shotgun blasts. Just like that, in less time than it takes to tell, we massacred five gangbangers. I did my job and stayed outside the bank to keep control over the elevator area. Meanwhile Vince and Big Ed started stuffing cash into duffel bags as fast as they could. There were various shouts from the first floor below. Someone was yelling frantically into a walkie-talkie broadcasting in the bank room, but I couldn't make out what they were saying.

Less than a minute. Whoever was talking on the walkie-talkie must have given a warning, or maybe it was just luck, but Vince and Big Ed came rushing out of the bank room with bulging duffle bags on their shoulders just in time. I guess the gangbangers had at least one AK-47. A barrage of bullets came ripping through the floor into the bank room. A blizzard of hardwood floor splinters filled the room. It was the kind of thing you see on TV or in a movie and it's so exciting and dramatic and all that shit, but when you're standing next to it and it's real, it's just scary as fuck. In all of human history I doubt there has ever been a time when three men went up a ladder faster.

We were fast enough. We managed to get across the roof, down the ladder, and into the brush before the gangbangers were able to sort out what was going on. We made no attempt to use the flashlights on our escape. We plowed right through the thorns and mud. We moved faster than the mosquitos could keep up. By the time we made it back to our car we were a muddy, bloody mess.

We decided to dump the shotguns into the drainage ditch as we made our escape, stepping on them to force them down into the mud. This was a calculated risk, but we figured the gangbangers wouldn't be able to drive over to that side fast enough to catch us even if they caught on right away and tried. Vince and Big Ed were both packing handguns for backup anyway, so it's not like we would have been sitting ducks. Full-length shotguns aren't very manageable once you're inside a car anyway; pistols work better. We intentionally drove out from the alley behind the strip mall next to a bowling alley, which, of course, was still open and busy at that time on a Friday night, so we could just blend in with the traffic coming and going from there.

It was about a thirty-minute drive from the job site back over to Shillelagh's. Dead quiet. Minds and bodies working overtime to climb back down off the adrenaline mountain. Not one of us said a single word the whole way over. I had my car parked there, packed and ready to go. I stayed at Shillelagh's just long enough to change into clean clothes, then get rid of the job clothes in a burn barrel Mack kept out back. From there, I headed north.

In a wide swath across the Northern part of Michigan's Lower Peninsula sits the Huron-Manistee National Forest, a massive chunk of public land. The nice thing about the National Forests is that you can just show up whenever you want, plunk down a tent anyplace you can get to, and camp without having to get any kind of a permit, or make any type of arrangements ahead of time.

So, that's what I did. I more or less just randomly picked a spot in the forest far enough from a main road to be private, but close enough to not be too hard to find in the dark. I managed to get there about an hour before sunrise, found a pull-off spot just off some unmemorable dirt road, hiked in about 150 yards, and found a nice, level, sandy spot under some jack pines to pitch my tent. (I still had all my camping gear left over from my time in Boy Scouts.) My plan was to just stay out in the woods long enough to establish at least a half-baked alibi. Then, after a night or two, to find a motel.

I ended up staying out in the woods all week. I loved it. I could walk all day and never leave the public land and never even see another human being. I went a solid week and never heard a siren wailing in the distance a single time.

I did some squirrel hunting. In the city you could just about hunt squirrels by walking up to them with a baseball bat, but not out in the country. Ghosts of the trees. You can sit dead still watching the same trees for an hour, then one will appear from nowhere. Just as quickly they can turn to smoke and drift away through the treetops. They are fun to kill. The best is when you shoot one out of the very top of a tree. They make the most satisfying plop when they hit the ground. About the best stew meat I've ever had. Nice, rich flavor and the meat doesn't get all mushy from long cooking like most meat does.

I also did some fishing. I got a hot tip from the lady at the little country store I was buying supplies from about a spot below a dam on the Au Sable River. She told me to put a minnow on a hook with two small split shots about a foot above and let that bounce around the rocks on the river bottom. I caught a bunch of rock bass. They are only about as big as my hand, but have a thin, white filet that fries up nice and crisp. Makes a superb fish sandwich.

After a week I called Big Ed to check in. The media was having a Roman orgy over the story. "Gang War!" The cops seemed convinced of that angle and were bringing in gangbangers left and right to grill them for clues. Even the gangbangers seemed sold on the idea; southeast Michigan saw a marked uptick in drive-by shootings and other such gang-on-gang violence. This caused the typical feedback loop. The more the gangbangers fought, the more convinced the cops and the media talking heads were that our raid had been part of a drug war. It became a self-fulfilling prophecy type of thing. Big Ed thought it was safe to come home.

I almost didn't. I seriously considered just never going back. Well, I mean, I would have to go back to get my cut from the raid and to clear out my safe deposit box, but after that I would have enough money to get by for a couple of years at least. I wanted to just stay out in the woods. At some level I knew I *should* just stay out in the woods.

But I didn't. I went back, and I stayed. I wish I hadn't done that. It *was* a big score. My cut was…well, what the fuck difference does it make? How much is enough to justify five cold-blooded murders?

Chapter 9

Ben Avery. Owned a smallish landscaping company. He kind of inherited it from his dad. Back in the '60s his father had taken the small family farm in Northville Township and converted part of it into a sod farm, then added a nursery growing trees and shrubs for the exploding suburban landscape trade. From there Ben took it the next logical step to skip the middleman and hired crews to install the landscaping directly. Over the course of a somewhat reckless youth and a nasty divorce, he had to sell off much of the farm, but still had the landscaping business. He had, in recent years, gotten that fairy tale second chance in life, marrying a beautiful, caring, sensible woman fifteen years his junior and having the most adorable little girl with her. Life was good.

You would think a wonderful family and a good enough business would be enough. For some unexplainable reason, it wasn't. Ben Avery was a neurotic mess. Jekyll and Hyde, but on a leash. Manic-depressive, but not quite at the dysfunctional level. Small business owners seem to be like this. I have often wondered if only assholes become small business owners, or if owning a small business turns you into an asshole. I believe it is mostly the latter. It's yet another of those great fantasies of the American Dream. Apparently, all kinds of shit involved "that isn't in the brochure" ends up giving all these guys their own special form of Self-Employed Psychosis.

What all Ben did, with or for who within the mob, I don't know, but it was always just a little dabbling here and there. Most recently he had been given a piece of one of the myriad of mob-controlled municipal contracts. This particular one had involved a "revitalization" of the Telegraph Road corridor. Ben's company got the contract to landscape the bland, nothing-but-boring-grass medians along a ten-mile stretch.

I was never on the money side of things, so I'm not entirely sure how the scam worked, but I think it mostly involved overselling, then under-delivering. So maybe Ben had in the contract to plant one thousand redbud trees of a certain size, then substitutes the next size down. The contract calls for six inches of hardwood mulch, Ben puts down four. It doesn't sound like much, but multiply that out over the course of thousands or hundreds of thousands of units, and it adds up. Meanwhile, the mob has the right people on the payroll, or whatever, so these little differences never get found out, and for that they get a cut of the extra profits (which, in essence, have been stolen from the hard-working taxpayers).

Within the world of organized crime, Ben existed at the outermost fringes. He wasn't even a small fish in a big ocean, he was a brine shrimp in a tidal pool. Every so often he got to mix in with the ocean fish, but just long enough to serve a purpose, then the tide went out and back into the isolation of average Joe tidal pool life he goes.

But Ben didn't see it that way. He became enamored with the romanticized image of the Hollywood mafioso. His fantasy became some kind of -otic/-osis delusion. He decided he *was* a gangster. He started throwing around weight he didn't have. He started bragging about connections and abilities that existed only within the la-la-land of his own mind. He made threats backed by thin air. He asked for favors that could never be repaid. He claimed power and prestige that were as real as the Emperor's New Clothes. He simply decided he was "mobbed up" and expected everyone to treat him as such.

Obviously, this kind of shit just can't be tolerated. A large part of it was the insult of a "stolen valor" type of thing, but it's worse than that. Even real mobsters weren't allowed to strut around flaunting it like this. Back in the old days, yes, at least to an extent, but not anymore. Especially after the RICO Act became law, low profile became the *modus operandi.*

Ben Avery "needed straightening out." Initially the job fell to Big Ed. Big Ed had a connection with the guy. Some years earlier Big Ed had done a five-year hitch at Jackson State prison on an assault beef. When he got out but was still on probation, Ben gave him a job as a foreman on one of his landscaping crews. This wasn't some bullshit, "no-show" job like you hear about mob guys getting sometimes, it was a legitimate job. Big Ed worked for Ben for about two years, and while he agreed the guy was a total nut-bag, he did genuinely like him. More than that, he really admired Ben's second wife, Amy, who he described as "a great lady." Now, some of you hear that and are having dirty thoughts. It wasn't like that. Big Ed knew he was a hideous ogre of a man and didn't even bother to hit on women. He got a hooker once a week. The way he looked at it, it was like going out to eat: He had a basic physical need and the most expedient way to satisfy it was to hire the job out.

Anyway, Big Ed went and explained to Ben that he needed to cut this shit out. Ben assured him he understood. That understanding lasted only about a week. Big Ed went to see him again for some real fire-and-brimstone-come-to-Jesus preaching. That lasted about three weeks. Big Ed made one last attempt. He told Ben in no uncertain terms this was his final warning, "After this it's out of my hands. I can't protect you here." Ben again promised he understood it was time to shut up and sit down. But like an addict who is so convinced today he no longer needs that needle, but then each passing day the urge gets stronger, and he relapses, Ben Avery was hopelessly addicted to that delusional persona he had created.

So that's when Big Ed brought me in. The problem was, though, he was being wishy-washy on what, exactly, he wanted me to do. "Straighten the guy out" may have meant something to him as a well-seasoned mob enforcer, but it didn't mean shit to me. After some aggravating back and forth I finally got fed up, "What are you asking me to do here, Ed, kill the guy?"

Big Ed was still struggling with it himself, so he took some time to answer, "Go talk to the guy. Feel him out. If you feel like he still isn't getting it…" And a deep sigh. "Yeah, take him out."

Still murky, but it seemed like that was as clear as the instructions were going to get. I told him I would get right on it.

Step one was to go see Mack for a drop gun. He opened the drawer of his office desk and took out a set of car keys, then led me out to his junk car area. Stopping at one of the rust heaps, he unlocked the trunk and rooted around inside. He came out with a big, clunky, snub-nosed .38 revolver. "These were so popular back in the '70s," he said. "No one wants the damn things anymore and they're a dime a dozen. They're shit for accuracy, but that's fine for doing up close work." He hefted the gun in his right hand, "They weigh about a ton, but that's good if you wanna use it as a club—if you decide to just fuck the guy up but not actually kill him." He swung the gun by the grip loosely so it hit his open left palm with a loud smack, "Like that—bust his fucking teeth right outta his head." Taking the pistol in both hands he extended his arms to point it right at my face, "Yeah, about peed your pants, eh? It's just a mean-looking piece of hardware—good if you decide just scaring the shit out of the guy is good enough."

Oh, nice of him to give me the opening. "Speaking of stuff like that…I'm… Well, I'm not real clear on what, exactly, I'm supposed to do."

"What'd Big Ed tell ya to do?"

"Straighten the guy out, he tells me. I asked what he meant. He says talk to the guy and if it still seems like he isn't getting it, whack him."

"Well, there ya go, then."

I tried not to fidget and look at my feet, but I did. "How the hell am I supposed to know? I mean—I don't wanna fuck it up—" I tried not to let my voice tremble, but it did.

Mack patted me on the shoulder, "Okay, kid, take it easy, take it easy. You watch too much TV. On TV, anyone makes the tiniest mistake, kablam, the boss whacks him. Ain't like that, kid. If it was, every one of us would be in the ground— ten times over! You got good instincts, kid, trust your gut."

I nodded, but was still looking at my feet.

Mack put his hand to his temple, "Look, if you wanna make it simple—Big Ed already gave permission to whack the guy—if you want simple, don't say nothing, just plunk the guy in the head and be done with it."

Step two was doing the surveillance work to figure out how and when I could get the mark alone. That turned out to be easier than I expected. The actual office for the landscaping business was the old farmhouse. Next to that was the old barn, now used as a garage for the business trucks. Scattered here and there behind the barn was an assortment of other outbuildings of various sizes and constructions, used to store this, that, and the other things needed for the landscaping crews. Off to the side was a large "storage area," which was really little more than a private landfill for all the trash the business generated. All of this was spread out over four or five acres, enclosed with a six-foot-tall chain-link fence. It was a simple matter to park in the strip mall next door, climb the fence, then find a convenient hiding spot in the mish-mash of outbuildings, equipment, and junk where I could spy on the office.

It only took a few nights for a clear pattern to emerge. After everyone else left for the day, Ben would stay another hour or two working in his office, then get in his mint condition white Ford Bronco parked next to the back door, and leave. On the third night, I decided there was no point dilly-dallying about it and it was time to just get the job done.

Big Ed had warned me that as part of his "gangster lifestyle" Ben had taken to carrying a gun. A .45 auto. A super-bad-ass-gangster gun. But being a large, heavy piece of artillery, instead of having it on him he usually kept it tucked down between the seats in that fancy Ford Bronco. On my way in to see him, I decided to check. The car door was unlocked. Dumbass. The gun was right there between the seats, just like Big Ed said. Moron. Well, might as well use it instead of that .38 in my pocket.

Before I went into the building I checked to make sure there was a round in the chamber. On TV and in the movies, they always show the shooter rack in a bullet after he walks into the room. Good for dramatic effect, but bullshit. It is asinine to carry around a gun that you may need to use at a moment's notice without a live round already in the chamber. I mean, seriously, who's that dumb? Pull your piece, flip the safety off, and let the lead fly.

I had never shot a .45. I wondered how much it would kick. I wondered how big of a hole it would blow in good old Ben. I figured it could just about blow a guy's head off at close range. I figured that, seeing as that Ben was a family man, I should shoot him in the chest so his wife at least had the option of an open-casket funeral. I mean, even when you do need to kill a guy, no point in being a dick about it.

I slipped in and surprised Ben, sitting at his desk. His eyes about popped out of his head as I came through the door with that .45 pointed at him. He stammered a little like he was starting to say something, but I cut him off, saying, "Shut the fuck up. Don't say one fucking word. Sit still. Keep your hands on the desk where I can see them." I sat down at a chair across the desk from him and put the butt of that .45 on the desktop, barrel pointed at his chest, my finger on the trigger. Then I just stared at him, letting an awkward silence smother him. Finally, thick with annoyance, "What the fuck is wrong with you? Why are you so insistent on having us kill you?"

He started to stammer again, but I stopped him with a quick bang of the gun butt on the desk, "Rhetorical question, asshole. Three times already…*three* fucking times you've been warned. The last time our mutual friend tried to make you understand if you didn't straighten out someone like me was coming. Now it's my fucked-up problem. I don't like problems. When I have a problem, I look for the easiest solution. Seems to me the easiest solution is to use your own gun to blow a hole through you big enough to drive a Mack truck through."

His face had gone sickly pale. Eyes wide and wet. Beads of moisture streamed down his face. How much was sweat and how much was tears, I couldn't tell. Shaking like a washing machine with an unbalanced load. Very pitiful. Really just a damn depressing sight.

On the wall behind him was a large portrait of what, I expect, was his wife and daughter. I don't mean a large photo, I mean an actual, professionally painted portrait. I don't remember what his wife looked like, other than that she was a beautiful woman, but his daughter—standing in front of his wife. Looked to be four or five. Joyful blue eyes. Long, dark hair in pigtails. She was wearing a lightweight summer dress, white cotton with pink polka dots. Holding a bouquet of goldenrod. The most adorable little smile. About the cutest little girl you could imagine. Up there on the wall, just staring right at me as I was one gentle squeeze away from killing her daddy.

Ben took my pause as his opening. In a gush came the long stream of begging, pleading, promising—I don't remember what all he vomited out. I didn't listen past the first bit of blubbering. You might think that someone like me, I mean a guy that did work like I did, would get off on this kind of thing. Watching a man squirm as he begs for his life. What a power trip! But no, I hated that kind of thing. It didn't make me feel powerful, just nauseous. I almost shot him just to shut him up.

But I didn't. After calmly explaining to him what would

have to happen if I had to come back, and more hemorrhaging from him of promises and assurances, I let him go. I'm not really sure why. Maybe it was the portrait of that angelic little girl staring right at me. Maybe it was a tinge of regret over the pointlessness of the murders I had already committed. Maybe I was going soft. Maybe I was just turning into a big ole pussy.

I briefly considered keeping Ben's gun to give to Mack to add to his stash. I realized, though, that wouldn't be a wise choice. As much of a "gangster" as Ben may have thought he was, I had little doubt the gun was legally purchased and registered, which made it about worthless to real gangsters. Mack would have to carefully obliterate the serial number, one letter and number at a time, with a drill bit. More trouble than it's worth. Easier ways to get a clean gun.

On my way out I returned it to Ben by smashing it through the driver's side window of his posh Ford Bronco. Then like those squirrels I was hunting in the woods up north, I just turned to smoke and drifted away.

Well, it worked. Ben finally got the message. He shut the fuck up and sat down. My mission was a success, for the thugs I represented, that is, while for me, personally, not so much…

It was not even quite two months later when Big Ed showed me the newspaper story, without saying a word. Shocking, horrific, tragic. Local businessman kills wife and young daughter, then turns the gun on himself in a murder-suicide. I couldn't bring myself to actually read the whole story. If they said he did it with a .45 auto, I think I would have lost it.

Now, I have no doubt a shrink would assure me this wasn't my fault. He would tell me the guy obviously had much deeper mental illness issues. Certainly, there's no way of knowing if my encounter with him had anything to do with pushing him over the edge. But for me that wasn't the problem. My gut feeling going into the deal was to kill Ben and be done with it. If I had, his wife, and—mother of God!—that adorable little girl, would still be alive. I cut the guy a break. I showed mercy. And this was the payoff. "No good deed goes unpunished," or whatever fucked-up, jaded cliche you want to toss out.

In my mind I knew there was no way I could have known. But in my heart, every year at the end of summer when I drive by a field of blooming goldenrod, I can't help but feel a little sad.

Chapter 10

It's odd the stupid little shit that we whip up into a dramatic froth. It's odd the insignificant crap we glom onto and decide it's a major problem. I suppose it's just human nature. I suppose a shrink would say when we do this it is because whatever the little issue is, it actually represents some deep-seated physiological problem.

Humans seem to have a happiness quotient. We are only capable of so much happiness, and once that limit is reached, we just invent some bullshit problem. This probably comes from the long expanse of time we evolved in, during most of which, real life-and-death problems were a near-daily occurrence. Now in our marshmallow and bubble-wrapped modern world, our ancient minds just don't know what to do. It's like a race car designed to whip around the track at two hundred miles per hour, stuck in first gear puttering down a tree-lined residential lane. Our poor ancient brains just can't help but to keep mashing down that gas pedal even if all it does is rev up the engine producing nothing but noise and exhaust fumes.

Throughout all of this I was still working construction. I ended up being sort of a floater, working on whatever crew needed help. I became a real jack-of-all-trades, learning carpentry, siding, and roofing skills in addition to the masonry experience. I still worked closely with good old Serge, though, at least twice a week. I guess we sort of became friends. I mean, to the extent that I seem capable of it. In my entire life I'm not sure I ever actually formed a real friendship with anyone. Serge was kind of like a grandfather to me. As I said before, I had a deep respect and admiration for him. We didn't socialize outside of work, except for the one time he invited me to his fortieth wedding anniversary party. Like I said before, I usually find social engagements like this to be one of Dante's levels of hell in *Inferno*, but I couldn't say no. To borrow from Machiavelli again, I went to Tony's party out of fear, I went to Serge's party out of love.

Serge met the love of his life, Maria, while a teenager in Italy. After he moved to the States he remained steadfast to her, maintaining a long-distance relationship for two years until he felt like he was making enough money to bring her over. Theirs was a relationship of simple but elegant love. The kind of thing you see and it's just beautiful to look at, like a sunset or a flower. The kind of marriage that makes you believe there must really be a God to have so perfectly welded two together as one.

During the celebration one of Serge's sons made a toast. It was something like, "True wealth can only be measured by the quality of the relationships we forge while upon this Earth, so here's to Sergio and Maria, the richest people in the room!" I couldn't disagree. Serge was the true, simple, honest, American Dream. People like him always have been and forever will be the foundation that holds up the world. It is said the meek shall inherit the Earth. Why would they want it? They already own Heaven.

Maria took a shine to me. She seemed convinced I was a fine young man and it was time for me to find the right girl and settle down. She delighted in tromping me all around the room to meet every one of her young, single, female relatives. I am capable of being properly social, if not outright charming, but it comes at great effort. I guess I took a shine to Maria too, because I was happy to go along with it and it was easier than usual to muster the effort.

A few of the girls were reasonably attractive. One in particular, Theresa, I think it was, was tempting. I don't usually go for redheads—I don't know why—but she just had one of those brickhouse, bodda-boom bodies that makes a man think of just one thing, done with great vigor. We did flirt a bit, but I didn't pursue it. I had too much respect for Serge, and now too for Maria, to try to bang their grand-niece. These were good people. I liked them. The kind of people you might say, "I would die for," but in the case of someone like me, the flip side of the same coin was, "the kind of people I would kill for."

Anyway, it was a couple months or so after that and I'm working one day with Serge, and he just seems out of sorts. He was usually a happy, upbeat kind of guy, but that day he was just sort of mopey. I asked him about it. He said he was having some trouble with his next-door neighbor.

Apparently, the guy had recently gotten a dog. A great big German Shepherd. A hyperactive, demon-possessed hellhound. "It a… It stays in the neighbor's yard, you know. It's a… Well, there's a fence, you know," he said, talking with his hands as much as his mouth, "But anyone come near the fence—it run over and jump up and down barking, snarling," he bounced up and down to demonstrate. Both his hands and mouth started talking louder, faster. "He's already plenty a big enough standing—head and shoulder over the fence already. Then he gets a bouncing and… What's that movie about that crazy dog? That scary movie?"

"*Cujo*? Stephen King?"

"Yeah, yeah, *Cujo*. That's what I got now. Cujo next door."

"That does seem annoying."

"Oh, yeah, but for me, it's okay. But my little grandkids! Oh! You know I build for them this very nice play set. I got the swings, the slide, the curly kind, you know, and the straight kind, and a castle. And once they loved it, but now—too scared. I tell them, dog is fine, won't come over fence and get them, but, you know, they're just little kids. They just see— what was it?…oh, Cujo. They just see Cujo and he looks and sounds so terrible. And, you know—just little kids—"

Serge's house sat one house in from the corner. This neighbor was the one with the corner lot. When his grandkids were visiting, one thing Serge always did was to take them for a walk around that corner and down a block to a gas station with a convenience store. "So, you know," Serge said, slower, sadder, "my grandkids come, I spoil them. We go on our walk. I buy them candy bar, chips, Faygo pop. But now? No good! Sidewalk goes right by other side of yard. Cujo dog comes running over, jumping up and down, arr arr, arr! They're just little kids—too scared! So, now, they come over, nothing to do. They don't want to visit no more. My wife— my sweet Maria, she needs to see her grandbabies. It just… Oh, it just so breaks my heart."

"So, being the decent human being I know you are, you talked to the neighbor about this?" I asked.

"Oh, yeah, sure, sure. He was… He wasn't a bad guy about it, but…he doesn't see—he says, 'yeah the dog is hyper, but harmless. He never gets out of the yard. He's actually very friendly,' you know, like that. So—"

"Have you considered putting up a privacy fence on your side?" but I realized as soon as I said it, it was a dumb question.

"But you know how it is in my neighborhood. The front, it's very short, but then the side…two hundred feet back that goes. Holy Mother!, a small fortune that cost me. And still, arr, arr, arr on the other side. Still scary. And still no help on the other side. No walks. No candy and Faygo pop."

I couldn't think of anything to say to help him. I hoped just letting him vent was helpful. Still, it gnawed at me. He was stuck. Old-timey Catholics like Serge accepted stuff like this as the type of suffering one must faithfully endure. I think the general thought process is something along the lines of the more you suffer on Earth, the more you are rewarded in Heaven. People like this actually seem like they *want* to suffer because if they have too easy of a life, they will go to Hell. So, Serge saw it as just a cross he had to bear.

I didn't. Fuck that. The mixer in my brain got cranked up to high. A cup of milk and a dash of sugar got worked up into a big bowl of whipped cream. If anyone was going to put up a fence, or build a kennel, or do whatever to deal with this fucking dog, it should be the goddamned neighbor, not Serge.

At this point in my life I had come to the conclusion that there was one thing I was truly good at. One thing I had a natural talent for. One innate gift, whether from God, or, perhaps, from Lucifer. In the simplest terms, I had a real knack for using fear and violence to convince people to do things they otherwise wouldn't. I fully intended to go see the neighbor and bring him around to my way of thinking. Since this kind of deal usually goes better with two guys, I mentioned it to Vince, to see if he was interested in helping out. That turned out to either be a really good idea, or a really bad one, depending on how you look at it.

Vince jumped on the idea—that is, in the way you jump on the brake pedal when a puppy darts into the road in front of your car. He read me the riot act, "Sorry, buddy, but no. Maybe if the guy was selling drugs on the corner, or something like that, but just your average law-abiding citizen—um, no, this shit doesn't work that way. He *will* go to the police, either after you threaten him, or, certainly, if he gives you shit about it and you have to bust him up. It *will* end up blowing up in your face. Then what? You willing to face a felony assault rap over a fucking dog? If you were Tony and one of your guys went off the reservation and got pinched on some bullshit felony, what would you do? With what you've done and what you know, don't you think that makes you a major liability? Over a fucking dog? You have to understand, Joey, what makes you so valuable is that you have no criminal record and no one knows who you are. You're a fucking ghost. That's pure gold, baby! And you're willing to throw that away *over a fucking dog*?!"

Of course, I knew he was right. Not that that actually helped any. Emotion is high trump. When emotions stampede logic gets trampled into the dust. What really irked me, though, was the realization that I had all this power but wasn't allowed to use it. It's like you're a millionaire, but have to eat SpaghettiOs every night for dinner. What's the fucking point of having all that money then? I was this bad-ass mob enforcer but I couldn't help out a friend dealing with some asshole neighbor? What was the point then? The money? I did have a lot more of it than I would have just from working a regular job. By that time I had it piled up in three different safe deposit boxes at three different banks. The reason it mostly just sat was because I didn't really have much use for it. The way it works for most people is you get all this money then use it to buy expensive stuff to show off to everyone else and raise your social status. For me, the less people noticed me, the happier I was, so that wasn't a motivation for me. Which, again, raised the "what's the point?" question. It's like struggling to climb to the top of a mountain and once you get there you find yourself looking all around and realize there's nothing there you actually want.

I continued to stew on it. One day I was sitting with Mack in his office and started bitching about it. He listened a bit, then, in his typical, gruff way, cut me off, "Jesus-Fucking-Christ." And he walked out of the office through a side door that led to a storage room. I heard him shuffling and banging around in there for a minute or two. He came back with this ancient-looking ball-peen hammer that looked like it had spent the past few decades in the bottom of a toolbox. "Here you go. One night when no one's around, you walk up to that fence. When that dog comes over and sticks his head over the fence to bark at you, wham!" And he slammed the small end of the hammer down on the open palm of his left hand. "Straight down, right on the top of his head. Right between the ears. Put some oomph into it. Don't limp wrist it! Done right it will hit him harder than a bullet. Turn his brain into pudding. Won't feel a fucking thing, just lights out." Then he tossed the hammer into my lap and walked out without another word.

Now, I already know what most people are thinking by this point. Now who's being emotional? There are a great many people out there who would sooner put me in jail for killing a dog than for killing a drug dealer.

I like dogs just fine, they're cool animals and all that, but animals aren't people. Oh, but pets give you "unconditional love." So basically, they don't judge you. Even though you're a fucked-up asshole, they love you just the same. Look, I hate to break it to you, but the reason for that is because they lack the mental capacity to judge you. It isn't so much unconditional love as it is ignorant love. What's really happening is the love of the owner is being reflected back to him from the pet. It's only slightly more evolved than the special relationship a little kid has with the Teddy Bear or security blanket he's inseparable from. A cup of reflected love, a teaspoon of true affection from the animal, and a big heap of self-delusion. All of which is fine. We all have and all need our own personal self-delusions. The issue comes when you try to force your delusion into my reality.

So, yes, I decided to whack the goddamn dog. I just needed to work out the logistics. At night, obviously. Also, on a night I knew Serge and Maria wouldn't be home. Part of this was the risk one of them would just happen to see me. The bigger part was I wanted to make sure Serge wouldn't be accused of doing the deed, so I had to make sure he had a strong alibi.

This left two possible nights. I knew Serge had his bowling league every Wednesday night. Maria always went along. She didn't bowl, but would go to visit with the wives of the other bowlers and gossip while they cheered their men on. The other option was Friday night when Maria went to play bingo in the gym of Madonna College, over in Livonia. Serge would go along to also play a little bingo, but mostly to go outside with the other husbands to smoke cigars and bullshit. I decided on Wednesday night.

It rained that night. That is always a big advantage on a deal like this. Fewer people around. Less likely people will notice what's going on outside. It was, more or less, just like Mack had said. I just walked along the fence on the sidewalk side of the yard until the dog came ripping over and stuck his head over the fence to bark at me. I put some oomph into it. I cracked him good and solid right in the middle of his head. One dull thud, and I knew I had done it right. His body went rigid, then he fell on his side. His hind legs flailed while his whole body convulsed. Blood came pouring out of his ears and nose. A lot of blood. Maybe as much as a gallon. It was apparent he wasn't coming back from it. Then I just tossed the hammer into the yard, lowered my head to obscure my face, and calmly walked the two blocks back to where I had parked my car.

I never said a word about it to Serge. He never mentioned the dog issue ever again. It was as if it had never happened. I imagine he suspected it was me. He was observant enough and smart enough to have figured out by that time that I was involved with Tony Mano in some way other than just as a helper on his construction crew. But that was none of his business. He didn't need to know. He didn't want to know. He would never condone such behavior. He simply didn't live in that world. Maybe I forced my delusion into his reality. Or did I force my reality into his delusion? Shit—it can be hard to tell sometimes.

Chapter 11

I can't remember the little prick's name. It was something really common like John Smith or Jim Jones or something like that. I just called him Little Napoleon. He was short, like maybe five foot two. And he did bear a striking resemblance to portraits you see of Napoleon Bonaparte, that is if you lightened the hair some and added a cheesy '70s-era porn star mustache.

He was, sort of, an emperor in his own right. During most of the 1970s and 1980s he owned the lion's share of the pay phones in the Detroit Metro area. If you dropped a dime or a quarter into a pay phone anywhere near Detroit during those two decades, it was probably one of his phones. In 1989 he turned fifty-five and decided to retire. He sold out for somewhere in the neighborhood of ten to twenty million dollars, depending upon who you ask, but was a multi-millionaire regardless.

What really made him Napoleon-esque was his massive ego. He considered himself the quintessential American success story. A brilliant businessman. A risk-taker. A tough and savvy negotiator. A banty rooster strutting around the barnyard and crowing from the fence post, "Look at me! Look at my success!" I suppose, at least to an extent, it is human nature to see our successes as being because of what we did, while our failures are the fault of some outside force beyond our control. I don't doubt the guy was smart, tough, and hard-working. So what? So were a thousand other guys who didn't end up millionaires for it.

The truth of the matter was a good-sized dose of luck helped him along. He got into the business while pay phones were a fairly cheap investment. In the early '80s as pagers became popular, pay phone use exploded. Then he sold out just before cell phones took off and effectively killed the pay phone business. Of course, if you were to ask Little Napoleon, he would claim it was his brilliance that allowed him to ride that brief economic wave with near-perfect timing.

Anyway, he retired and moved up to Traverse City. This allowed him to be a big fish in a small pond. He was rich enough to be in the top tier of society there. And he made sure he had the nice house, fancy cars, boats, and twenty-year-old, blond, blow-job babes to show it off. But he also made sure to sprinkle a little cash on every charity and fundraiser in the region, making himself somewhat of a local hero. Little League team needs new uniforms? Done! Local animal shelter is having a pet food donation drive? Send over a truckload! He managed to get his picture in the paper about once a month for some "good deed" or another. All of this was, of course, to feed his own ego. They say you can't buy love, but you most certainly can buy a good reputation.

It only took a year and a half and this started getting old. He was, after all, Little Napoleon, and he had to find new lands to conquer. He somehow linked up with the owner of Lakeland Concrete Company. They were a decent-sized regional concrete company covering most of what is called central Michigan, but were not in the Detroit market. Little Napoleon put a chunk of his cash into the company as a partner. He was confident he had the connections to get into the Detroit market where he could double his money with one good contract.

The Detroit metro area, at the time, (and probably now, and probably forever) always went through an insane amount of concrete on road projects alone. Part of this was just due to growth in the area and new road construction, but much more of it was the constant need to fix existing roads. Detroit, compared to other northern areas, doesn't get all that much snow. But, when they do, they assault it with military-style might and precision. After a blizzard you could fly a plane over Michigan and clearly see Wayne County (which makes up the bulk of metro Detroit) as the dark area in a sea of white. Untold tons of rock salt. An armada of plow trucks. Both are good to get the cars moving in the short term, but both are pure hell on concrete.

So, there was an obscene amount of money in play, and where there's that kind of cash, organized crime is going to find ways to get their tentacles into it. According to Mack, it was a major source of revenue for the Detroit Family. I don't know how far this went, but the point is that to get a contract to supply concrete for a road project it would be helpful to have a mob connection and a willingness to play by their rules.

Little Napoleon already had such connections. Pay phones are an all-cash business. This is very attractive to criminals. As I understand it (again, according to Mack), during his reign as the pay phone emperor of Detroit, Little Napoleon assisted various mobsters in laundering their ill-gotten gains. In a nutshell, he "sold" large blocks of pay phones to mobsters on paper. This allowed them to launder their dirty money by claiming it as income from pay phone routes. Meanwhile, in reality, Little Napoleon still maintained those phones and his guys collected the actual money they generated. It was a relatively easy matter, then, for Lakeland Concrete Company to get added in as a supplier on one of the mob-controlled paving contracts.

Again, I was never on the big money side of things, so I'm speculating some, but basically the way the scam worked was by setting up a situation where the concrete supplier could get paid for supplying more than was actually delivered. If each load is just 5 percent short or the contractor is credited with just a few more loads each week than were actually delivered, it's easy to see how fast that can snowball into a pile of extra profits. The key to it, though, is always strictly controlling things to maximize profits while still keeping it subtle enough to not raise red flags and blow the scam.

The first problem Little Napoleon caused was to violate these strict controls and boost his own profits by shorting the contract beyond the accepted limits. Each time he was warned about this he ignored it. When warnings turned to flat-out threats, he basically told the mob to fuck off. He was a high-profile, well-respected businessman who lived well outside of Detroit, and the mob couldn't touch him.

But, even this level of audacity isn't as dangerous as the movies and TV shows often make it out to be. It's just a run-of-the-mill business dispute, so the mob's recourse is just to stop doing business with that supplier and take the next hungry guy in line who's willing to play by the rules. So, that's what was done. That's when Little Napoleon made his second, and much more serious, mistake.

Little Napoleon did not accept this. Lakeland Concrete Company *would* continue on as a supplier on the project, and *would* get future contracts, or he was going to rat them out. Yes, the little shit actually had the gall to try to blackmail the Detroit Mafia. This was a mortal sin. It was like that banty rooster deciding to chase the farmer out of the barnyard. At first, the farmer backs off, but only long enough to sharpen his hatchet and wait for a chance to snatch up that little bastard and turn him into chicken soup.

As I understood it, word came down from the Boss himself. Little Napoleon needed to go to the guillotine, quickly, but with the utmost secrecy. This created the first two logistical nightmares that would need to be sorted out. On TV and in the movies, the Don says, "whack the guy" and an army of highly skilled assassins hits the streets and the guy's dead the next day. In reality, that isn't even close. Taking out some average, low-level fellow thug usually involved at least a few weeks of cat and mouse until the right opportunity presented itself. Getting at a high-profile "civilian" usually took months or even years, if it could be done at all.

The second part of the problem was that this was a respected, wealthy, connected businessman. There was going to be a major investigation, likely involving the resources of the state police, and, probably too, the FBI. Along the way, Little Napoleon's mob connection was going to be discovered. This had to be a very clean hit, done such that the trail of breadcrumbs couldn't lead back to any of the top guys.

It was at this point that I was brought in. Initially, I was just to see what kind of recon work could be done to try to figure out a way to actually get the job done. This is when the next set of logistical nightmares became evident. To begin with, Traverse City is four hours away from Detroit, so an eight-hour round trip, minimum. I would have to travel there and camp out in a motel room, or something like that, for days or weeks at a time.

The bigger problem, though, was that Little Napoleon lived in an ultra-high-end gated community. To get in, you had to stop at a guard house where your name, license plate number, and who you were going to see was recorded. So, it wasn't going to be possible to just drive into the neighborhood and watch his house. Sitting outside the gates to watch for his car and tailing him wasn't going to work either. In a well-populated area, you can easily find ways to hide in plain sight, but in a small-town setting like this, I would be sure to draw suspicion. I was in over my head.

But, the whole point of organized crime is to gather together people and resources to accomplish what an individual can't do alone. As it was, Mack wasn't just good at getting the various stuff needed to do jobs, he was also skilled at getting background information and at planning.

After doing some research, he had me meet him at his office, "I think I got a way to at least get your foot in the door to start gathering the needed intel. Come with me." He led me out into the garage area and over to a workbench. Putting on his reading glasses, he bent over a map laid out on the workbench. Tracing his finger over the map, he got his bearings, "Okay, here we go. That gated community sits all along the east side of this lake." Tapping the spot on the map, he continued, "Now, let's see…so over here is Traverse City, so it's out in the country a little ways."

He returned his gaze to the lake and tapped it with his finger again. "Now, get ready for me to educate your dumb ass. Here's the deal: All of the lakes in Michigan are natural formations, left over from the last ice age. Because of that, the waters themselves are considered public property. What I mean is, while the land around the lakes can be private property, the open water itself belongs to everyone. So, technically, if there's someplace to put in a boat, you can boat right over to this guy's place, and you ain't trespassing until you get off the boat. But, I think there's an easier way."

Moving his finger down to the south end of the blue blob on the map, he tapped there, twice. "A marina here. The same developer put it in when he built fancy-pants land. You know, rich folks got boats—need someplace to get 'em fixed, store 'em in the off-season, so makes sense. Now, more schooling: The state don't like when fancy people buy up all the land around a lake and block us common folk from the public waters. So, to swing the deal to build the marina, the developer had to put in a public boat launch, connected to it, here," he said, and traced his finger over the map to show its location. "So, at least it's a place you could legally park without looking too suspicious, and possibly gain access into the community."

Mack reached under the map and pulled out a smaller map, placing it on top of the first. "So, now, this is a map of the gated community itself. As you can see, the houses sit all along here, not right on the water. There's a…well, kind of a low ridge that runs all along there…so, the houses sit up on that, look down on the lake. Let's see…" He moved his finger to the legend at the bottom corner of the map. "Looks like, maybe two hundred yards from the houses to the lake. These hash marks," he said, pointing, "those are steps that go down from each house to this…well, a terrace I guess you'd call it, that runs all the way along here, below the ridge the houses are on. That's where all the richy-riches have a…outdoor entertainment area, I guess you'd call it. You know, swimming pools, tennis courts, a big patio, shit like that. Some place to have their swanky outdoor soirees, you know. Then," pointing to another set of hash marks, he said, "another set of steps that go down to a little strip of beach. Then, of course everyone's got a dock, or two, or three, for their boat, or two, or three."

He drew his finger back and forth across the edge of the lake, "So, this—let's call it the beach area—that goes all along here. So, here's how it goes in communities like this: Each strip of beach is privately owned, it goes with the house, you know, but it's common practice that all the residents can use the strip of beach right along the lake, it's, sort of like, treated like common property. You know, like for jogging, dog walking, romantic strolls, or whatever. And then I got you…" He lifted the maps aside to expose several more sheets of paper. He flipped through them. "Shit, ain't here. But I got it…maybe in my office still. Anyway, I got you the name of the guy that owns the house about ten doors down from your guy's place. The way I figure it, you sneak in from the marina/public access area and just jog along the beach. Anyone asks, you have a name to drop. He's your uncle, say, and you're staying with him for a few days."

"And if that doesn't work?"

"Probably they'll just call security to bounce your ass. Worst case, the cops come and give you a trespassing ticket. No big deal."

"Looks like it's a ways from the boat launch to this guy's house."

Mack looked back at the map. He held his index finger and thumb apart over the scale in the legend, then transferred his measurement to the map. "Yeah, looks like—well, figuring for the curve of the shore, I'd say a little under a mile."

I nodded and shrugged, "Well…yeah, at least it's something…worth a try."

So, I headed north to Traverse City. The first two days just involved cruising around the public boat launch every few hours to scout that out. This was late April, spring in southern Michigan, but still more like winter up north. I was pleased to find that most of the ice was already out on this particular lake and there were even a few die-hard fishermen already venturing out. This was good in that it helped me blend in some.

The marina was already up and going for the year, busy getting things ready for the fast-approaching boating season. I noted that they were always closed up tight by six p.m., though. Better yet, behind their building was a great mish-mash of parked boats, piles of boat parts, stacks of pallets, and other such cover that could be used to sneak over to the fence that divided the gated community from this realm of the lowly commoners. I also decided my best option was going to be to park behind the marina where my car would be more hidden. I figured with a public area like a boat launch the cops probably cruised through every so often and my car just sitting there for hours at a time each night was going to look fishy.

The first night went well. Just scale the fence, then follow it down to the shoreline, and make my way along the lake. There was plenty of natural light reflecting off the water and the beach was made up of this bright white sand. At first I thought it was some fancy shit the rich folks had trucked in, but it extended so far up the slope it must have been natural. The first trip in I had myself outfitted in an all-black jogging suit for camouflage, but after that switched to light gray, which actually blended in better.

The set-up was better than I had hoped for. Between the beach the terrace above sat a natural area allowed to grow up with clumps of tall grass and bushes. Looking out from the backs of the houses gave a clear view of the lake, but only a patchy view of the beach itself. Whenever I felt like I was in one of those open patches, I made sure to go into full-on jogger mode, the rest of the time I just walked. By counting the number or stairways coming down to the beach I was able to get a good guess on which house I was looking for. Then I had to sneak up to the front to confirm the address, but only on that first night.

From there it was just many long hours of being huddled in the darkness, watching. I did have one thing going for me straight away: The whole point of having a fancy house on a lake is to take advantage of the scenic view. So, the entire back of the house was a series of large windows and a sliding glass door that led out to a deck that spanned across the entire back of the house. As long as the lights were on inside, I could just hunker down in the dark and watch everything going on in the house.

I had hoped to establish some kind of regular travel pattern that would allow a shooter to ambush the mark as he came home, like in that toenail moon hit I did. That didn't look promising. He didn't seem to have a regular pattern, and worse, when he came home, he opened the door to his attached garage by remote control, pulled into the garage, and then immediately closed the door behind him. That didn't leave much to go on. I headed home to sit down with Mack and hash out the options.

I met with Mack at his office at Shillelagh's, as usual. He

wasn't about to discuss any incriminating details in his office, as usual. It was a nice spring day. Behind his office he had made a makeshift patio area, just six square feet of flagstones laid on the ground, with a small glass table, two lawn chairs, and a barbeque grill. We sat down there. "So, I imagine you had sense enough to check his doors after he went to bed, like maybe he feels safe enough out in the country, in a gated community?" Mack said.

"Yeah, no dice."

"I figured. Never that damn easy. Too many years living in the big city, too much of a habit, I guess. But, tell me more about this garage thing. Any chance a guy could just slip in before the door closes, .22 him in the head as he gets out of his car?"

"Not seeing it. No good place to hide close enough."

"Okay, good, so you've given it some thought…"

"Yeah, a lot of windshield time between here and Traverse City."

"So what you thinking?"

"Well…I was thinking, I figured with the lights on in the house, and dark outside, I could walk right up to the sliding glass door while he's watching TV, and just blast him through the glass."

"Huh…yeah, kid, you watch too much TV. That don't actually work like they show it. Thick glass on a sliding glass door. Deflect the bullet more than you think. Would probably take several shots…yeah, no good." He paused and rubbed his jaw. "The way around that would be a rifle—or a shotgun. But, no, don't like it. Too big of a boom in too quiet of a neighborhood. Someone will call the cops and they will roll out, in force—put on a good show for all the rich folks. That leaves you trying to escape from a mile behind enemy lines. Too risky. I wouldn't give a goddamn Green Beret good odds!"

Now, I know what many of you are thinking, and the idea came to me too: On TV and in the movies they always show all these assassins running around with guns outfitted with silencers. They make it look like these are just run-of-the-mill hitman tools. So I asked Mack about that. He shook his head, "Yeah, I wish, but no. Really hard to get. Really expensive. Possession alone is a federal offense. And then, the silencer has to be matched to the gun—the barrel perfectly machined to receive it. Then after you use it, then what? You wanna keep it, cause it's super hard to get and expensive, but—rule one, kid, you never, never, never keep a gun the cops can make a ballistic match on to a murder. So, you gotta toss it, then hope you can get another one? Wouldn't really help here anyway. You gotta figure it's gonna take a few shots just to break the glass, then maybe you just wing him and gotta try to chase him down. All he needs is a few seconds to get a phone and dial three numbers—your ass is cooked!"

Mack stared out into space and drummed his fingers on the table for about thirty seconds. He turned back to me, "I notice you keep going back to this…to this, ah…he's sitting in a chair watching TV at night thing…"

"Right, that's the one, well, sort of pattern, I could make out. Almost every weekday he's home alone at night. Then he always has this…I don't know what to call it…decompression time, I guess, from about ten to eleven where he sits in his recliner and watches TV. That room is just off the deck, so… so you can walk right up to that sliding glass door, and he's just sitting there, like ten feet away."

Mack leaned back in his chair and got a devilish grin, "And when he's not alone? All that time lurking in the dark

I've bet you've seen some good shows. I mean, c'mon, guy like that—gotta have at least one fine, bonny young lass—"

"Oh, shit, Mack. Dirty old man. Yeah, maybe. Not telling you. Your old ass—get overstimulated—have a fucking heart attack."

"Ha, ha… Yeah, fuck you, kid. Getting back into it, it seems the way to go—if there's some way to get him to come outside—I mean out the back, where no one could see—then kill him quiet."

"Actually, I've thought about that too. May have a way…"

"And?"

"Well…since we're just talking hypothetical anyway: It's…iffy, in that it may or may not work. But if it doesn't it isn't something that would spook him either—not blow the deal—still have another chance. I need to think on it more. Assuming I get him outside…"

"Ever done any knife work, kid?"

"Um…no, but how difficult could it be?"

"Well, another one of those Hollywood problems, kid. They make it look like you just poke a guy and, boom, he drops dead. Ain't like that. Usually, I mean. If you really know what you're doing—don't fuck around with it—it can be like that. But, the other trouble is—done right, I mean, you gotta be right up on the guy, and then—done right—the blood really gushes. You get covered in it. That's where the term 'wet work' comes from, kid, from doing knife work." Mack paused again to gaze into space and finger drum, then snapped his head back to me, "Hold on a sec here… I thought you were just doing recon on this. You're talking like…you get the contract, kid?"

"Well…no, but…I've already snuck back and forth into there a dozen times. And—from what I've been told—this needs to be done very quiet. Cops don't even know I exist—no one gonna come knocking on my door."

"It's a big—think you're up for it?"

"Yeah."

"Want me to ask Tony?"

"Yeah."

Mack leaned back in his chair, crossed his arms, and smiled. "Okay, kid, but first," making a rolling motion with his hand, "give me some of those Peeping Tom details."

"Fine…fine. Blond. Couldn't be but twenty. Gorgeous. Ba-boom!" And I cupped my hands out in front of my chest. "Going down on him like a sewing machine on high speed. Had his brains blown out in under a minute. The girl has talent!" I noticed Mack had closed his eyes. I couldn't help but laugh.

Opening his eyes, he cried, "That it? C'mon!"

"Shit, what do you expect? He's an old coot like you, how much more could he handle?"

"Yeah, yeah…fuck you. Oh, and…fuck you again."

"So you'll talk to Tony?"

"Yeah, kid, I'll talk to him. What you say makes sense. I'll talk to him."

It was only a couple more days before Mack called me in again. I had the contract. Most hits got assigned like this. If I got pinched and turned rat, I couldn't testify that Tony Mano told me to do anything. All I could say is "Mack said Tony said," then the defense attorney yells, "objection, hearsay." It may not seem like much, but it is another wall the prosecution has to find a way around.

Mack and I went back and forth on the various methods to kill someone silently, and picked one I felt comfortable with. Mack went to work right away on making the needed tool. Actually, I had him make two so I could practice with it ahead of time.

Time was of the essence. It was now mid-May and getting more springlike. Every passing day it became more and more likely people would be using the waterfront, or otherwise just milling about outside. I went in on a Monday, same as a dozen times before, walk-jogging down the beach. No issues. No one around. Very quiet.

Little Napoleon had the same type of outdoor entertainment area on the terrace below his house that all the houses there had. The first place you got to on his, when coming down the steps from his back deck, was a large brick patio ringed with ornate stone benches and a large, stone firepit in the center. I figured that if I built a fire in that firepit, he would clearly see it from his living room, and, I hoped, come out to investigate.

Now, I already know what many of you are thinking: No way some hoity-toity rich dude is going to bother, he's just going to call the cops or the security guard at the gatehouse to come over and deal with it. Most, likely, would, but I was banking on a tough old banty rooster from Detroit to handle it himself. If he did, instead, call out the cavalry, I would see their headlights and hear them talking and have plenty of time to slip away in the darkness. Then they would just figure it was some kids or drunk fool neighbor messing around and not think too much of it.

One thing every Boy Scout damn for sure learns is how to make a fire. It was a simple matter to gather up a heap of dry twigs and sticks and set it ablaze. As soon as I heard the door onto the deck slide open I crouched down behind a bush next to the bottom of the stairway. It was just barely big enough to hide me.

One, two, three steps onto the brick patio and he was in perfect position. I had practiced the move at least a hundred times in my apartment before coming. I had stuffed a pillow into an empty trash can to hold a broom with the head pointed up, then put that on a chair so that the head of the broom would sit right at the height Little Napoleon's head would be. Then I crouched down and sprung up practicing the right movements until they became one flawless, fluid memory. The tool itself was as simple as they get, just two sawed-off sections of broom handle connected by a couple feet or so of picture-hanging wire.

I had never garroted a person before. A couple of things surprised me. First was how fast and easy it worked. No doubt, I had practiced and had the move down pat, and no doubt I was much bigger and stronger than Little Napoleon, but I had prepared myself for more of a struggle. I don't think it took much more than twenty seconds for him to go limp, although I held on a while to be sure.

The second surprise was a problem. I didn't have any idea how easily a thin strand of wire like that cuts through a guy's neck. I maybe put too much muscle into it. I damn near sliced his fucking head off. The wire was buried in his neck so deep it wouldn't come out. This was fine in that I planned on leaving it behind anyway, but what I hadn't planned on was all the blood. I guess I sliced through his jugular vein. I was soaked. Enough to go through the thick cloth of my sweatshirt and sweatpants and get on my skin. A huge blood stain that was clear as day on that light gray jogging suit. Shit. Not good.

My first instinct was to head for the lake to try to get cleaned up. That was stupid. Of course, it didn't get the blood out, although the wetness did help hide it some. But, fuck, that water was cold! So now I'm soaking wet, shivering uncontrollably as hypothermia quickly sets in, and a mile from my car. Brilliant, just fucking brilliant!

I ran for it. What else was there to do? No bullshit walk-jogging, a steady run until my lungs gave out, walk a ways, repeat. By the time I got to the fence, between the exertion and the cold, I struggled to get my muscles to work well enough to make the climb.

Back at the car I had clean clothes to change into. Even without planning for the blood, I wanted every bit of clothes that could have even a single grain of that distinct-looking white sand from the beach off me and bagged up tight before I left. It was a struggle, but at that point I was going on full adrenaline, so I stripped down naked, wiped the blood off my skin as best I could with my wet clothes, triple-bagged it all, put on dry clothes, and got the fuck out of there.

I drove straight back home with no stops along the way and never more than five miles an hour over the speed limit. Actually, not home, but back to Shillelagh's. I had to drop off the car. I had to burn those bloody clothes. Of course this was still in the middle of the night, so no one was there. We had arranged a signal. I parked the car where Mack would see it when he came in to work in the morning. If the keys were left under the seat, that meant the job was done. If they were behind the sun visor that meant I had hit a small snag and came back to regroup.

Then I went home, took a long shower, and slept for fourteen hours straight. And when I woke up, life went on as if nothing happened. I never was asked for any details. I never discussed it with Mack, or Tony, or anyone. That I know of, the police didn't come around to question anyone from our crew. I intentionally went into a news blackout for the next few weeks, so I don't know what kind of orgy the media had over it. Like I said before, as soon as it's done, it never happened. That's just how it has to be.

But it was a major hit. It was a major accomplishment for the Family, and Tony Mano was the guy who got the credit for that. With what was about to happen, this had major significance. Me taking out Little Napoleon may very well have ended up saving Tony Mano's life.

Chapter 12

Carl Cassini, but people who knew him well called him Cass. Now, you would think this came as a shortened version of his last name, but no. It was short for his nickname, Casanova. Every man has some hobby he spends too much time and money on. It is a natural, healthy thing. For Cass, it was chasing women. He was a world-class ass-wrangler. If picking up women was an Olympic event, Cass would be a gold medalist. By the time I met him he was already in his fifties, and hadn't slowed down one bit.

He was part of the Cowboy Crew, but worked directly under Mike Picano on the money side of things. For example, in that sweetheart landscaping contract I mentioned in the Ben Avery story, Cass was the mob guy running that scam. Being on the muscle side of things, under Tony Mano, I knew him only vaguely, having met him here and there at various social gatherings, like the cookouts Tony threw. He was hardcore, old-school mafioso, so to be respectful, I always called him Mr. Cassini, but since he's never going to read this anyway, and just for fun, I'll refer to him here as Cass.

He had an interesting history. He was from Chicago. As a teenager he somehow got involved with the Family there. He did well as a full-time wiseguy during the late fifties through early '70s, which was a real heyday period for the American Mafia. Then he fucked up. No surprise, there was a woman involved. He had an affair with the wife of a Made Man. Going all the way back to the rules established when the American Mafia was formed, this was taboo. And, it was considered a death sentence offense.

Before the contract could be satisfied, Cass fled to Toledo. Somehow, he hooked up with Mike Picano there, and started working for him. It took eight or nine months for the Chicago boys to figure out he was in Toledo, which was—beyond question—part of the territory of the Detroit Family.

They did the right thing. They went to the Chicago Boss, who went to the Detroit Boss and requested that he carry out the contract. The Detroit Boss then went to Picano. Somehow Picano talked the Boss out of it. Cass was a real hustler and a "good earner." The Detroit Boss informed the Chicago guys that he was not going to honor the contract. The Chicago Family recognized his divine right to do so. As long as Cass stayed within the confines of the Detroit Family's recognized territory, they would leave him alone. So, in essence, he was in exile. When Picano later moved on to Captain of the Cowboy Crew, he brought Cass with him.

In high school history class you learn that World War I started after Archduke Ferdinand was assassinated in Sarajevo. The teacher then goes on to explain how this seemingly minor event was so important because it touched off a "powder keg" in European politics that was just waiting for the fuse to be lit. I guess the situation within the Cowboy Crew was kind of like that. On the one hand you had Mike Picano who was the official Captain, recognized by the power and authority of the Family. On the other hand you had Tony Mano, the de facto Captain who actually got things done and controlled the small army of enforcers and hitmen. So, maybe not exactly a powder keg, but at least an M-80 firecracker. Not enough to start a World War, but enough to make some noise and hurt anyone standing too close. Someone just needed to light the fuse.

Charlie Robinson owned and operated The Eagle, a little bar and grill up in Orchard Lake. He was this big black guy, about fifty years old but in better shape than most men half his age. He was kind of a local hero. But, not like that cocky fucker Little Napoleon, a legitimate hero. First, he served three tours in Vietnam as a Marine, earning a variety of medals. Then, back home he continued his service to his community, not by throwing around a little cash here and there, but by actually committing his time and energy. He coached for, then ran, a local basketball league. He was a mentor to countless young men as part of the Big Brother Program. Most recently he had started The Real Warrior Program, which went into the worst of the gang areas in Detroit to try to persuade the young guys there that the biggest, baddest gang they could join was the U.S. Military. On a plain, unpainted, and unadorned sheet of plywood on one wall of The Eagle were over a hundred hash marks in Sharpie marker, representing each kid Charlie Robinson got out of gang life and into uniform.

Cass was a regular at The Eagle. One afternoon he stopped in after a round of golf with his hot-young-babe-*de jour* on his arm. She did something to piss him off and he smacked her, or somehow got rough with her. Charlie Robinson was a real man. Real men don't abide that kind of shit. He stepped in. Cass took a swing at him. Charlie promptly kicked his ass, threw him out the door, and told him not to come back. But Cass was an Archduke in his own right. And his pride had been assassinated. And, just like that, the fuse was lit on the M-80.

Cass came up on the rough streets of Chicago during a time when mob guys were well known, and both feared and respected, within their communities. Anyone who dared to look at one the wrong way, let alone lay hands on him, could expect quick and violent repercussions. It was lost on him that he was no longer in that time and place. This was Orchard Lake, for shit's sake, not some gritty urban turf the mob had ruled for generations. Even in the old-timey mob-controlled neighborhoods, wiseguys couldn't get away with doing whatever the fuck they wanted to, like they once had. Before RICO the mob was like a young bull, that, seeing a herd of cows, rushed in and fucked them all. After RICO the mob became a wise old bull that blended in with the herd as best he could and got what action he could, when he could.

Cass was furious. He wanted Charlie Robinson taken out. He went to Mike Picano. Naturally, Mike took it to Tony. Tony tried to talk them out of it. He thought the idea was insane. Criminals killing other criminals had always been, and probably to an extent, always will be, considered by law enforcement and the public in general as somewhat acceptable. Like I said before, it's like soldiers on the battlefield, they're going to be shooting at one another.

The problem comes when bombs get dropped on a civilian target. Charlie Robinson wasn't just a civilian target, he was practically a folk hero. He was that rare human being who tries every day to be a better person, and then actually has some success at it. He'd defended a woman, and then himself.

Even under the law of the jungle, both are considered noble and justified.

And Cass wanted him whacked for it? What the fuck? But Cass could not be reasoned with. And he was a very good earner for Mike. So Mike, as was his absolute right as Captain, ordered the hit. And, Tony, as his soldier, had the absolute duty to carry it out. Those are the rules. That's just how it has to be.

The next few weeks Tony did next to nothing. Every time Cass or Mike asked about it, he just said he "was working on it." He was hoping with a bit of time to cool off Cass could be talked out of it. Instead, the opposite happened. The longer it took, the more and more worked up over it Cass got. Meanwhile, the longer he had to think about it, the more and more Tony became opposed to it. He went from just thinking it was a dumb idea from a practical viewpoint to deciding it was just outright immoral. Harsh words were exchanged. Finally, Mike Picano had no choice but to call them both in for a sit-down.

I guess Tony had some inkling things wouldn't go well. He asked that me, Vince, and Big Ed be waiting for him at Franco's, this bar over in Farmington, so we could have a meeting right after. It was the middle of the week, so the place was dead. Me and Vince camped out at a table in the far corner. Tony came in and beelined over to our table. As he sat down, he asked, "Oh, Big Ed not here yet?"

"Talked to him about an hour ago," Vince said, "Probably not going to make it. You know, his mom took that fall. Not doing well. He had to run over to help her. So…how'd it go?"

"About like I expected, which is to say, not well. I flat-out refused to do the hit."

"Bet that went over well."

"Yeah, Cass had a fucking meltdown. Starts ranting and raving, 'I'll kill the motherfucker myself!' Then, he doubled down on what was already a bad bet, gets in my face, 'And then I'm coming for *you!*,' blah, blah, blah."

I was just a fly on the wall.

"So, how'd you handle that?" Vince asked.

"Fuck it, I just let him have his temper tantrum," Tony said.

"What about Mike?"

"Well…okay, look, I admit, this maybe wasn't the smartest move, but I'm just—fuck it—so before Mike even has a chance to weigh in, I go to him, 'Make a choice, him or me,' which—yeah, isn't the thing to say. But, fuck it."

Vince leaned in on his elbows, "Hell yes, fuck it."

"So, of course, Mike blows a fucking gasket, 'I already made my choice! I'm the Captain for shit's sake! You have no right to question it!' Blah, blah, blah. He's stubbornly dug in on his own position. Didn't see no point in arguing, so I just shrugged and told him, 'If that's how you want it, fine, but just don't forget, you picked this fight, not me,' and I walked out of the meeting."

Vince just nodded.

I just remained a fly on the wall.

So, I fibbed a little when I said Tony had done nothing about the Charlie Robinson situation. From the beginning he had me doing recon work. No, not on Charlie, on Cass. I got a break early on. I decided to tail Cass one Friday evening, hoping that instead of going out prowling he already had a regular Friday night thing. Cass drove a burgundy Cadillac, very similar to the one me and Vince took off that guy Andy when I was first getting started in The Life. (It's possible it was the same car, although I doubt it. Caddys were fairly popular among the well-to-do in Michigan at that time, and that burgundy color was somewhat common.)

Tailing someone in a well-populated area is both easier and harder than you would think. It's easy in that you can blend in with the traffic and not arouse suspicion. It's difficult in that you can lose the mark when you get stuck behind some slowpoke or they make it through a traffic light just before it turns red. Then all you can do is race on ahead and hope they haven't turned and you can pick them up again.

I managed to stick with him as he made his way further and further out into the country. This was bad in that I no longer had the cover of other traffic, so with each passing mile it became more and more apparent I was tailing him. That's when it dawned on me, at first as a shock, but once I thought about it, it made perfect sense. The area he was heading into was very familiar to me. I had a good idea where he was going. I peeled off from my pursuit, waited thirty minutes, then snuck into where I figured he had ended up.

A cute little bungalow off a washboard-rutted dirt road in Canton Township. And there was his burgundy Cadillac parked outside—right next to a little red corvette. It made sense. Barbara and Cass would have met at one of Tony's parties. And there is no force upon this earth that could keep a guy like Cass from hitting on a woman like Barbara. And Cass was the kind of guy who thought that the only reason to make money was to spend it on women, which was exactly the kind of stallion Barbara kept in her stable. It's maybe even possible he was the one who bought her that Corvette.

Hiding out in that brushy field next to her place for the next two Friday evenings showed that she kept Cass on the same type of regular schedule she kept all her studs on. At the time my orders were to pass along to Big Ed whatever I found out about Cass. I decided to take this information directly to Tony, along the lines of, "I know she is a friend of yours…" He was pleased. He got that big, horse-mouth, toothy grin on his face. He ordered me, "Keep this between us," then the hint that told me what was about to happen, "And no need to watch Cass anymore."

Big Ed Kowalski's specialty was knife work. His signature blade was either a British Special Forces knife, or something similar to it. Basically, a long, thin dagger. Its acute point easily penetrated, even through thick clothing. Its two razor-sharp edges doubled the opportunity to slice through vital blood vessels. Its narrow width then made it easy to rotate ninety degrees and extract, cutting another double wound tract on the way out. "Always pull the blade out, even if you plan on leaving the knife behind," he once schooled me, "gotta leave a hole for the blood to come out."

The blow-up at the sit-down was on a Wednesday night. That next Friday Cass kept his usual appointment with Barbara. Before he made it to her door a giant ogre of a man grabbed him from behind, pulled him in close, and plunged a dagger straight into his heart, rotated it a half-turn, and extracted. He was dead within seconds.

My next involvement was to help Big Ed get rid of the body. By the time I got there, he already had Cass in a tight bundle of plastic drop cloths and duct tape. Up to this point I had no idea how involved Barbara was going to be. I had no idea to what extent, if any, she was involved with Tony on the criminal side of things. I was a little surprised when I pulled in to find her standing next to Big Ed and the Cass mummy, as casual as if she was at a damn picnic, smoking a Virginia Slim.

As soon as I parked she got into Cass's Caddy and drove

it away. That didn't surprise me. I supposed she didn't want to take the risk I would say or do the wrong thing and tip off Big Ed that she and I were…well, whatever we were. She reminded me with some frequency of her strong desire to keep our…special friendship?…a secret. I never really understood why. Once, and only once, I challenged her on it. "Ooh, Joey…it's just…like this secret love affair. It's like this forbidden fruit kind of thing. Ooh, it just…ooh, it just makes me so hot!" she said, then pulled this move that always turned me to mush. She would take my right hand, lean in to nuzzle my neck, and just as her nose touched my neck, would pivot her shoulder so her right nipple just ever so slightly brushed against my arm. I swear, if she pulled that move on the president of the United States, then whispered the right words in his ear, she could convince him to push the button to start World War III.

She was, of course, the obvious choice to ditch the evidence. If she got caught with the car, or if it somehow turned up with her fingerprints in it, she could explain it away since they were fuck-buddies. I imagine she took it over to Shillelagh's and from there Mack had it at a chop shop with due haste.

Meanwhile, I helped Big Ed load up the body and take it…well, I promised Big Ed I would never tell. And, considering how things ended up going between us, I feel obliged to honor that promise even now. It *was* a brilliant place to stash a body. I'll just put it this way: They'll find Jimmy Hoffa's motherfucking body before they ever find Carl Cassini.

Big Ed was, of course, the obvious choice for a job like this. It wasn't just that he was Tony's most experienced and most loyal hitman. This hit had the potential to have major repercussions. Mike Picano was going to seek retribution. Big Ed had come up the hard way and had ridden this rollercoaster before. This wouldn't be the first time someone got pissed off and came gunning for him.

But Big Ed was a hard man to kill. He already had a wide network of hidey-holes and street contacts he could tap into. And, he really was a Goliath character within the Detroit criminal underworld. Few men would try to go up against him. Those who did would do it with some anxiety. Often the slightest hesitation is the only difference in who lives and who dies. So far in Big Ed's life, it had always been the other guy who was a half-step behind.

Chapter 13

Before the sun rose the next morning, Tony, Big Ed, Vince, and me were "on the mattress," which is old-timey mob lingo for in hiding because the shit has hit the fan. Mack, apparently, was considered safe. He was not, technically, under Tony. While they had a close association, Mack worked with all the crews on an "as needed" basis more along the lines of an independent contractor.

Big Ed stashed me in one of his bolt holes, a crappy little basement apartment in a seedy apartment complex down in Garden City. It looked to me like half the residents there were meth-heads and the other half crack addicts. I exaggerate, but not all that much. This was good, though, in that people like that mind their own business and have a severe aversion to any level of cooperation with law enforcement.

The apartment consisted of two rooms. When you first walked in, that was the living room area. Connected to it was a small kitchen area with a fridge, stove, sink, and a short section of counter against the back wall, then about ten feet of counter across from that, extending out from the side wall and dividing it from the living room space. Next to the kitchen, a door led to a tiny bedroom and adjacent bathroom. The only furnishings were an old leather recliner and a black-and-white TV. Not even a mattress! I took the sleeping bag from my camping gear and just slept on the floor.

Over the past couple years of hanging around Mack I had spent many hours being regaled by stories of the rise and fall of many colorful figures in mob mythology. It is amazing what a guy can learn when he just lets someone talk, and then actually listens. One recurring theme became evident: The most dangerous position a mobster can end up in is to get caught in the middle of a war where he needs to pick a side. Mob wars tend to be winner-take-all type deals, so pick wrong and you're basically fucked. Tony's hit on Cass was an act of war. How big of a war had yet to be determined. Not that that helped me much. I suppose a war is as big as your involvement in it. When you're one of the frontline soldiers where the bullets are flying, a small family feud or a full-on World War are basically the same thing. I was now a soldier in a war zone. Mack gave me a sleek little Walther P-38 to carry at all times.

Both Tony Mano and Mike Picano were in a bad spot. It would seem that the obvious next move for Tony would be to take out Mike. That would be a dangerous move. That really would be setting off the powder keg. From the beginning the rule had been established that a soldier cannot kill a Made Man without getting permission from the Boss first. Now, I don't know, technically, if Mike Picano was actually a Made Man, but that didn't really matter. He was a long-standing Captain in the Family and if Tony conducted an unsanctioned hit on him, there was going to be a serious issue.

Meanwhile, Mike had free rein to whack Tony at will. Mike's problem was, Tony controlled the soldiers within the crew who did that type of work. Mike was the head, but Tony was the arm. The head could no longer control the arm, but if the arm rose up and killed the head, the arm died too.

Mike's first move was to appeal to the Family for help. I don't know how far up this went and to what extent the actual Boss of the Family got involved. All I know is the little bits and pieces I gleaned along the way, combined with what I could reason out on my own. From what I could gather, the higher-ups told Mike they considered the matter to be an "internal issue" within the crew, and, as the Captain, they left it up to him to sort it out.

I think several overlapping and interplaying issues led to this. At the time the FBI was working overtime with surveillance, bugs, and wiretaps in an attempt to find a way to take out the leadership of the Detroit Mafia. They were having damn little success, but it made for a tense situation. The top guys didn't need any bullshit problems from this piss-ant little crew out in the hinterlands.

Meanwhile, they knew Tony Mano as the guy who had recently taken care of the Little Napoleon situation, which had the potential to be an exploding powder keg of its own. And, going forward, as the law brought more and more pressure on their enterprise, they knew they needed guys like Tony to deal with potential rats or other such lighters of the fuse. On top of that, Tony had just enough muscle to make a fight with him bloody and costly enough to end up a Pyrrhic victory, at best.

Tony saw this as a good development, in that it meant the weight of the Family wasn't about to fall on him. It still left him, though, in a tricky position. It still didn't amount to outright permission to hit Mike. For that Tony would need to have a sit-down with the Boss, or someone close enough to the top to speak for the Boss. The problem there was that the Boss then may decide that the most expedient way to deal with this problem was to arrange a meeting where Tony walked in, then was carried out, never to be seen again.

Tony decided it was a situation where it was better to ask forgiveness than ask permission. He had to let Mike make the first move. If Mike came after him, Tony would take him out. That's just basic law of the jungle-type self-defense. The Boss would probably accept that. Then his most expedient solution would be to let Tony take over as official Captain, with his crew of dedicated killers intact and ready to serve the needs of the Family.

So, then it came down to how Mike Picano decided to handle the situation. The smart, pragmatic move would be to just make peace with Tony and get on with life. As things stood, Mike was—at best—a part-time mobster. Moving forward in life he seemed interested in getting less involved with The Life, not deeper back into it. But, as I said before, people just don't work that way. Emotion is high trump. He tripped over his pride and ended up so deep in the thicket he couldn't see the forest for the trees. He just started wildly swinging that machete, cutting a pathway deeper into a jungle he didn't even want to be in anymore. It's like that guy in high school who is about to break things off with his girlfriend, then he sees some other guy hitting on her, so instead, he professes his undying love and gives her his class ring. It's amazing how the smartest animal on Earth so often does such stupid shit.

Mike knew that the key to the whole thing was Big Ed. He couldn't get at Tony without getting Big Ed on his side, or if that didn't work, getting Big Ed out of the way. So, Mike went to Big Ed. Big Ed was respectful, but firm. He told him no. I know this because Big Ed told me about it, while he was checking up on me in that rathole apartment he stashed me in—as he did every few days—although he did leave out the details of the actual conversation. He went on to tell me the reason he refused to go against Tony, "So, you've probably already heard, some years back I got jammed up."

"Yeah, on an assault rap, was it?"

"Right. Assault and battery. What happened was I tracked some deadbeat debtor to a bar and went after him for payment. The guy had a couple buddies in the bar who jumped in to help him. Full on brawl—right out of an action movie. Tables busting, shit flying everywhere. Anyway, I beat the living shit out of all three of them. Put 'em in the hospital. They claim one almost died. No big surprise, got arrested. Fucking prosecutor—draws up a list as long as his arm of felonies to charge me with, including attempted murder. This is just the game these rotten-ass pricks play to force a plea deal. So, fuck it, I'm jammed, I take a deal for five years at Jackson State Prison."

I just nodded along. Good story.

"So anyway, I'm inside and word gets passed to me that there's a contract out on another con there. I get the order to take the guy out. This ain't good—between a rock and a hard place. On the one hand, not allowed to say no on a deal like that. You do, you're marked for death. So—not trying to be all dramatic, that contract probably doesn't get pushed, but— you know, it's out there, hanging over your head. It means I at least need to leave the Detroit area once I get out. But then on the other hand, if I do the hit while inside—that's just damn hard to get away with. Probably gonna end up in prison for life. I don't know how he did it. Tony, he convinced whoever he needed to that I was much too valuable of a soldier to burn that way. I got let out of the contract. Not to be too mushy about it, but, the way I see it, Tony saved my life. So, that's it—ain't going against Tony, no matter what. If that means I get whacked, oh well, too bad, so sad for me."

Mike Picano's next move was to go to Vince. Vince called me afterward and asked to come over to my hideout apartment to talk. As he walked in he took one look around the place and whistled, "Holy hell, Joey, when you said the place was a rat hole, I thought you were exaggerating. Could you imagine…you pick up a chick and bring her back here? No way a guy gets laid in this dump."

"Yeah, I doubt a hooker would stay."

"Yeah, one look around and she's 'fuck it, not even if he pays double,' and out the door."

As he walked past me to come in, I could smell the alcohol. Day drinking. Bad sign.

"Got any beer?" Vince said.

"Nope."

"Oh yeah, you don't really drink."

I pointed toward the kitchen, "Wouldn't help anyway, fridge is busted."

Vince started pacing.

I sensed he needed a nudge, "Okay, so what does Picano have to say?"

"Not what I was hoping to hear, but…well, short version: The Family fully backs Mike, they're just giving him a little time to try to resolve the situation on his own. Tony's a goner. His ship is sinking, just a matter of who he takes with him, etc., etc., like that. Then he gives this cute speech, 'There are rules. Tony has broken them. I'm the Captain. Those soldiers that follow the rules and loyally back me will be rewarded. Those that don't, die,' etc., etc., like that. Then he goes full-on Sunday homily on me, 'That is how it always has been, is now, and forever will be.' Holy shit." Stopped pacing to look me in the eye.

Needed another nudge? "And?"

"And, well, I mean, let's face it, he isn't wrong." Pacing again. "I mean, I know with all the time you've spent with Mack, you've heard the stories. Hell, more like lectures, history lessons."

"Yeah, that guy shoulda been a college professor."

"Yeah, so you know—going all the way back, this thing has always had a—always had a set structure, always had set rules. And—I mean, let's face it, Tony—well, shit, he as much as admitted it. Remember over at Franco's, right after his sit-down? He as much as said he went too far. He as much as admitted he crossed the line. Then he whacks Cass?" Pacing faster, arms swinging.

"So where does that leave us?"

"It leaves us holding a flaming bag of dog shit is where it leaves us!" Vince stopped pacing and leaned against the kitchen counter, "We got no choice, Joey. We gotta pick a side."

"I already talked to Big Ed. I know he's made his choice."

"Yeah, and he—well, I understand where he's coming from. I respect his loyalty, but—"

Shit, shit, shit. Now *I* needed a beer. "But you disagree?"

Vince started wearing out the carpeting again, arms folded across his chest, "I hate to say it—would have never in a million years thought it could happen—I just don't see any other way. If we're gonna survive—if we're gonna continue on and get ahead in this thing—I just don't see another way."

He stopped pacing, leaned on the counter again, and locked eyes with me. Bombs away, "There just isn't another way, Joey. I was hoping you would be willing to help me set up Big Ed—you know—"

Hail Mary, full of grace…

Just the two of us, all alone in that crappy little basement apartment. Did he just—? Yeah, he did. He *asked* me if I was willing to help him set up Big Ed for a hit; didn't use his typical assumptive close sales technique.

That told me all I needed to know. In that moment, with just the two of us alone in hiding, there was no possible way I could say no. If I did, I have little doubt Vince would have pulled a gun and plunked me in the head right there on the spot. It wasn't just that I would be an enemy soldier at that point that he would eventually have to take out anyway. The much bigger issue was that the only hope Vince had of getting at a guy like Big Ed was to take him completely unaware. If Big Ed found out about the plot, Vince was fucked. By *asking* me he created a justification in his own head. If I said no, at least he gave me a chance, so then having to kill me wouldn't seem like such a ruthless violation of our friendship.

So, of course, I said yes. And, just like that, the M-80-hot-potato ended up in my lap. Now I was the lynchpin. The fate of the Cowboy Crew was in my hands. It was up to me to decide who would win and who would lose. It was up to me to decide who would live and who would die.

Decisions like this get massively over-romanticized in books and movies. There is no thrill of a power trip, it's more like a nightmare you just desperately want to wake up from. There really is no way to *know* what to do. But you have to do something. I didn't overthink it. I trusted my instincts. I felt what I needed to do. I told Vince it would take a few days but that I would go to Mack for the needed tools and get it all set up.

A few days later, Vince came back to the apartment for a dress rehearsal. As soon as he walked in, the first thing he saw was a shotgun, laid across the kitchen counter, pointed toward the door. "Okay," I said, "here's the setup. Big Ed comes by every few days to check up on me. Next time is tomorrow afternoon. You'll be over here," I walked over to the counter, "crouched down behind the counter with the shotgun. I'll be over here," I walked over to the recliner, "sitting down, that .38 Mack gave me in my lap. As soon as Big Ed is all the way in the door, you blast him—"

"Wait, wait, don't you have to go to the door and let him in?"

"No, it's his place, got a key, lets himself in. I'm sitting in the recliner, his focus will be on me." I walked to the middle of the room, I spanned out my arms, "So plenty of space, I'm off to the side. Let him get all the way in. Go center mass, in the chest. One, no chance of missing, two, I want all of it in him, no buckshot through the wall into the hallway. As soon as you shoot, I jump up out of the chair, run over, slam the door shut, and put one in his head from the .38. Simple."

"What about the body?"

"Fuck it, leave it. We scoot right after. Lock the door behind us and get the fuck outta dodge."

Vince rubbed his chin then started to pace.

I knew what his concern was and jumped on it, "I have no known ties to this place. Have all day to do a good clean-up. When you come—"

"Yeah, yeah, gloves on, start to finish." Done pacing, hands clasped together, "Yeah, I like it. Simple. Simple."

It was about three o'clock on a Tuesday afternoon when

Big Ed walked into the trap. Everything went as the co-conspirators had planned. As soon as he was all the way in the door, Vince pulled the trigger on the shotgun. There was a tremendous explosion from the gun. Vince was violently thrown backward, slamming him into the kitchen stove. He crumpled in a heap on the stained linoleum floor. I sprung out of the chair, rushed over to Vince, and shot him in the head before he could recover.

Vince had forgotten the lesson of the raid on the gangbangers' bank, that what can work in one direction can just as easily be turned around to work in the opposite direction. The idea for the rigged shotgun came from yet another story told by Mack. I don't remember the exact details, but it was about one mobster who pulled a hilarious prank on another by shoving modeling clay into the barrel of a shotgun, then inviting the other guy to a friendly skeet shooting contest. The way Mack told it, the guy that got pranked just got knocked on his ass when he fired the plugged-up gun, and everyone had a good laugh.

For my version I used Silly Putty. Three "eggs" worth, and put in a shell containing birdshot instead of buckshot—if you ever want to try it. But, don't. What Mack didn't tell me was that with modern shotgun shells in a modern shotgun, doing that causes the barrel to burst. I was damn lucky I wasn't hit by any wild shrapnel, although it did look like most went up into the ceiling. Still, not something I would ever try again, at least not when I'm going to be so close to the explosion.

Big Ed couldn't help but chuckle. He wiped his brow, "Whew, can't believe that actually worked—"

"Yeah, sometimes simple ain't best," then we just locked the door behind us and got the fuck outta Dodge.

There was one other huge advantage to setting up Vince

like this. It showed there was no question he had turned on us. He had a gun pointed at Big Ed and pulled the trigger, fully expecting to murder him. Our consciences were eased. Our guilt was assuaged. Our hands were…well, as clean as I guess they can be with shit like this. What else could we do? Vince clearly had made his choice. It was kill or be killed. Maybe Vince was going through his own Icarus Phase. I just wish it didn't have to be me who melted his wings. He was, at least sort of, my friend, and my mentor. Maybe some would see poetic justice there. As he sowed, he reaped. *Rest in peace, Vince DeLuca. When we meet one day in hell I'm sure you'll shove a pitchfork up my ass. I guess I deserve it.*

The next part of the plan was just like the aftermath of the gangbanger massacre, I fled town. If Tony and Big Ed had figured right, Mike would now be in checkmate and would have no choice but to sue for peace. In that case, I wasn't needed. Or, there was still a small chance the higher-ups would decide to jump in and rain fire and brimstone down on Tony and Big Ed. If that happened, having one more soldier with them wasn't going to help much anyway, so I just needed to be out of the way. I was very much the "ghost" Vince one time described me as. Mike Picano knew I worked for Tony, but I doubt he ever knew how far involved I was. I am almost certain no one higher up knew (or cared) that I even existed. So, as long I was out of the area, it was unlikely anyone would ever bother to come looking for me. I did as before. I headed up north. I went back out into the woods.

My instructions were to call Big Ed every few days to check in. After a week and a half of this, he told me the war was over. Everything Mike had told Vince had been complete bullshit. It is claimed no one ever retires from the mob. This is not entirely true. Most never have the chance because they end up dead or in prison. Of the few remaining, most never have the desire to give up the power and money of the lifestyle. Mike Picano was the exception. He was allowed to retire and move to Florida. In that sense, while it could be said he "lost" the war, he really did end up getting what he wanted. He was burned out on The Life. He may, very well, have been one of the few "winners" thug life ever produced.

Big Ed told me it was now safe to come home. Tony was now the recognized Captain of the Cowboy Crew, and he had big plans. I told Big Ed I was "enjoying my vacation," and asked for a few more days. "You earned it, Joey, I'm sure Tony won't mind."

But, I lied. I had no intention of going back. I had planned this as soon as I knew I had to kill Vince. I had emptied out my safe deposit boxes, took what few possessions I needed, and just walked away from the shitstorm. I was done with it. This time I really was just going to stay out in the woods. I didn't tell Big Ed or Tony any of this. I just never called either of them again. I made like a squirrel. I turned into a wisp of smoke and just drifted away into the trees.

Chapter 14

Well, shit, you didn't really think it was going to be that easy, did you? I mean, it was, for a couple years. Initially, I went back up to that area I had camped in after the gangbanger massacre. But I soon decided that wasn't far enough away and drifted my way up into the Upper Peninsula, eventually settling a little ways up the coast of Lake Superior from Marquette. In books and movies and TV shows when someone is looking to disappear, they always have the character go to some exotic location out of the country. No need. There are vast areas of rural America one can easily melt away into. Places where no one cares who you are or where you came from. Places where no one would even think to look. Places where you can tune out the outside world and simply be.

I found a local real estate management company that rented cabins and cottages for the summer tourist season. I worked a deal to rent one of the little eight-hundred-square-foot cottages they had. Since they could only hope to rent it out six months out of the year, they let me have it for a year at what they could get if it was booked solid for five months. It was a good deal for both sides. It was also a good connection to have. With the jack-of-all-trades skills I picked up as a floater on the Mano Construction crew, I was able to find plenty of odd jobs with them, and whoever else needed help, which helped stretch the pile of cash I had stashed from my bad old days. Not that I needed much. I found I could live on almost nothing.

For five or six months up that way everything is frozen solid and you're ass-deep in snow, so there isn't much work available. During the winter there are really only three things to do: snowmobile, drink, and ice fish—done in that order. First you get on your snowmobile and ride it over to the bar, because, well, there just isn't any other way to get there. Then you get good and liquored up, at which point you decide the thing to do is go out on some frozen lake, cut through two feet of ice, and sit there for hours on end on a five-gallon bucket with a miniature fishing pole hoping to catch a fish. After all, it's only ten below!

There's something about spending half the year that way that just addles the brain. The locals are all complete whack jobs. People think Southern Rednecks are the craziest rural denizens, but those boys got nothing on the Northern Wood Hick. I mostly avoided them. I was, largely, a hermit. I came to understand my dad better. I had the same mental illness he had. I created a space where I could simultaneously exist and not exist. I just left out the alcohol.

It was exactly two years, four months, and three days. The cruelty of it was, it was just long enough for me to start having hope. Hope that I really had gotten away. Hope that one of those skeletons in my closet wasn't going to spring back to life, grow flesh, and seek vengeance. I was returning home one random afternoon when I saw the car parked outside my place. A little too nice for the area. State government license plate. Some guy in a frumpy suit leaning on the hood, waiting for me. Middle-aged, about average height with a prominent gut, balding head, and a thin, dark mustache. As I got out of my car he badged me and introduced himself as, "Lieutenant Don Purdue, Michigan State Police." I thought for certain the next words out of his mouth were going to be "I have a warrant for your arrest," but instead he asked if there was somewhere we could sit down and talk.

I directed him to a picnic table in the yard. We sat across from one another with a large manilla envelope he had been carrying placed on the table between us. All that stuff Little Louie had told me all those years before about how to deal with the cops started swirling around my head as Don Purdue started his spiel, "I work in the organized crime division of the state police. Didn't know we had that, huh? But, yeah, we deal with the smaller criminal groups in the state the feds don't have time to mess with. I've been working my ass off for a little over a year with one goal. I'm looking to take down your old boss, Tony Mano. You're gonna help me. Here's why."

Wait…what?

Then he went full Tommy gun on me. He reached into the envelope and pulled out a photograph, placed it in front of me, and tapped the picture with his left index finger, "This is the gun you used to kill Vince DeLuca." Then in quick succession he pulled page after page out to add to the stack, "And this is the ballistics report that matches the slug that went through his head into the kitchen floor to that gun. And this is the report showing a partial fingerprint found on the clip inside that gun's handle, and a second, more complete print found on a round inside that clip. And, I took the liberty of stopping by some time back while you were out and pulled your prints off the doorknob here. As you can see on this page, they match."

He paused to see my reaction. Me, nothing, stone cold. He continued on, slower, no Tommy gun, "So, as you can see, I have you dead to rights for the DeLuca murder." Another pause.

Still no reaction from me.

"So, what it comes down to is simply this: Do you want me to arrest you for murder, or do you want to help me take down Tony Mano?"

Holy shit. Like in one of those war movies when the commando sneaking through the jungle bumps up against a trip wire and hears the "click" of the mine being armed. I guess it was poetic irony. The job that finally convinced me to give up The Life was now the one screw-up that was going to force me back into it. This is how you know God is a guy. He fucks with you like one guy fucks with another guy. Good one, Lord, good one!

"What did you have in mind?" I asked.

Lieutenant Don gave a satisfied smile, "Do you have any direct knowledge or any hard evidence you can give me that implicates Tony Mano in any crime?"

"No."

"Okay, I expected that. I believe you. I've been up the guy's ass for a while now and I know how cautious he is. That's why I need a man on the inside. That's why you're gonna go back to work for Tony, get me the evidence I need, then take an immunity deal and witness protection."

I'm going to do what now? Deflect, deflect. "What makes you think Tony would take me back? I mean, I basically just walked away—just abandoned him. If he's a normal guy, and I just show up after all this time and ask for my old job back, he's going to tell me to fuck off. If he's really the guy you think he is, he's gonna put a bullet in the back of my head."

Don shit-eating grinned, folded his arms, and leaned back in his seat, "I don't think so. To begin with, I think the guy owes you. I've only been able to piece together so much, but: Vince DeLuca gets taken out—*by you*—then almost right away Mike Picano decides to retire and Tony Mano takes his place. That doesn't seem like a coincidence. Even without that, he *will* take you back, and here's why: From the moment he took over he's been recruiting new muscle. I think he's trying an Albert Anastasia-style, 'Murder Inc.'-type deal, on a smaller scale. He needs...well, guys like you. It isn't a coincidence I showed up now. I've actually been sitting on this evidence I have on you for a while now, waiting for the right moment. Tony just lost two guys. They were trying a rip-off on a drug house, but they didn't know about the hidden room with the guy with an uzi. It was a fucking mess. A third guy got away, but we're fairly certain he took at least one bullet. So, Tony just happens to be shorthanded right now. I think he'll welcome you back like the Prodigal Son."

I was thinking about what Little Louie had told me. About how skilled cops like Don Purdue were at playing their game. About how they would flat-out lie to you to manipulate you.

Don must have anticipated this too, because after a brief pause he continued his sales presentation, "Look, Joe, I understand, this is a lot of shit to dump on you out of the blue like this." He placed the papers he had presented me back into the manilla envelope and slid it over to me, explaining, "These are your copies. Hire your own lawyer to look them over and see what he thinks about the case I have against you.

I can give you one week. In one week, at exactly this time, I'm coming back here to see you. Now, at this point, I should give you some bullshit about how I'm going to be watching you like a hawk, so don't even think about running, but I won't. Choose to believe this or not, but if you work with me I promise I'll always play it straight with you. I just don't have the resources to babysit you, especially out here in buttfuck Egypt. But, believe this: If you aren't here in one week, I'm going to immediately get a warrant for your arrest and file a copy with the U.S. Marshals Service. Sooner or later, we will catch up to you, then you're going to look that much more guilty and there's no hope of you getting any type of deal. You hear me?"

"Yes."

We shook hands, and he left.

So, I decided getting a lawyer to look things over was the prudent thing to do. I figured I would need to go down south to one of the bigger cities to find someone who could give me solid advice on such a major charge, but saw no harm in looking through the Marquette Yellow Pages first. I was surprised how many goddamn lawyers there were! That whole area, at the time, had maybe fifty thousand residents, but there were pages and pages of lawyers listed. Must have been at least five hundred. Who knew American society could support such a big parasite load?

Anyway, I found one who mentioned in his ad that he had done twenty years as a prosecutor in Ingham County before switching to private practice. I figured that was my man. I don't remember the guy's name. I called his office and asked to buy an hour of his time.

He only needed about ten minutes. The thing about Midwesterners is that we are blunt, straightforward, practical-type people. He looked over the evidence file and didn't hem and haw or pussyfoot around any. "Well, it depends what else they have, but with just this, I would plead it down and take a deal for fifteen to twenty," he said.

Not what I wanted to hear, but it was what I expected. It was (too much) just like that deal where I had to decide which side to back in "the war." There was no good choice. I had to decide between the lesser of two evils. In the end, I decided that going to prison would be the worst option. For me, that would be a fate worse than death. I agreed with Don that running wasn't an option. I had already tried that once and it seemed God, or Fate, or whatever, was hell-bent on not letting me off that easily.

I will confess, I did consider suicide. Like I said, better dead than decades as a caged animal cheek to jowl with other caged animals. I figured my best option would be to blow my brains out. I found, for example, that there is this spot right where your eye socket meets the bridge of your nose that a gun barrel fits into perfectly. But, it feels like there's a thick ridge of bone right there, so maybe not. I mean, the last thing you want is to fuck it up and end up brain damaged instead of dead. I figured the barrel in the mouth, shooting straight up through the roof of the mouth, was the tried-and-true method. What it very simply came down to, though, was that I just didn't have the balls. If death was the way to escape going to prison, I was going to need some help.

So, one week later when Don came back by to ask if I was in or out, there really was only one possible answer. I called up Tony and told him something along the lines of, "I'm coming into town for a few days and was hoping to see you." He seemed surprised, but genuinely pleased, to hear from me. He invited me over to his house, "around two next

Saturday afternoon."

I was going in blind and unsupported. This first contact was critical. If I was found wearing a wire, or if backup was close enough to be spotted in the area, the whole deal would be fucked. If Tony held a grudge, or smelled a rat, or whatever, and decided to take me out, there wasn't anything I could do about it. Part of me hoped he would. I just hoped it would be as quick and as painless as possible.

My concern was heightened when I knocked on Tony's front door and it was answered by Big Ed. He was cordial enough, and invited me in. As soon as the door closed, though, "I'm sure you understand. I have to pat you down."

As he checked me for wires and weapons, I noticed a large wedding photo on the wall of Tony and—holy shit, Barbara! As Big Ed finished his search, I asked, "Tony got married?"

The answer came from Tony as he stepped in from an adjacent room, "Yeah, me and Barbara decided to give up our wild ways and settle down about a year ago."

Hmmm…well, that certainly complicated things…

Then he gave me his big horse-mouth grin and shook my hand. Before he had a chance to ask why I was there I reached into my pocket and took out a note I had prepared. Not knowing what kind of surveillance may be in place, it simply read, "You're being spied on by state police. Somewhere safe we can talk?"

Tony handed the note to Big Ed without a word. He put his hand on my shoulder, "I've made some additions out back. C'mon, let me show you."

There was a small niche off Tony's back patio where the patio met the house. Originally, he was going to put a shower in there for people to rinse off before or after going in the swimming pool, or possibly put in a bar there, but he never got around to it. He now had it walled in and only accessible by a heavy steel door. It looked like one of those Cold War-era bomb shelters. "We call this the Bat Cave," he said, as he unlocked the deadbolt and motioned me inside. The room itself was maybe eight feet by eight feet. Hanging down in the middle of the ceiling was a cord with a single, bare lightbulb. That was it. Completely austere. Bare cinder block walls. Not even a chair to sit on.

As he closed us in, he said, "That door stays locked at all times. I have two security cameras pointed at it. And, as you can see…" Gestured at all the nothing in the room with a wave of the hand. "There's no place to hide a bug anyway."

Big Ed came with us into the Bat Cave. I couldn't help but notice that it would make an ideal place to murder someone.

Before either had a chance to speak, I spilled my guts. I told them every detail of my encounter with Don Purdue and what he wanted me to do. I told them how close I came to just blowing my fucking brains out, "But I didn't have the balls. Still, I'd rather be dead than be a fucking rat. I'd rather be dead than in prison. I fully understand that the smartest thing for you to do would be to make me disappear, permanently. In a sense, you'd be doing me a favor—"

Tony cut me off with a pat on my shoulder, "Now, now, Joey, we aren't there—not yet, anyway. I appreciate your loyalty. With that thing with Vince, and, even more, now. That really does go a long way with me. Okay—okay, look, look, go back to this Lieutenant Don Purdue character and tell him I seem open to the idea of bringing you back, but I need a week or two. Need to—to mull it over, say. Meanwhile let me use my connections to dig deeper into this guy and what he has cooking. Maybe we can find a way to swing this around to our favor."

Big Ed just stood there, a gargoyle statue on a Gothic cathedral.

Tony paced back and forth once, talking and walking. "The elephant in the room question, though, is how the fuck did the cops get that gun? What'd you do with it?"

"Yeah, guess I fucked up there. After I shot Vince I traded guns with him, leaving the murder weapon in his waistband. I…well, you know, we still had a war on, and I didn't want to be unarmed. I thought it was a clean gun, and I figured they would think it was his and not run full forensics on it. Guess I fucked up."

"Yes, but how did they connect that gun to *you*? What made them think to even try to match your prints to the ones on the gun?"

I just shrugged, "Yeah, I've been wondering that too!"

That was a lie, but a necessary one. I remembered exactly what had happened to that gun. You do recall all this happened on a Tuesday? Well, on my way out of town I just couldn't help but make one last stop. Where the mind is willing, the flesh is weak. I left that gun with Barbara. I figured that after seeing how involved she was with the Carl Cassini hit, she could be trusted to properly dispose of it. I don't know why she kept it. I couldn't even imagine how or why she would give it to the cops. I most certainly intended to find out, but her now being married to Tony made the whole thing quite the sticky situation. I was going to need to get that sorted out.

And, that was it; he let me go. But, I have no doubt I came very close. No doubt Big Ed had a knife in his belt. With one nod from Tony, in less time than it takes to read this, he could have sent me for a reunion with Vince. Maybe it would have been better if he had.

Meanwhile, there was nothing to do but wait. I tried to

talk Don into letting me go back up north, but he wanted to keep me close. He stashed me in a safehouse in Swartz Creek, a little ways west of Flint. This gave the state police techs time to set me up with a new surveillance system they had been working on. I was given what looked like an ordinary beeper to keep clipped on my belt. When the beeper was turned on, it activated a bug inside. The broadcast range was fairly short so they stashed a receiver under the dashboard of my car that would record whatever conversations the bug picked up, on an ordinary cassette tape. Since the tape could only hold sixty minutes of sound before being changed, it would be up to me to decide when to turn on and turn off the bug. But, a set-up like that is limited, so what Don was really banking on was that I would be able to get more sophisticated bugs planted in key locations once I was fully accepted back into the crew.

It took almost two weeks for Tony to call me back in for another meeting. Again, at his house. This time alone. I took that to mean he probably wasn't going to have me whacked, at least not right then.

No Barbara either, and that I counted as a win. I hadn't figured out yet what to do about her. It's amazing how quickly the love/hate switch can get flipped. Not that I had been in love with her, but I had cared deeply for her. In the least I had considered her a close friend. If, back then, she had asked me to kill someone for her, I wouldn't have hesitated to do it. Now, I wanted to kill her. That was an odd feeling, actually *wanting* to kill someone. In the past murder had just been an unpleasant job I had to do, like taking out the trash or shoveling the driveway after a snowstorm. I blamed her. I had gotten free. I had, to the extent I could, found some level of peace and contentment. And her actions snatched all that away. This felt uniquely shitty, hating someone so much to want to kill them.

Anyway, I had arranged a signal with Tony ahead of time. As soon as he welcomed me in he said, "Oh, I meant to ask you before, how is your mother doing?" If I responded by also using the word "mother," like, "My mother is doing fine," that meant I was wired. I told him I wasn't wired, but wasn't offended when he searched me anyway. Then he shunted me off to the security of the Bat Cave for an in-depth discussion.

Tony had been busy. He had spent many hours and an obscene amount of bribe money to work every source he could find for information on what Don Purdue and the Michigan State Police were up to. What he found, or more so, what he didn't find, was remarkable, "No one I talked to can find any information on an open investigation of me or anyone associated with me. This Don Purdue character is legit, but he has a reputation as a maverick. What I think is, the only way I can figure it is, he's kinda doing his own thing here, you know, 'off book,' so to speak. I think he somehow stumbled onto you, still don't know how, and is now trying to parlay that into a career-making bust, without his superiors knowing about it or signing off on it as an 'official investigation.' That's good for us, just need to find a way to turn it around on him."

I told Tony about the bug in the beeper deal the cops were setting me up with.

He took a keen interest in that, "So they're counting on you to record…whatever, then just turn it over to them on a tape?"

"That's how I understand it."

"Huh…I would think a defense attorney would have a field day with the lack of control on the chain of evidence. But, I guess if they have an expert do the voice matches, and then have you testify…yeah, I guess it could work. At some point I need to have a closer look at that set-up—there may be an opportunity there. I need to think about that some. Meanwhile, you report back to Purdue…oh, let's see, like, 'I have my foot in the door but Tony is proceeding with caution. It will probably take a few months for me to prove myself and get all the way back in.' You handle that, Joey?"

"No problem."

This bought Tony time to see if and how he could go from being the mouse to being the cat. Or, if that didn't pan out, it kept me close enough to put a bullet in the back of my head at a moment's notice. I still expected it to go that way.

Step one was to hire me back onto the Mano Construction crew. I guess I shouldn't have been surprised to find that Big Ed was the foreman of the crew I was assigned to. I wondered how long it would be before he had me stay late to dig another grave just before the concrete got poured for a basement. I wondered if it was going to be me going into the hole. Then again, I was on good terms with Big Ed, and, in a sense, had saved his life, so he probably wouldn't be a dick about it and make me dig my own grave. Not that it really mattered.

I suppose it's human nature to get all angsty about one's inevitable end. It is yet another case where emotion beats down logic. The how, when, and where are unknowable and largely uncontrollable. How will I be remembered? Who will get my stuff? What will my legacy be? Dead is dead, so what difference does it make? Either there is no afterlife, so I won't know, or there is an afterlife and I will be so far beyond earthly worries that it is insignificant. When my time comes, how could I possibly care what people have to say about me or what they do with my stuff? Life belongs to the living, let them sort it out.

One of the first things I learned upon my return to my

old life was that Serge was gone. A mere six months prior to his retirement he had a massive heart attack and dropped dead while laying brick for a house wall. I could only hope he died with a trowel in his hand, containing a big glop of mortar, mixed just right—like-a-butta! It bothered me some that I hadn't known and had missed his funeral. I wondered if I should go see Maria and pay my respects.

But no, it was too late for that now. I suppose that's the problem with running away from something, you have to be willing to part with both the bad and the good. It made me think about this knick-knack-type thing my mom had that sat on the top of the bookcase in the hallway outside the bathroom in the house I grew up in. It was a sculpture of an open book sitting on a wooden stand and across the pages in fancy calligraphy was the prayer of Saint Francis, "God, grant me the serenity to accept the things I cannot change, the courage to change the things I can, and the wisdom to know the difference." I suppose every human struggle comes down to that one simple sentence. It's always been that last part that I've struggled with the most.

It took a few weeks for Tony to come up with his opening move in the real-life chess match with Lieutenant Don Purdue. He instructed me to go to Don and tell him, "The only way Tony is going to let me back in is if I prove my loyalty by doing a hit for him. What do you want me to do?" He wanted to see how Don would react. If he really was a rogue cop, like Tony suspected, he wouldn't object. Naturally, Tony needed me to use the beeper bug to record Don's reaction, then give him the tape.

So, that's what I did. Don's reaction was, more or less, "Look, Joe, you've got to understand the situation. You're my CI, that's it. I have charges pending on you I'm willing to hold back on in exchange for your cooperation on a bigger case. I understand you're a bad guy, and out there in bad guy land you will be doing bad guy stuff. But, if you think I'm giving you permission, or some kind of free pass to do whatever the fuck you want to, that's not it. Any crimes you commit you're on the hook for. My hope is you working with me is going to end with you being valuable enough to get offered immunity and protection. That's it."

It is amazing how two people can look at the same thing and see it in opposite ways. I thought Don's response was a disaster. It struck me as what you would expect any legitimate cop would say to any scumbag CI he was working. If nothing else, he seemed to do a good job threading the eye of the needle and staying in the gray area. Tony saw it the other way around. He thought it proved Don Purdue was "off the reservation." He just couldn't see any way a legitimate cop would look the other way when told a murder was about to happen.

This, then, led to Tony revealing his "master plan" on how we were going to turn the tables on Don. His plan was nothing short of wacky. It was so far-fetched and crazy-sounding, I'm reluctant to even try to explain it. But, then again, oftentimes it's the craziest ideas that get the job done. Sometimes simple ain't best.

As best I can explain it, this was Tony's idea: From time to time he would supply me with tapes to give to Don, along with when the taped conversations took place and who was saying what. But, here's the catch: The tapes would be bogus. Instead of real mobsters the voices would be actors playing the part. (Really?) The "crimes" discussed would be a mix of complete fabrications and real events, but only ones that had happened in the past.

After this had gone on long enough Tony would set me up with an ace attorney who would march me into the FBI office in Detroit to report how I was being blackmailed by this corrupt cop into creating false evidence to frame Tony, et al. So, the endgame would be that I would "turn rat," get immunity, and be put into witness protection, but as a witness against Don Purdue and corruption in the state police, not as a witness against the mob. The beauty of it was that—if it worked—it didn't just get rid of Don Purdue, it also tainted everything the organized crime division of the Michigan State Police already had, or would develop in the future, to use against the Detroit Mafia. "Elegant," Tony called it.

How insane the idea was and what hope it had of working didn't make any difference to me, at least in the short term. As far as I was concerned I was still a "dead man walking" and what this basically amounted to was like a stay of execution from the governor. On the one side Don Purdue had no reason to charge me because he would think he was getting the information he wanted, while on the other side Tony had no reason to kill me because he thought he could use me to get the state cops off his back. And there I was just stuck in the middle between these two great millstones, trying not to get crushed into dust. I reflected back on what Tony had told me at our first meeting, the part about the Croatians, about how they had spent nearly their whole existence under the thumb of one superpower or another, but had held their own. I guess that's what I now needed to figure out how to do too.

Meanwhile, what Don had said about Tony being shorthanded and needing soldiers was true. Tony saw no reason not to put me back into play and get what work he could out of me, while he could. So, just like that, I was tossed right back into the cesspool. Treading water. Trying not to drown. But this time I knew too much, had, perhaps, matured too much, or thought too much, and couldn't pretend the shit didn't stink. The sluice opened, water rushed into the raceway, and ever so slowly the millstones started to turn…

CHAPTER 15

Dmetri Petrovich. To say he was a complete piece of shit would be a serious understatement. A textbook psychopath. A natural-born sadist. The epitome of the cliched Hollywood mob henchman who delights in maiming and torturing. Soulless. Not that you could tell. He was young, good-looking, well-mannered, charismatic—everything you would expect of a fine, upstanding young man. The boy next door. The guy you wouldn't object to dating your daughter. Then, when no one is looking he steals the family cat and tortures it to death in the garage. I have no idea where Tony found this nut bag. In a sense, it's probably good he ended up a mob enforcer. It channeled his darkness. At least with that he was mostly hurting other bad people. Without it he probably would have ended up a serial killer. The other guys on the crew called him "D," but, privately in my own head, I called him "Demented." He was to be my partner on the first serious piece of work I had to do.

There is a fine old tradition of barn burning in America.

Going back to colonial times, when someone seriously pissed you off and needed straightening out, one party sent a clear message: Under the cover of darkness you would get together friends and kinfolk, and go put a torch to the motherfucker's barn. Then, if that didn't get the message across, it justified a full-on feud and the musket balls could get-ta-flyin'. It was just plain bad manners to start the actual killing and maiming without a stern warning first. Or, it was just a coward's act of terrorism carried out by someone who didn't have the balls for a man-to-man fight. I guess it depends which side of it you're on.

The majestic Alcott estate was perched on a terrace above the north bank of the Clinton River, near Mount Clemens. Its current occupant was John Xavier Alcott III, the latest in a long line of old money in southeast Michigan. The Alcotts owned dozens of businesses dealing in damn near everything, but their real bread-and-butter trade was in pharmaceuticals. How they ran afoul of the Detroit Mafia, I don't know. I heard it had something to do with a labor dispute. As I've already said many times before, those kinds of details weren't my end of it. The bugler sounds "charge" and the troops move forward—that's all they need to know.

A crown jewel of the Alcott estate was a magnificent ten-stall horse stable, although at the time, it housed only nine animals. Among these were two thoroughbreds of noted Kentucky lineage and two rider-jumpers from a fine Virginia pedigree of fox-hunting mounts. The value of the horses alone surpassed the cost of a nice house in Detroit at the time.

Doing this job meant I had to deal with something I had been dreading: I would have to go see Mack. I didn't know how he was going to take my Prodigal Son stunt. I certainly couldn't blame him if he was pissed off. In the least, he would be curious. As a precaution I took along some back-up: I stopped at a liquor store on the way to see him and picked up a fifth of Bushmills single malt. As soon as I walked into his office at Shillelagh's, Mack sprung up from behind his desk and rushed me. "Damn, kid! Good to see ya, good to see ya," he grumbled, patting me on the back.

Whew! I handed him the bottle.

He set it on his desk, "Sit down, kid, sit down. Ain't you sight—about gave ya up for dead. Where the hell you been, Siberia?"

"Just about—the U.P."

"Yeah, that is damn near Siberia. So how the hell did you end up there?"

"Well, you know, after—after that thing, I went up north for a—for a break, I guess, and well, it's a long story, but I just keep on going and…and, I guess I just got stuck for a while."

"Stuck awhile, eh? In the U.P.?" After a short pause, he smacked his forehead with the palm of his hand, "Oh, oh, I get it! Of course, of course, only one way that happens: a woman!"

"Maybe…maybe."

"Yeah, and she must have been one fine piece to keep you that far away for so long. Let's have it, kid, details, details…"

"Nope. Sorry, old man, gonna have to live vicariously through someone else."

Mack reeled back. "Oh, c'mon now…"

"Look at it this way, Mack: If I'm back now, something must have gone horribly wrong…"

Blank stare.

"As in, the wounds are still too fresh…don't want salt rubbed in them…"

"Oh, oh. Yeah, yeah, sure, kid, I get it, I get it."

Sometimes lies are oil, a few drops keep things running smoothly.

"So what is it that brings you around?" Mack asked.

"I need some help on a little project."

Mack sprung out of his seat again and started to usher me out the door, "Sure, sure, kid, but first let me show you my latest project."

He led me around the side of the office toward his junk car lot, then stopped in front of an RV parked there. He said, "There she is. A little rough, yeah, but she's an Airstream. Will be real slick once I get her fixed up. C'mon, I'll show you the inside." Mack opened the door and we went inside the Airstream. He sat down at a small table with padded, bench seats on three sides. As I sat down next to him, I pulled a map from my back pocket. I opened it on the table and pointed with my finger, "Right about here is this big, fancy estate. Next to it is this big, fancy horse stable. The job is, burn down the fucking stable."

"That it? Shit, what do ya need me for?"

Confused look.

"What I mean is, a horse stable is about the easiest building there is to burn."

"Yeah?"

"Sure, kid, think about it: The thing about a horse stable is that it's basically a pre-built bonfire waiting to be lit. The structure is all wood beams and planks. The floor is covered with straw or sawdust. And then you have the big stacks of hay bales and paper bags of pelleted feed, all of which burn jim-dandy."

"Okay, good," I said, "but set that aside a minute, we'll come back to it. He's where I'm jammed: Kind of like that deal, up north, that gated community deal. No good access.

Stable is, well, that part's okay, far enough from the house we can sneak in, no problem. But, only way in is down this long-ass driveway, like a quarter-mile, at least, right in view of the house. So, I poked around some. No good place to stash a car out on the main road. Don't really want to have to escape that way anyway, figure…picturing fire trucks and cops pouring in from that side. So then I remembered what you told me before, told me how open waters are public, and this fancy place is right on the Clinton River. So, I was thinking maybe a boat…"

Mack slapped my knee, "Read my mind, kid, read my mind. But not a boat, exactly, a canoe. Ever use a canoe?"

"Sure, when I was a kid—in Boy Scouts."

"Okay, good. Like riding a bike, kid, nothing to it. Quiet. Easy to transport. Sneaky. Let me see here." He leaned over the map. "Okay, so the Clinton flows this way, east. You want to go in from the east, downriver, that is. That way you paddle upstream to get there, which is fine, plenty of time, then you can escape downstream, much faster. See these little squiggly blue lines? Those are feeder creeks that go into the river. Drive these roads that intersect them and I guarantee, you'll find a pull-off spot where you can stash a car near one of them. All a canoe needs is a little water—knee-deep, say. Paddle down the feeder to the river. Hug the bank," he examined the map again, then pointed, "Okay, good, see these marks? Look like clumps of grass? Those show marshy areas along the river. See, all along there, lots of 'em. That's good. If there's any boats on the water, you'll hear 'em a long ways off, and see 'em—boats gotta have lights on 'em when running at night. Then you just paddle into one of them marshy spots and hunker down. They'll blow on by—never see ya."

I nodded, "Yeah, I like it, I like it. So you can get a canoe?

Oh, and some way to haul it?"

Mack snapped his fingers, "No problem, kid, two, three days."

I leaned back and nodded. What else? Oh, right, "So, getting back to—yeah, this arson thing—it's new to me."

"Yeah, well…ain't much to it. Like I said—horse stable, that's easy. The mistake most guys make is, they overdo it. It don't take much, and once she's get going, get the fuck out, fast! Don't need you turning into a toasted marshmallow, kid. Use gasoline, but just a little. Get a can of lighter fluid, dump that out, and put in gas. That's more than enough. But—not exaggerating here, kid—she's gonna go up quick." He reached over to pat my cheek, "Look at that pretty face, don't burn it off, kid."

"Okay, good stuff. Anything else?"

Mack thought for a moment, then, "Yeah just one thing. Out on the water. You got a partner on this, yeah?"

"Yeah."

"Right, so noise. Some clunking around with the canoe, that's not so bad. But be real careful about talking. Sound really carries on the water—the human voice is very distinct."

I um-hummed and nodded.

Mack drummed his fingers on the table and looked out the window of the Airstream as he ran through the list in his head, then, "So, I guess that's about it. Am curious though, who you going in with?"

"Some new guy, I mean, new to me. Dmetri—"

"Oh, shit."

"Yeah? Uh-oh—"

"Well…no, kid, I don't mean it like—ah, shit, I'll say it, I just don't like the guy."

"What's wrong with him?"

"I dunno…he just strikes me as a complete whack job."

"Then why'd Tony bring him in?"

"I dunno…I dunno…ain't my business. Something about 'he's a stone-cold killer' and 'that's what we need right now.' I dunno. He's—he's either really arrogant or really dense, hard to tell which."

"One seems as bad as the other."

"Yeah, that's what I'm saying. Just watch out for that prick. I don't have a good feeling about him."

There is a special time of night when it is best for doing the devil's work. This is between two and four a.m. Even the hardcore night owls are usually in by two, and even the most chipper of early birds seldom get going before four. I wrapped tape around the paddles' shafts where they may clunk against the canoe. I warned Demented to speak in a whisper, if at all. It was a beautiful night. Warm, but not too hot. A clear, star-studded sky ruled by a crescent moon. A symphony of bugs, buzzing, whirring, chirping, singing, so loud you could barely hear the splash and drip of the paddles. So beautiful. So peaceful. It was almost a disappointment when we reached the small dock and landing area that sat on the river below the Alcott estate.

Inside the stable it didn't take long to find the spot I wanted. The one empty stall was being used to store bales of hay, with loose hay on the ground below them and many more bales stacked up in the loft above. Perfect. I had brought along a lighter fluid can, but with the lighter fluid replaced with much more volatile gasoline, just like Mack had advised. I soaked the hay bales stacked in the stall with the gas, but high enough up that it would take a bit of time before the flames from the loose hay below would ignite the gas.

Then I started going down the line of stall doors to unbolt

each door. We hadn't discussed this ahead of time, but to me it was just common sense. One of the basic laws of barn burning is that you make sure any animals kept there have a chance to run out. I mean, what kind of sick fuck burns up a bunch of caged animals? I only got the first bolt loose before an exasperated Demented hissed, "What are you doing?"

"Unlatching the stall doors…"

"Fuck that!"

Before I could react he lit the match, a second later, followed by a loud whoosh and a blinding flash. It was amazing how fast the fire took off. I only managed to throw open the bolts on two more stall doors before I had to make my escape.

We ran at a full sprint back to the river, then half ran, half slid down the bank to the canoe. That took, maybe, thirty seconds, but even by then the fire lit up the night sky. As Mack said, a horse stable is a giant bonfire just waiting to get touched off.

Between the adrenaline and the benefit of paddling downstream the return trip took only a quarter of the time it had taken to paddle in. At the mouth of the feeder stream, where it spread out to meet the Clinton, there was a shallow, marshy area. We paddled the canoe up into the cattails, hopped out, and working together to tip the canoe sideways, filled it with water and sunk it under the reeds. Then we just spear-chucked the paddles into the marsh grass and waded out to walk the few hundred yards along the creek to where the truck was stashed.

As we slopped our way out, Demented stopped, threw his head back, and with a loud inhalation, "Ah, I love the smell of roasting horse flesh on a summer night!"

I was glad at that point we had already gotten rid of the

canoe paddles. I don't know that I could have stopped myself from beating him to death with one of them. Sick fuck. (It would have been a good place to hide a body.) As things turned out, I wish I had just killed him right then and there.

In a blinding flash the Alcott stable was reduced to ash and six horses died a horrible death. And in a blinding flash all of the reasons I had turned my back on this lifestyle came back to me. In the past I had been somewhat able to deny—to even maybe justify—what I was doing. But, no, that was just naive bullshit. I was a terrible person doing terrible things to benefit even more terrible people. Again. Serenity? Courage? Where was the wisdom? I needed to sort this shit out.

Meanwhile, I was supplying Don Purdue with regular tapes I had been given by Tony, per his master plan. I never bothered to listen to what was actually on them, and Don never questioned me about their content. He understood, and made me understand, that we were playing the long game. He expected it to take several months to get anything worthwhile at all, and many more months to get enough to build an actual case. "Patience is a virtue." I don't dispute it, it just happens to be one of those virtues the Good Lord saw fit to bless me with very little of. I was looking to move things along a bit faster.

Chapter 16

It was only a matter of time before the Barbara situation would come to a head. I was a regular visitor to Tony's place, going about once a week for a staff meeting type deal in the Bat Cave. Barbara never seemed to be around, which suited me fine since I still didn't have a plan on how to deal with her.

Most times I would get to these meetings on the early side and had to wait on the patio outside the locked Bat Cave until everyone else arrived. Looking at the door from the patio side, a defect jumped out at me that bothered me more and more every time I looked at it. When the frame for the Bat Cave door was installed, it didn't fit flush against the rough natural stone the wall and patio were made from, so the remaining odd spaces were mortared in.

When Serge originally built the patio and adjacent wall he put a colorant in the mortar to give it a muted grayish brown color. This made the stonework look old, like ancient ruins in Rome, or some shit like that. But, by the time Tony made the renovations, Serge had already passed. The mason

Tony used did his best to match the color using commercially available mortar dyes, but he couldn't get it quite right. His mix was a little too yellow, and too bright and new-looking. It was a stupid little thing, but it just bugged me.

I mentioned it to Tony. I told him I had a good idea how Serge had gotten that color, and offered to redo the mortar work. Tony didn't seem all that interested. I persisted, "Let me do it as a tribute to Serge. I feel bad for missing his funeral. You know he's gonna haunt your ass for fucking up his stonework…" Tony agreed to at least let me bring him samples of what I thought was the "proper" mortar, and if he really saw a difference, I could do it.

The trick Serge used to get this aged mortar look was to add coffee to the mix, one gallon of strong coffee per ten gallons of water. I scaled down to a small batch, mixed it up, let the mortar set, and took it for comparison. A near-perfect match. Tony still thought it an unnecessary change, but said, "You are right that it's the kind of thing that would drive Serge nuts. Yeah, go ahead and fix it."

I told him I would get everything together and do it that Saturday afternoon.

"Oh, but I'm playing golf then," Tony said.

"All the better. I can do all of it from outside—don't really need you looking over my shoulder the whole time anyway."

So, that's what I did. I showed up around one Saturday afternoon, went around back to the patio, and just got to it. First I had to use a hammer and cold chisel to chip out all the wrong mortar. This exposed a gap one to three inches wide around the sides and top of the doorframe. From there I could see that the mason had packed the gap with wadded-up newspaper to provide backing and support for the mortar before it set and could hold itself up. I pulled most of this backfill out, to replace it with new, fluffy material that would better support the new mortar. Doing this showed that the gaps on the inside of the door frame, visible only from inside the Bat Cave, had been left unfilled. Nothing unusual there.

I had just finished packing in all the new newspaper when Barbara appeared to check on me and see if I needed anything. Damn she looked good. But in a snap that impulse was washed away by an overriding desire to take my hammer and just beat her fucking brains in. Not that I could do that right then and there.

As I said before, mid-Westerners tend to be blunt, straightforward, just rip the band-aid off-type people. So I just let it rip, "Look, Barbara, I know we're on camera here, so be careful how you react. The only reason I'm back is because you kept that gun I gave you and then gave it to the cops. That really fucked things up for me. I need to know what the deal is with that."

Turning her back to where the cameras were, white as new snow and with a trembling voice, "Oh, shit, Joey…you don't understand—"

"This isn't the time or place. I'll be done in an hour. Meet me at that park a few miles down the road?"

"Sh-sh-sure."

"First picnic shelter on the right, leave a few minutes after I do."

"Sure, um, yeah."

So, she met me at the picnic shelter near the entrance of Rotary Park, off Six Mile Road. She was still scared shitless. Still snow-white and trembling. She started with, "You have to understand, Joey, I thought you were dead! I mean, with all the shit going on then—with Vince getting killed—then you just up and disappear. And every time I asked Tony about it, all he keeps saying is he doesn't know where you disappeared to. I mean, shit, that really looked like you got taken out and your body was stashed. I thought you ended up like Carl! I mean, what else could I think?"

She went on to tell me the long, sad tale of how the gun I left with her ended up in the hands of the state police. Barbara had a brother, eight years younger, who everyone called Danny Boy. Danny Boy was what I refer to as a professional fuck-up. If you could go to college to major in screwing up, Danny Boy would have a PhD. It seemed no matter how much he tried to go straight, how much people tried to help him, or how many breaks the system gave him, he always found a way to trip over his own feet and end up face down in trouble.

"It was about a year after you disappeared—Danny Boy got out of jail—" Barbara said.

"For the umpteenth time." I couldn't help making the dig.

"Yeah, sure, but he's my little brother. So, being a good sister, I tried to help him out. So, I talked to Paul—my boss—at the flower shop, you remember? I talked Paul into taking Danny Boy on as a delivery driver."

"Should have known better. You can't fix people. People can only fix themselves. Danny Boy—"

"You're right. You're right. But, my little brother, so—so, yeah he screwed me. Decided that delivering flowers was the perfect cover for moving drugs. At first, just a little pot. Then, next thing you know, bigger bags of pot. Then various other hard shit tossed in for extra cash. And, you know, the kid isn't exactly a criminal mastermind, so it didn't take very long for the cops to catch on."

"And the shit hit the fan."

"Exactly. And, his distribution route covered over a

dozen different localities, so the state police were brought in. And, yeah, the shit hit the fan. Danny Boy got popped with enough dope to face a pile of felony counts. The delivery van got impounded. Then, if that isn't bad enough, search warrants get served on both the flower shop and my house. And the cops don't know—they think maybe this is some big drug ring, so—a fucking circus, Joey. They're looking at me—they're looking at Paul. A fucking mess! So, ultimately we're cleared of any involvement, of course, but—but then, of course, I got fired."

I couldn't help but laugh. Not that I was trying to be a dick about it. Okay, maybe I was. "Yeah, too bad Paul's gay. Otherwise I have little doubt you could've used your—well, let's say, use your considerable feminine wiles to—to convince him to not fire you."

"Yeah, sure. That a dig or a compliment? But, yeah, so, basically just out on my ass."

Yes, out on her gorgeous, perfectly pert ass. But I wasn't going to say that out loud. Hell, I was trying to not even think about it.

"Okay, so, how does this tale of woe lead to the gun thing?" I asked.

"So, Danny Boy's facing several decades worth of prison time. And—he's my little brother, you know—so I still had it—that gun, you know—and—" She started to cry, "And I knew it was—"

"You knew it was *the* clue in an unsolved homicide, so you traded it. You played let's make a deal with the cops."

She was sobbing now, hands over her face, and could only nod.

I gave her a minute, then asked, "So how'd that work out?"

She collected herself, but still with a whimper, said, "It

worked out. He got eighteen months and one of those—what is it? Yeah, drug treatment programs."

"Okay, fine, but, I gotta ask: Why on God's green Earth did you keep that gun to begin with?"

Oh, shit, here comes the waterworks again. Through the sobs and heaves, she explained, "I don't know—I don't know—it was just such a chaotic time! I guess I—I guess I just forgot about it."

Okay, that sounded a bit bullshitty, but a moot point.

She ended the same way she started, "You have to understand, Joey, I really, really thought you were dead, otherwise I would never have done that! Can you ever—"

Then, well, you know, wah-wah-wah. I let her have a good cry.

Well, shit. I had to admit her explanation made sense. I had to admit that if it had been the other way around, I probably would have done the same thing. When I was a kid my mom always made me go to mass every Sunday (and Holy Days of Obligation, of course!), like a proper Catholic should. I remember one time the priest was giving this homily about forgiveness. One point he was trying to make was how holding a grudge was like carrying around this heavy burden and part of what forgiveness was all about was setting down that burden so it didn't drag you down anymore. Adulthood happens when all that wonky-wonk, blah-blah shit you were told as a kid suddenly comes back to you and makes sense.

So I forgave her. And, yes, it was just like setting aside a heavy, smothering weight when I put my hand on her shoulder, and told her, "It's okay. I understand now. We're—we're good, okay? No reason Tony needs to know any of this, okay?"

She nodded, then really broke down. I let her put her

head on my shoulder and gave her a one-armed hug as she heaved and sobbed on for a while. I wanted to really embrace her, to really comfort her, to feel her body pressed against mine again, like—but, no. After all, she was married now, and the wife of my boss.

And that was the end of that.

Chapter 17

The Jimmy Hoffa job may well be the greatest mob hit of all time. In any event, it has to be somewhere in the top ten. Everyone knew the Mafia took him out. Everyone knew where and when it happened. The authorities had a fairly good idea who the key players were. The problem was, no one could actually prove a goddamned thing. A key element to this was that the body was never found. It was the Detroit Family's legacy. It was their deepest, most treasured secret that they would protect with vicious vigor for decades afterward. No one was allowed to talk about it. Even hinting that you had any inside information on the job was a death wish. The Family simply had zero tolerance on the issue. Claiming to know anything about Jimmy Hoffa was an almost guaranteed way to end up going to meet him.

Jeff Desmond was nobody. He was a twenty-six-year-old, mid-level, keyboard-tapper, pencil-pusher in a two-hundred-cubicle office building doing some little mundane thing for some big mundane company. He was not a mobster. At any level. Never had been. But, his uncle…

As Mack told it: At one time his uncle, who Mack would refer to only as "JP," was an important but clandestine player in the Detroit Family. His job had been, more or less, the same type of role Mack now held. He was the supply, logistics, and planning guy. The mechanic. The quartermaster. As such, he probably did have some level of involvement with the Hoffa job, at least with the transportation and hiding of the body part of the deal. Jeff had a close relationship with his uncle. Jeff's father was killed in a car accident when Jeff was quite young and JP stepped in to fill that role. JP had passed away several years earlier, but it was reported that in his final months he did suffer some dementia. It was possible that if he really did have any details on the Hoffa job, he let them slip to Jeff.

Now why, exactly, several years later, Jeff would start flapping his gums about it is one of those questions no one could ever answer. He probably just craved the attention. Jeff hung out at this hole-in-the-wall bar in Royal Oak called the Grapevine. When he started telling tales of his mobster uncle and how he was in on the greatest missing person case in Detroit history, the other patrons took notice. The guys would buy him beers. Somewhat attractive girls would somewhat pay attention to him. To a poor schmo-drone-worker bee like Jeff, it was nirvana. Now, whether or not he ever gave any actual details, or if any of it was ever actually true, is unknown but also irrelevant. Jeff Desmond had become a squeaky wheel, and he needed to get greased.

The job went to Tony. He filled the rest of us in with the thumbnail sketch background at one of our regular meetings in the Bat Cave, then, "Big Ed will be handling this, but only in the get-it-done sense. I don't want him doing the actual job. Once the cops start investigating, they're gonna find out about—well, a possible mob connection, they'll call it. Big Ed is what they call 'known to law enforcement.' Known to be a Family guy, you know. So, he needs to stay in the background. So that's that, but—" Tony stomped his foot. "That sound you just heard was the other shoe dropping. There's a wrinkle. As you guys know, the Family is under close scrutiny right now. It's been decreed from the top that they don't just want guys whacked, they also want the bodies to disappear. Now, before anyone starts bitching, I get it, it makes the job much more complicated. There are all kinds of situations where you can slip in, pop a guy, then slip away. Those are fairly easy to come up with. But when you add in needing to load up, transport, then hide a body, that's a whole 'nother ball of wax. Fortunately, the Family is helping out on that. Big Ed's already up to speed, but Joey, D, you guys need to go see Mack, like quick, like sometime this next week. He'll bring you up to speed on it. I'll let Big Ed take it from there," and Tony left the Bat Cave.

Big Ed began, "Okay, so like Tony said, I'm running it and you guys," he pointed to me and Demented, and said, "are doing it. D, I just need you as the shooter. Joey, you are recon. Me and Joey got details to discuss, but D, you can go."

"Don't want me to stick around, help out?" Demented asked.

Big Ed extended his hand like a gun and made the trigger-pulling motion, "Can you do that?"

"Uh…yeah," Demented answered.

"Good, right now, that's all you need to know. Scoot." As Demented was about out the door, Big Ed added, "Oh, and D, be sure to go see Mack."

"Yeah, yeah," Demented answered, and he left.

Big Ed had me jot down what background information he already had on Jeff Desmond, then told me, "You can take it from there."

"What kind of timeline we got on this?" I asked.

Big Ed pondered a moment, then, "Well…sooner better than later, Joey. Nothing official, but the longer this takes, the more bitching about it I'm gonna get."

I just nodded and headed out to get started.

The starting point on any hit is scoping out those known locations the mark frequents. These were Jeff's regular, known hangout, the Grapevine, his workplace, and his home. I didn't like what I found. I went to visit with Big Ed at one of the Mano Construction sites. Out by the scrap lumber pile, I laid it out for Big Ed. "I started with the bar. Nope. The Grapevine sits in the middle of a block surrounded by other bars, nightclubs, restaurants, like that. Always super busy, people everywhere, ya know? It would be a tough spot just for a blast and run, never mind getting a body out. Then, his workplace—shit, even worse. I mean, sure, he's in and out on a regular schedule, but with a big herd of fellow office drones. So, that ain't it. So, I go scope out his apartment—"

"Yeah, that's—well, I was hoping—you know, a lot of the time, the simplest way to hit a guy is to just knock on his door, then when he answers it, either blast him, or if you need to be quiet, force your way in and stab him or knock him over the head."

"Yeah, but in this case, not seeing it. He lives in this big-ass apartment complex, in a middle apartment on the second floor. Again, a very busy-type environment, people coming and going all the time. Even if we find an opening to push in and whack him, actually smuggling the body out would be damn near impossible."

Big Ed scratched his head, "Well, shit, so much for easy. It is what it is. You know what this means…"

This left me stuck with the long, tedious task of having to follow Jeff around, looking for some place in his routine that would work. This took several weeks, during which Big Ed was bitching nonstop about how long it was taking. As I pointed out to him, there were any number of times while following Jeff around that I could have discretely popped him in the head and left the body, but if the job specs were to make the guy disappear, that was more mountain than mole hill. I eventually found an open spot in Jeff's routine that looked like it could be made to work. This was during the time that ATMs were becoming popular. Like most younger folks at the time, Jeff would stop at one to get loaded up with cash before a night out on the town.

I met with Big Ed to hash it out, again at the construction site, out there where only the scrap two-by-fours could overhear. I laid it out, "So, past couple Fridays, I'm tailing the guy, and both times, he stops by this ATM at a Bank of America branch a few miles from the Grapevine, then heads to a diner down the street from the bar for dinner, then on to the Grapevine."

I could see Big Ed start to fidget and shake his head so I jumped ahead of what I knew his objections would be, telling him, "Now, before you object, let me map it out: This particular bank has a fancy, ah, ornate type front entrance. So, can't mess that up by adding an ATM. So, instead, put it on the right side of the building. That side has its own little parking lot, off the main parking lot, you know. And, all around that, just enough trees and bushes and landscaping shit to make it pretty well hidden."

Big Ed folded his arms across his chest and nodded, but

then, "Okay, but still…an ATM on a Friday night—"

I held up my hand to stop him, "But wait, there's more. Both times Jeff hit the ATM right around 7 p.m. This is good. Yes, Friday night is a busy time for ATM use, but that 7 p.m. time sits in a sweet spot—there's a lull. I mean, think about it: Most people either use it right after work, say 5:30 to 6, or just before hitting the bar, which is like 8:30 or later."

Big Ed nodded. "Okay…okay, we're getting somewhere…"

"And here's the rest of it: Both times, same way: pulls into one of the parking spots in that side lot, parks along this low, grassy berm, the other side of which is a church parking lot. Then he makes the short hike over to the ATM, gets his cash, and walks back to his car. So, assuming we could catch him while no one else happens to be around—"

Big Ed smiled, "Yeah. Ambush him as he gets out, put a bullet in his head, then drag his ass over the berm to a car parked at the church. Yeah, yeah, throw him in the trunk, and scoot on outta there. I like it. Get it done."

I met with Mack for the needed tools. He supplied me with a car and a crappy little, Saturday night special-type .22 revolver. I couldn't help but to rile up Mack a little, "Shit, old man, what the fuck is this? A cap gun?"

But Mack gave as good as he got. "Damn, kid, ain't you dumb? As usual, it falls on me to educate your dumb ass. Twenty-two handguns are *it* for this type of up-close work. They're cheap and easy to get. They make less noise—more of a pop, or crack, not that drama-shit boom that Hollywood special effects always uses—what most common folk associate with a gunshot. Then, the key to it, kid, is you use these," and he held out a box of hollow-point bullets. "Plenty of power to penetrate the skull, then bust up and bounce around in there—turn the brain to mush—leaves just small bits of lead inside that make a ballistics match nearly impossible. Shit, kid, more pro hits have been done with .22s than all other calibers combined."

I took the gun and ammo from him.

Mack rubbed his chin, "Let's see, what else? At an ATM, huh? Banks got security cameras. Let's see…well, at least one pointed at the ATM…and no telling how far into the parking lot it sees. Shooter better be disguised. Let me get ya a ski mask."

So, that's what we did. We got lucky. No one else was using the bank when Jeff arrived, and the church was also vacant. Jeff got unlucky. He didn't even get his car door closed before a figure all in black materialized from the shadows and plunked him in the head. Up, over the berm into the open car trunk, and that was it.

But that was the easy part. Any big game hunter will tell you, the real work starts after the kill has been made. Now, at this point you would think we would use the cover of darkness to go dig a grave in some out-of-the-way spot to stash the body. That is the dramatic mainstay of hitmen on TV and in the movies. Actually doing it that way, though, is fraught with danger. Human beings are not good at seeing in the dark. You have to use headlights to drive into the spot. Once there, flashlights or lanterns need to be used to see what you're doing. Digging a grave takes time. Light can be seen from far away. Anyone who sees it is going to be suspicious. If Farmer Brown looks out his window and sees lights out in a field a half mile away in the middle of the night, he's going to call the sheriff. Of course, the fear during the day is that someone is going to roll up on you and ask what the fuck you're doing out there. So, the ideal situation is to have some secluded spot you have some legitimate access to, and then do the work during the day when no one cares or has any reason to take notice.

The Detroit Mafia had a long history of investment in real estate. It was a safe, easy place to park piles of illicit money. In recent decades they had gotten into the habit of buying up large chunks of farmland, mainly in southern Michigan and northern Ohio, and converting them into corporate farms under the name "Michigan Green." On paper, me, Demented, and god-only-knows how many other thugs were employees of Michigan Green. (Eventually we even had company ID badges.)

Prior to the hit, as Tony had ordered, me and Demented met with Mack to be schooled on how this helped with the new way the Boss wanted things done. At the tool shed behind Shillelagh's, Mack began the instruction, "Okay now, kiddies, pay close attention, need to know this chapter and verse. As much ahead of time as possible, you let me know. I get with the company and find the right spot. Ideally, like now, crops already harvested, empty fields, so easy. Otherwise, always a few here and there left fallow. That means not planted that year, dumbasses. I supply you with a map of the selected farm along with a specific field to work in. Stick to where I send you! Get it?"

Me and Demented both nodded.

Mack continued with detailed instructions on how to do things, "If anyone comes poking around, they won't, that's the whole fucking point, but if someone questions you, a grave is a pit to 'examine the soil profile.' Say it back to me."

"A pit to *examine the soil profile*." Like fucking kindergarteners.

"Good, good. Gold stars for both. Now, every time, *every time*, children, you have one of these," and bent down to open a big, orange case full of measuring devices, soil test kits, etc., "Open it up like this. Have it sitting there next to your work site, all official-looking. Got that?"

More nods.

"Okay, good, last part, but most important. Don't fuck around with this. Don't shortcut it, or half-ass it, okay? Every time, children, every fucking time, you dig the hole like this: First, leaf rake." He held one up, like we really were kindergarteners and didn't know what a fucking leaf rake was. "Rake aside any loose stuff on the surface. Then, lay out your tarps." He gestured toward two large plastic tarps, laid out on the ground with about six feet of open space between. "Now, the digging part, one way, and one way only! First, all the topsoil, that goes on one tarp. You'll be able to tell, very dark, loose, fluffy. Don't forget these are farm fields. That topsoil is gold! Then you hit the sterile layer below that. Usually sandy or clay, but you'll see, it's lighter colored, different dirt. That goes on the other tarp. We good? Okay, so then, no one around? Good, hustle that body into the hole. Then reverse it, sterile, light-colored soil, then topsoil, then rake all the loose stuff back over. Abracadabra, they've been disappeared!"

So that Saturday morning me and Demented planted Jeff Desmond in the middle of some field in the middle of nowhere. I took the gun from Demented to dispose of elsewhere. Yeah, it's tempting to just toss it in the hole, but on the off chance the body is found, no point in leaving a key piece of evidence with it.

I think the next rotation on that field was corn, so I guess the poor sap ended up as animal feed, or taco shells, or one of the thousand other things the magic of modern science can turn corn into. And, I guess, the big muckety-mucks all had smug grins of satisfaction that they had protected The

Family legacy.

I thought it was just pitiful, petty nonsense. I doubt the poor guy actually knew anything. Even if he did, one stern warning would have shut him up. I doubt it would have even been necessary to rough him up much. But those weren't my decisions to make. I was just a pawn, moving one square at a time, hoping neither side would notice me and decide to wipe me out.

Chapter 18

Of course, throughout all of this there was the need to make money. The whole point of the mob was to generate wealth for its members. You had to hustle. You had to earn. You had to kick money up to the Captain so he could kick money up to the Boss. Everybody's gotta eat. Most of this type of stuff I did under Big Ed, who always had some kind of scheme going.

I got to do some truck hijacking. This has always been one of those bread-and-butter mainstays of mob income. I suppose that goes back just about forever. It's easy to imagine a group of cavemen finding a deposit of flint, then spending all day chipping out the good pieces only to get jumped halfway back to their village by spear-toting thugs who rip them off for it. I guess as long as people have been moving valuables from one place to another there have been bad guys looking to steal it along the way.

Big Ed's method was the simple, tried-and-true style. It started with at least some level of "inside information" to determine what trucks to hit, when, and where. At times it was entirely an inside job with the truck driver just meeting us at a prearranged location on his route where we could "rob" him. Mostly, though, it was the more typical armed robbery-type deal. We would find someplace on the truck's route that was narrow enough to box in the truck, but also secluded enough to not make a scene. A follow car would trail the truck until it got to the trap location, then call on a walkie-talkie to the guys in the block car up ahead. From there it's simple. The block car pulls out across the road to block forward movement while the follow car turns sideways across the road just behind the truck. Then the front car guys jump out with guns and force the driver out. Our driver gets into the truck, the hold-up guys get back into the block car, the follow car…well, follows, and the hijack crew drives off leaving the poor sap trucker on the side of the road. Done right, the whole deal is done in a minute.

Me and Demented were the stick-up guys in the block car. We used a "Jimmy the Gent" style, although I doubt he's the one who actually invented it. After getting the driver out of the truck, we would have him take out his wallet and give us his driver's license, then give him a hundred-dollar bill in exchange. This combined the carrot-and-stick approach. The trucker knew we then knew who he was and where to find him, so he better be careful what he said, but at the same time was compensated for his inconvenience.

We always wore ski masks. Part of this was just in case any witnesses happened along. Mostly, though, it was a courtesy to the truck driver. He could then honestly tell the cops he couldn't identify the hijackers and not end up in trouble with either them or us. Big Ed was always in the follow car. This was because he was such a big guy, and also had those really distinct pale blue eyes, so that even with a mask on, he risked being identified. Along with Big Ed was this guy I knew only as Nicky, who was our truck driver. (I think he was an up-and-coming member of the Cowboy Crew, but I only ever dealt with him on these truck jobs.)

We mostly targeted shipments of electronics, like TVs, stereos, VCRs, that kind of shit. Valuable enough, easy to unload and move around as needed, easy to store, and easy to re-sell. Big Ed handled all that. He paid taxes to Tony on the take, then kept half of what was left, gave 20 percent each to me and Demented as the serious-felony-armed-robbers, and 10 percent to Nicky as the driver. We did, maybe, somewhere around one or two a week for about six months.

The last one we did was kind of comical. Me and Demented were staked out in the block car, waiting. Usually when I had to spend any time alone in a car with Demented, I would play the radio, a touch extra loud, to discourage him from striking up a conversation. I had already concluded he was an asshole, and wasn't worth talking to. That wasn't an option in this particular case, though. We needed to listen for the message to come over the walkie-talkie that it was time for us to pounce. Out of the blue Demented turned to me, and said, "You don't like me much, do ya?"

Hmm…looks like the machine needs a little oil. "It isn't that, D. It's just—tunnel vision—focus. When I'm on a job, all I'm locked in on is the job," I said.

"Uh-huh…uh-huh…yeah, I get that. I hope this deal don't take too long—got this yummy mummy I been seeing—don't have the kids tonight. If we can get this shit wrapped up quick enough I can slip in and—well you know, slip one in."

Ha-ha, fucking hilarious. More oil needed. "See, that's exactly what I mean," I said. "See, me, personally, I can't let myself think about stuff like that. If I'm distracted—if I'm just trying to get on to something else—that's when mistakes get made. For me, I mean."

"Sure, sure, I get it."

Normally, that's when I would reach for the volume knob on the radio. Instead, the walkie-talkie saved me.

The actual hijacking was boilerplate. We trapped in a large, unmarked box truck on a lonely shortcut road through an industrial area. Out of the block car lickety-split, .45 autos pointed at the truck cab, "Let's go, out, out! Hands up, hands up!"

The driver climbed down out of the cab and put up his hands, then with an odd smile, "I think you guys made a mistake. This isn't the truck you—"

Demented snapped. In two giant strides he was in the driver's face. He put the muzzle of his .45 right on the guy's forehead, finger on the trigger, "Shut the fuck up! One more fucking word, your brains are all over the road."

I was afraid the crazy son of a bitch was about to actually do it, so I jumped in. Taking the driver by his coat sleeve, I manhandled him off the road into a shallow drainage ditch. I snapped my fingers, "Wallet, C'mon, quick." The driver took out his wallet and started to hand it to me. I stopped him, "Just take out your driver's license." He handed me the license with a slight tremble in his hand. I took it with my left hand, right still holding my gun, down at my hip but pointed at his gut. "Now, without saying a word, you understand why I'm taking this?" I asked. He nodded. I put his license into my shirt pocket, and in the same motion, took out the C-note. I handed it to him, "And we'll leave the truck someplace it can be found. All you need to do is stay deaf, dumb, and blind." I reached over and patted him on the cheek. "Capeesh?"

He nodded.

I waved in Nicky. He came up at a trot and jumped in the truck cab. Just as I was leaving, I looked back at the driver. He was just standing there on the side of the road with a big shit-eating grin. That seemed odd, but, no telling how people react to stress, so I didn't think much of it.

Once back at the warehouse Big Ed had arranged for the drop-off, we opened the back of the truck and—what the fuck? Lobsters! Live lobsters. Crate upon crate upon crate. I think every fucking lobster caught in Maine that season was crammed into that goddamn truck. Big Ed smacked his forehead, saying, "Shit, shit, shit!" And smacked his forehead a few more times.

"What the hell is this?" Demented asked.

Big Ed tensed up and turned to Demented like he was about to sock him, but then turned away and dropped his head, "Oh, mother of…yeah, guys, sorry, my fuck up. I got this connection over at the trucking company, you know. Got sloppy—yeah, got sloppy. Just had 'em look at the dollar amount put on the shipper's form as the insurance value of the cargo."

I tried to help him out, "Well, shit. They are—I mean, they're fucking lobsters, but, hey, they're still high-dollar shit."

Big Ed leaned against the truck and hammered its side with his fist, "Yeah…and yeah, people will buy 'em, but—perishable. This ain't just boxes of stereo equipment we can stack up in the warehouse waiting for a buyer." Big Ed slammed the truck shut. "Shit! You guys go home, I'll—shit, I got a lot a phone calls to make." Big Ed worked non-stop for the next two days to unload that haul. By that weekend every seafood place from Detroit down to Toledo was running a special on fresh Maine lobster.

After that, Big Ed got out of the truck hijacking racket. Not because of the lobster fiasco, although his actual timing was probably influenced by that. He dropped the racket because that was just how Big Ed operated. During his lifelong criminal career, he made money just about every illegal way you can think of, but only short-term. His approach was to go in, make as much as he safely could as fast as he could, then drop the whole thing and move on.

The subject popped up one weekend when we were over at Tony's for one of his cookouts. I was sitting with Big Ed smoking cigars and sipping rum. Well, that is, Big Ed was smoking cigars and gulping rum, I was nursing mine and people-watching. I guess the rum was working on him. He was more chatty than usual. "See, Joey, it's like this: Criminal investigations take time. Cracking something like a hijacking ring usually takes many months if not years of—you know—investigation, cop shit. By then, whoosh, I'm gone. It leaves the cops what I call 'fishing behind the school.' It doesn't matter how good of fishermen they are, or how good their bait is, the fish ain't there anymore! Can't catch what ain't there!"

"Yeah, makes sense."

Big Ed leaned back in his chair, blew a big puff of cigar smoke into the air, and watched it drift away for a few seconds. With just a hint of slur in his voice, "Everyone thinks you have to climb to the top of the mountain. They forget that the higher up you get—more exposed—more dangerous the climb gets. Then, what's on top of the mountain? A bunch of fucking rocks! And the wind never stops blowing, and the lightning strikes, and…fuck that! Climb up high enough to have a good view, then climb back down and find another mountain."

This provided an opening to ask about something I had

been wondering about, so I asked, "So, is that why you got out of the ripping-off-druggies thing?"

"Yeah, Joey, exactly, exactly. That's the perfect example. I dropped it, but some other guys—" It took two cigar puffs and a swig of rum to bring Big Ed back on track, "It was D and two other guys that are gone now. That's such an odd thing. Don't know who made the rule. One of us bites it, poof, just gone, like he never was. It's like we're some primitive tribe where it's considered taboo to speak the name of the dead."

"Yeah, I've noticed that. Like Little Louie."

Big Ed leaned back and grinned, "Oh, shit, yeah, Little Louie. He was a—yeah, Louie was a good guy. I miss that fat fucker." He raised his glass high, "Here's to Little Louie!"

A brief pause to refill his glass from the fifth of Bacardi Gold on the table. I took a sip from mine, then lit a cigarette, my abandoned cigar already dead in the ashtray.

"So, anyway," Big Ed continued, "They have this sweet deal. Got some narco squad cop on the take. He's feeding them intel on houses to hit. But—" he tapped a finger to his temple, "But, you gotta use your fucking brain. Trouble there is, all the info he has is just in the precinct he works in. Small area, you know. So, yeah, they fucked up. Got greedy. Hit too many places too fast in too small of an area." He tapped his temple again, "Druggies ain't dumb. Gonna figure it out. Gonna hit back. So, one night they make what seems like an ordinary raid. But as soon as the druggies hit the floor— musta had a guy hidden, waiting, you know. Lights the place up—uzi, we think. D was lucky to escape, just a 9mm hole all the way through his left thigh. The other two—" He raised his glass up to the sky, and toasted them, "permanently retired from The Life."

Which isn't to say Big Ed wasn't ready to snatch up a pile

of drug money, if the right opportunity came along. Rick and Sammy Munoz, first cousins from somewhere down in Texas, offered such an opening. They were buying bales of marijuana smuggled over the border from Mexico and distributing it throughout south Texas. While visiting family in Michigan, they saw a business opportunity. The pot on the streets there was both more expensive and of lower quality than the stuff coming over the border into Texas. They started by just cramming a couple bales into the trunk of a car and heading north. That went well and they started bringing in more.

That's when they hit a snag. At the time, much of the pot trade in southern Michigan was controlled by a biker gang, the Dark Knights. They had little tolerance for competition. Two nobodies from out of state had little hope of going up against them. If the Munoz boys wanted to continue with their enterprise, they would need some major help.

How they got linked up with Big Ed, I don't know. He offered protection two ways. One, with his wide network of safehouses and hidey-holes where the product could be stashed, using a different location for each new shipment. Two, by using his considerable underworld clout to get the bikers to back off.

Now, at least on the surface, this would appear to be a violation of the Detroit Family's no-drug-dealing rule. Big Ed, and, more importantly, Tony, felt they were safely in the gray area there. To begin with, all Big Ed was providing was protection. At no point was he involved in the actual transporting or selling of the drugs. Also, this was just marijuana, which was a bullshit, "soft" drug, not coke or heroin or one of the real, "hard" drugs.

The way the public perception of marijuana has changed just in my lifetime is nothing short of comical. When I was growing up they called it "devil weed," a "gateway drug," smoked only by "burnouts" and "losers." Getting caught with just one joint was a trip to jail and a permanent stigma on your record. Meanwhile, cigarette smoking was everywhere.

In just a few decades that got turned around and the two almost switched places. Tobacco ended up getting demonized. Even slight exposure to occasional secondhand tobacco smoke was declared a major health risk. But pot? Well, we decided it wasn't nearly as bad as it was made out to be. In fact, as it turns out, it is a magical panacea, good for just about all that ails you.

Anyway, the real reason that Big Ed's involvement with the Munoz boys wasn't considered a rule violation was because he never intended it to be anything other than a short-term scam. Under his protection, they were able to import larger and larger loads. When they got to the point where they were bringing in as much as they could resell, Big Ed encouraged them to continue hauling in more. He had the places to stash it and assured them he could use his wide network of underworld contacts to expand their distribution base.

This was a lie. As soon as Big Ed felt the pile of pot bales was as big as it would get, he was just going to steal it all. He had planned it that way from the start. When that day finally arrived, Big Ed intended to meet Rick and Sammy at the stash house, help them unload, then whack them. Big Ed was like that. He was what, I guess, I would call an "amoral killer." It was, very simply, a matter of what was practical and expedient. If the weeds are crowding your lettuce plants, you pluck them out. If you need to steal from other criminals, why give them a chance to seek revenge by coming after you or ratting to the cops? Just pluck them out and toss them in the compost pile. Ain't nothing personal.

It was at that point that I got pulled into the deal. It was during one of our regular meetings in the Bat Cave. Big Ed needed my help getting rid of the bodies. He barely got started laying it out when Tony stopped him, "Hold up a sec. Been doing some thinking on this. Got another idea on how to get rid of these guys. Here's the way I figure it: Since we got a 'rat' in our house anyway, might as well try to get some mileage out of it." He tapped my arm and horse-grinned, "No offense, Joey. What we do is, have Joey go rat to his cop buddy, tell him that if Rick and Sammy Munoz set foot in Michigan, they're gonna to get hit."

Big Ed grumbled and shook his head.

"Hold on now," Tony continued, "I'm just getting to the good part. Look, Purdue can only react in one of two ways, either of which is good for us. One, he could ignore the tip and let things play out. Of course, Joey's gonna record the whole thing, so that if he goes that route—I mean, what more is needed to prove this guy's a rogue cop? And we got the asshole on tape. Then, yeah, do the hit—really puts the nails in his coffin. Two, Purdue could pass word down to the cops in Texas. They warn these guys off. Make them think they barely dodged a bullet. Make them too scared to cause trouble."

Big Ed had taken on what I called his Goliath pose, standing tall and rigid, feet apart, arms folded across his chest.

"We win either way," Tony said.

Big Ed relaxed his pose, "Well, seems simpler to just whack 'em, but, hey, you're the boss."

Tony turned to me and asked, "Well?"

I shrugged, "Like the man says, you're the boss. You say 'jump,' I jump up into the air and don't fucking come back down until you say so."

Tony laughed.

So, that's what I did. Somewhat to Tony's disappointment, Don picked option two. Authorities with the DEA in Texas warned off the Munoz cousins. In a nutshell, they told them that not only would they be keeping a close eye on them, but also that the Detroit Mafia "had a contract out on them" so they better stay as far away as possible.

This then left Big Ed with a big enough pile of pot bales to get every man, woman, and child in the Detroit metro area stoned, twice. So, now how does he get around the no-drug-dealing rule? Again, one of those details he had covered from the start. The Dark Knights hadn't backed off the Munoz boys just because of Big Ed's "considerable clout" or some fear of going up against "the mafia." They were in on the scam. Big Ed sold the whole heap of hay to them at enough of a discount for both sides to make a killing.

I was given a few grand as a "facilitator," having saved Big Ed the trouble and risk of adding two more life-sentence-no-statute-of limitations-felonies to his resume. It was also a rare opportunity for me to somewhat feel good about my fucked-up situation. I had actually managed to save a couple of lives. But what little hope I gleaned in that moment was quickly snatched away. The next job may well be the worst thing I've ever done.

CHAPTER 19

I think the guy's name was Darren. I can't remember his last name. It may have been Johnson, or something like that. He was just about to start his senior year at the University of Michigan, which he was attending on a full-ride basketball scholarship. While not a superstar, he was a rock-solid starter on the team, and fully expected to go on to a career in the NBA. At this point I should give some dramatic backstory about how he beat the odds to rise up out of poverty in some hellhole, drug and gang-addled Detroit neighborhood to find success and salvation on the basketball court. That would make what ended up happening seem all the more tragic. But I won't. I don't know what his back story was. And what was done to him was tragic enough all by itself.

Now, on the surface, this guy seems to be an unlikely target for a mob hit. As usual, nobody ever gave me any details on who ordered the job or why he was targeted. It was yet another case, though, where I got the distinct impression the order came from someone higher up the ladder than Tony.

As such, there must have been some serious problem this guy was causing, and/or a huge pile of money involved.

It was only years later when I happened to catch one of those "true crime"-type shows that a probable explanation came to me. The TV show was about how these mobsters in Philly had found a way to tap into the insane money generated by professional sports in America. They had either set up or bought into a perfectly legal, legitimate sports agency, as in, the guys who represent and manage professional athletes.

The illicit side of it was, they would identify promising high school athletes, then use typical mob tactics like bribes and extortion to get them full-ride scholarships at schools where they could really show off their talent. In exchange, the athletes were then obligated to sign with the mobbed-up sports agency if they went pro. These types of semi-legitimate-semi-illegal businesses were typical. Tony Mano was a good example. Of course, I have no way to know for certain, but would be confident in saying, at least half his income was completely legitimate, 25 percent was clearly illegal, and 25 percent was in that murky gray area in between.

Of course, the main problem with this kind of arrangement is that, being at least partially illegal, no formal contract is involved. So if the athlete decides to renege, it's not a matter of going to court to sue for breach of contract. The mob then has to resort to…well, you know, typical mob tactics. If I figured it right, there were probably dozens of guys like Darren who were, basically, on the hook to the mob. And, seeing that they made these deals when young, dumb, and just out of high school, there must have been at least a few, now getting ready to enter the mega-bucks realm of professional sports, that were regretting the deal. With tens of millions of dollars in agent fees at play, these contracts had to be enforced. In all likelihood poor Darren was selected because he was valuable, but not super valuable. He would be the sacrificial lamb, slaughtered to bring the rest of the herd in line. He would be made an example of. Machiavelli would nod in approval from hell.

Now, this makes it sound like the mob decided to whack Darren. No. What they wanted done was, it could be argued, even worse. They wanted him crippled. They wanted to send a clear message to any other sheep that were tempted to stray that either you play for them or you will not be able to play at all.

Big Ed had me meet him one evening at a construction site in Northville, inside a nearly complete garage the construction crew had set up as a break area. They had lawn chairs and lawn tables set up café-style around the cement floor. It being the dog days of summer, they then put a small generator outside to run box fans to cool off. Big Ed fired up the fans, and we sat down to talk. He laid out the job.

Shit! Looking at my feet, I said, "Jesus, Ed. That's some sick shit. Why you bringing this to me? Sound's perfect for D, right up his alley."

"Yeah, I agree, but don't got time. Got a small window of opportunity. Oh, wait—yeah, you probably don't know. D's doing thirty in County."

"Oh?"

"Yeah, dumb shit. You know how he is—bit of a screw loose. So, one night he goes to some bar he hangs out at. Parks on the street out front. He drives that big-ass LTD, you know? So, comes out to find some asswipe has parked in front of him, too close, you know, can't get out. So, what's he do? Smashes the guy's window, gets in the guy's car, puts it in neutral. Then, uses that big-ass LTD to just shove it out onto the street. Okay, fine, but—dumbass. It's up on a hill, so gets rolling, takes off down the hill, bounces off two other parked cars, then slams right into a house. Some old folks sleeping there, about have fucking heart attacks. Course, D thinks this is just fucking hilarious."

"Huh. Only thirty days for that?"

Big Ed just shrugged.

I shifted side to side in my lawn chair and gave Big Ed the puppy dog look.

He shook his head, "No, Joey, can't be me. Doing the deed? Yeah, no problem. Getting away? There's the sticky part. Hell, it would be easier if you could just whack him. Dead guys don't raise no fuss. But hurt a guy? Gonna be screaming his fucking head off. And—picture the scene— college town, week before school starts—gonna be people all over the place. So, right away, a crowd. Cops called. Imagine it—all those dumbass college kids doing all their dumbass college kid shit—gonna be cops everywhere. I figure, two minutes, tops, first one is on it. Then, not much longer for a whole army of boys in blue to swoop in and drop a dragnet over the area."

I looked at my feet again and shook my head, "Well! That just sounds fucking awesome…"

"Yeah, but that's what I'm getting at. Set-up like that, you don't even try to get away. You just, um, blend in, you know, just get a block or two away and join the crowd. So, get it? Look at me, then look at you. I ain't blending in none with no bunch of college kids, you fit right in. Get me?"

"Yeah…yeah."

"It is what it is, Joey."

"Yeah…yeah. Is what it is. I need to have that put on a fucking plaque—hang that on my fucking wall."

The set-up to ambush Darren was simple enough. This was the week before classes started back up, and Darren was there early to attend daily workouts and practices for the basketball team. The last practice session ended at nine p.m., which then put Darren back at his off-campus rental house at about 9:30. When he came home, he would walk up onto the front porch, unlock the door, then go inside. Along the front of the house, and extending right up the porch, were these really thick yew bushes. Even in the middle of the day you could crouch down behind them and be invisible. Now, of course, Darren had a pile of roommates sharing the house, some of which had already moved back in. But, the whole point of moving back to college the week before was to have a few days to party your ass off before classes started, so his roommates were unlikely to be home at that time of night. Yeah, it looked simple enough. Probably. Maybe. It would take some luck.

Thursday night. I was hunkered down in my hidey-hole like a cottontail rabbit in a brush pile. Right in the corner where the porch stuck out from the front wall of the house. Buried in yew branches. I was in an all-black tracksuit over my regular clothes. That made it uncomfortably hot. I hoped Darren didn't keep me waiting too long. He didn't.

A little after 9:30 he arrived at the front door, his knees about level with my head if I stood all the way up. Perfect. I placed the barrel of a .45 auto right up to his left knee, pulled the trigger, and obliterated that crucial leg joint. Darren dropped on his left side and started screaming bloody murder.

The first thing that had to go was the gun. I dumped it right there behind the bushes. From there I went into flushed rabbit mode, scuttling between the bushes and front wall, then around the corner and down the left side of the house. Just before popping out into view in the backyard I straightened up, and went into a casual walk, like I was just taking a shortcut between the houses. Behind the house was an old garage, then an alley. Stepping out into the alley was my first spot where I had to worry about witnesses, who, at that point, would report seeing a man all in black near the scene of the crime.

From there I turned right and headed down the alley, quick, but casual. The next thing that had to go was my gunshot residue-coated gloves. On Mack's advice, I had worn a pair of thin, black, cotton gloves. The soft material would not hold any fingerprints on the insides of the gloves. As I made my way down the alley I saw another old garage with one side covered with thick vines, going up to its roof. I rolled the gloves into a ball and tossed them up into the mass of vines.

The alley led out to a sidewalk. As I stepped out there I knew people would see me, again, as a man dressed all in black. I kept it as casual as I could and made my way along the sidewalk, away from the crime scene. After a block or so, I saw the opportunity for the next phase of my plan. There were two houses side by side that looked unoccupied, with no lights on inside. I slipped between them, and once in the darkness far enough from the sidewalk, stripped off the tracksuit to expose a light gray tee shirt and blue jeans. From there I zig-zagged between dark houses out to the sidewalk on the opposite side of the block. Then it was just another block to my hide-out.

It was a decent-sized apartment complex that largely catered to the college crowd. In scoping it out ahead of time, I noticed it had hosted an active party scene the past few nights. This night was no different. I wandered around a bit looking for a big enough group to blend into. It didn't take much effort. There were three apartments in a row with doors wide open and a big enough party for it to be spilling out into the hallway.

Of course, the best way to blend in in such a crowd would be to grab a beer and join the festivities. But, I didn't want to drink. My plan was to just hang around for a couple of hours, then drive home. But, just standing around not drinking wasn't exactly "blending in," so to help that along I decided to chat up a pair of plumpkins leaning against a wall in one of the apartments. One of them, Mindy I think her name was, seemed to take a liking to me. She was a bit bigger of a girl than I generally like, but cute and well-built. Not that I had any intentions. I just needed to kill enough time for the heat to die down so I could get the fuck out of there.

Mindy had other ideas. When a tray of shots came around, she offered me one. I declined with a lame joke of an excuse, "I'll pass, drank enough last night to last two days, at least!" But Mindy was undeterred. The next time the shots came around, she took one and offered it to me by tucking the glass into her ample cleavage. Cliched yes, but, well, that's just hard to say no to. And it was just one drink. Mindy had other ideas. She kept them coming until my mind was unable to say no but my body could still say yes. Then she dragged me off to her apartment. Huh, I thought it was supposed to be the guy who gets the girl drunk and takes advantage of her. Hooray for women's lib! I guess.

The next day I felt like shit warmed over. Yes, a hangover, but that was the least of it. Regret. Remorse. Guilt. There had been tinges of them with past jobs, but not like this. Before, I had always found a way to justify it, to compartmentalize it, to seal it up in a box, put it on the shelf, and walk away. But not this time. What I had done was…horrific…inhuman. Killing a man is bad, but isn't killing his hopes and dreams even worse? Taking a man's life is certainly an affront to The Creator, but stealing a man's ability to use his God-given talent must be at least a shade of gray darker yet. I knew I couldn't go on like this.

I weighed my options. I could go to Don Purdue and tell him I was out, then hope that my attempt at cooperation would at least merit a lighter sentence. Or, I could, in essence, commit suicide, by going to Tony Mano and telling him I quit. After tearing my fucking guts out over it for a few days, I decided there was no reason to cross that bridge, at the moment. I would continue on and see what came up next. But, I was absolutely determined I was *not* doing another job like this one. The problem, though, when you draw a line in the sand like that, is that then Fate takes offense and calls the hand. It took only a few more months for another job to come up that was even worse than this one.

Chapter 20

Avia Perdiz. A natural beauty. A Puerto Rican goddess. The kind of girl who could snap her fingers and have a thousand guys lined up around the block willing to kill one another to get with her. Not that she would ever do something like that. She was a good girl, a good daughter, a good student, a good Catholic. Much more Madonna than whore.

So, what she did while home from college that summer between her freshman and sophomore years was out of character for her. She had a torrid affair. With a married man. No doubt, she was naive. No doubt, she thought it was true love. But, no doubt, it was wrong. If that's all there was to it, she could have moved on, learned some hard lessons, gone to confession, said ten Hail Marys, and be absolved of her sin.

But she got pregnant. And, he was an important man, on his way up in the world. The scandal would ruin him. He implored her to have an abortion. She refused. He offered piles of money. She refused. He made innuendos that became open threats. She refused. She would not kill her baby. And, she would not hide who the father was. He was going to have to man-the-fuck-up and take responsibility.

I don't know who this jackass was. His identity remained a guarded secret. I think he was either a politician or some high-up bureaucrat in the mob's pocket. He needed "the problem to go away." Whoever he was, he must have been perceived by those high up in the Detroit Family to be ultra-valuable. So much so, they were willing to do what even professional scumbags would consider deplorable. Avia Perdiz needed to disappear. And, the one guy The Family knew could get it done was Tony Mano. He got the contract. He knew he only had two guys who could carry it out.

Tony called me in for a meeting at the Bat Cave. Just the two of us. Concerning. He seemed tense. More concerning. As we walked into the Bat Cave, I could see Tony had placed two of those white, molded plastic deck chairs inside. "Better sit down for this, Joey," he said.

Okay, now I was more than concerned.

Tony gave me the background on the job, then took a deep breath, "Okay, so that's it. A seriously nasty piece of work."

"I thought—I mean, always been under the impression—we don't do shit like this."

"Yeah, huh? Me too. Never had to—shit, never even heard of it being done. I promise you this much, Joey, isn't a Family guy. No real man would—a woman? Carrying your kid? Asshole. Not right, but—not my call. Me, personally, I'd rather whack the asshole and leave the girl, but, not my call. And, sorry, Joey, not yours either. You know—"

I nodded, looked at the wall for a moment, then back to Tony, "Yeah, I know. And can't be Big Ed—"

"Right. Not on a civilian. Gotta be—gonna be a

big investigation."

"Sounds about right for D, though. He's a…um…"

"Psychopath?"

"Well…yeah."

"Maybe so, but he's *my* psychopath. No, I'm sure it wouldn't bother him none, but—well, to begin with, it's still a two-man job. But it's more than that. This one needs to be done, um…very carefully. I don't just mean—well, what I mean is—look, like it or not, it's gonna happen. That genie is outta the bottle. You can do it right. Quick. Painless. You know, like just pop her in the back of the head when she's just—just doesn't even know it's coming, here one second, gone the next, like that."

"Sure…sure. I just wish—"

"Too bad. Put that in a box, tape it up real good, and stick it on the shelf. Like I said, it's happening, with or without you. You say no, all that changes is there's two bodies in the hole instead of one. That's just how it is. You know—"

Oh, shit, please don't actually say it.

"It is what it is."

I am going to have that put on a plaque. Then I'm going to burn that motherfucking plaque.

So, just like that, my hand got called. I had to either cross the bridge or renege on the promise I made to myself. I went to Don Purdue and laid out the situation. As soon as he heard about it, he said what I was already thinking, "No matter what it takes, we absolutely, positively, no question, cannot, cannot, *cannot* let this murder take place."

The issue then became how, or more realistically, if, that could be done without blowing my cover. Ideally, Don wanted to keep me in the game as long as possible to get as much incriminating information on Tony (and the Detroit Mafia in general) as possible. I suppose it is basic human nature to want to "have your cake and eat it too." At the individual level, it seems just about every reasonably intelligent adult knows this isn't possible. But somehow, at the collective level, we constantly convince ourselves it is. Just about every politician in America gets elected by convincing the electorate that he can not only replace their bread with cake, but that they also can then eat the cake and, magically, a new cake will appear.

Anyway, this then led to a discussion on how best to handle the situation. Don started, more thinking out loud than talking to me, "The easiest, most straightforward, safest route would be to grab up Avia, and put her into protective custody. But, as soon as that's done, they would know there was a rat, right? So then I guess—"

"No need to guess," I broke in. "The way it works in the mob is that if there is even a suspicion a guy is a rat, he gets whacked. It doesn't matter if he really was guilty or not. The higher-ups feel like the problem has been dealt with, while the lower downs get the message to stay in line."

"Right, right. So, as soon as Avia goes into protective custody, the jig is up. We would need to yank you out too—put you under protection as well." Don paced back and forth, "That would be the prudent thing to do. Okay, but—how imminent is this thing, Joey?"

"Well, I dunno. Just landed in my lap. Usually—I mean, I can't see any way it doesn't take weeks, maybe months to get a job like this setup. It ain't like the movies where the Godfather waves his hand and bodies start dropping."

"Okay…okay, good. So, what you're saying is, it's highly unlikely Avia is in any immediate danger. We have some time."

"Yeah, that's about it."

"Okay, good. Let me think. Go outside and have a smoke.

Let me think about this some."

By the time I finished my smoke break, Don had a plan. "Okay, Joey, you continue on as usual, do the recon work, and set up the hit. Once a time and place are set, let me know. From there we have two options: Ideally, best-case scenario is, the set-up is such that we can sub in a female undercover agent for Avia, then, as you and Dmetri move in for the kill, have a posse of hidden officers pounce on you. If it works, that would then give us leverage on two fronts: First, we could at least attempt to bring some kind of charges against Dmetri. At least get him out of the way, hell maybe even flip him. Second, and more importantly, Avia accepting police protection and cooperating with us is voluntary. If we can clearly show there was a serious attempt on her life, she'll be much more likely to cooperate. Or, if the set-up for the hit is such that there's no safe or practical way to set up a sting, we are back to just pulling the plug and putting both you and Avia into protective custody. In any event, there seems to be no reason to think we don't have plenty of time to get this fleshed out. That sound okay with you?"

I shrugged, "Yeah, sounds like a plan." Ah, but what is that saying about the "best laid plans o' mice and men?"

As it turned out, we didn't have nearly as much time as I expected. Either someone else had already done the recon work, or, more likely, someone had inside information on Avia's schedule.

Avia was a student at Michigan State University. Like most students there she lived in one of the dorms on campus. Parking was at a premium on campus, so those students who wanted to keep a car couldn't park it at their dorm. Instead, they had to store it in a multi-acre student parking lot way down on the southern edge of the campus. For most students this meant a one-to-two-mile hike from the dorms.

Avia kept a car there. She was in the habit of driving home to Lincoln Park (near Detroit) every weekend to visit her family and take a break from the ruckus of weekend college dorm life. So, early each Saturday morning, with the vast majority of her fellow students still sleeping off their Friday night debauchery, Avia would hike out to the hinterlands, get her car, and go home.

So, really all me and Demented had to do was go scope out that parking lot, make sure it looked like a decent ambush spot, and confirm Avia's schedule. From that we could plan the actual hit for some future time. The next Saturday we got up ungodly early to drive an hour and a half to the MSU student parking lot. We had been told Avia usually left at about 7:30, and that she usually parked on the east side of the lot. We had a picture of her, a description of her car, and a license plate number.

We got there a little before seven and started by driving up and down the aisles in the lot to locate her car. It was a gray Chevy Nova, which didn't exactly stand out, so we had to really look. This was made slightly more difficult because she had backed into the parking spot and Michigan only required a license plate on the back, so once we found it, Demented had to jump out and go around to the back to confirm it was the right car. From there we just had to park a little ways off and wait and watch.

From what I could observe while waiting, whoever picked this as a possible ambush spot had been smart. It was almost a complete ghost town at that time of morning. And, this lot really was out in the hinterlands. Across the street to the east was a large woodlot. To the north was a thick, brushy swath where some railroad tracks went through. I couldn't see that far south and west, but it looked like just scrub and farm fields there.

Avia arrived right on time. We saw her coming from a ways off, walking south down the sidewalk from campus, which was the only way to get to this part of the lot. As she got close, Demented let out a long, low whistle. "Damn! That girl is hot!" All we needed to do from there was to let her get in her car and drive away, then take what we had learned and decide if we wanted to stake her out again next Saturday, or just hit her then.

But Demented had other ideas. As she was about to her car, he popped open his door, on the passenger side of our car, and started to get out. I grabbed his arm. "What the fuck are you doing?"

He pulled away and waved me off. "You need to learn to calm down, man. Just want to have a closer look." When I started to object he cut me off, "Don't worry, I'm not stupid, I know what I'm doing." Before I could stop him, he was out the door.

I watched as he walked over to Avia and started talking to her. I was too far away to hear what they were saying, but it looked amicable. Then Demented said something to her and pointed to the back of her car. She went around to the back of the car with Demented behind her, at which point they were out of sight from where I was sitting.

The next thing I knew, Demented walked back into view at the front of Avia's car and was motioning me to come over. I got out of our car and started walking over. Once I got close enough that Demented wouldn't need to yell, he told me, "No, no, I meant bring the car over." So I got back in our car and drove over, parking right in front of Avia's car. Then I got out to see what all the commotion was about.

Joining Demented at the back of Avia's car, I saw it—that beautiful young girl's dead body, lying there on the pavement with a few feet of quarter-inch, yellow rope wrapped around her neck. Shit, shit, shit! It felt like a punch in the gut. Demented shrugged, "Well, Tony said get it done fast, and I didn't see any point in fucking around with it."

I was pissed, at Demented, at myself, at the whole goddamn fucked-up situation. But that had to be set aside. Why the boat sank, or whose fault it was, are questions to take up after you've swam ashore. This was an example of that critical difference between fault and responsibility. It may not have been my fault we now had a dead body to deal with, but it most certainly was my responsibility. I kept my head in the game.

I recalled a number of "funny" stories Mack had told about mobsters who put what they thought was a dead body in the trunk, only to end up down the road a ways and hear thumping coming from the trunk. So, as a precaution, the first thing I did was to take that rope around Avia's neck, tie a taut-line hitch, and cinch the knot down tight around her neck. That would keep her airway sealed and ensure she wouldn't recover if she really wasn't quite dead. Then after a thorough scan all around, we loaded her into our car trunk and got the hell out of there.

The next big problem was what to do with the body. That kind of shit is supposed to be planned out ahead of time. I knew we had no choice but to call Mack and that he was not going to be happy about the situation. Since I figured this mess was Demented's doing, I told him he needed to make that call. He objected, "C'mon, Joey, you know that grumpy old coot *hates* my ass. He seems to like you okay. You seem to know how to handle him."

I didn't see any point in arguing. We stopped at a pay phone and I called Mack. He was not happy. Of course, I had to be careful what I said over the phone. Like most thugs, we had code for stuff like this. I told him something like, "That car you have me test-driving has some major issues. I can get it back to the shop in an hour."

Mack grumbled, let out a long string of cuss words, then, "Okay, fine."

When we got to Shillelagh's I told Demented he had better wait in the car while I went inside to deal with Mack. Once I told Mack what the deal was, he blew his top. It took a few minutes to calm him down and remind him of the obvious, "Look, Mack, I don't like the situation any better than you do. This got sprung on me too. But it is what it is, and we're stuck with it."

Mack looked like he was about to spout off again, but then, "Go out to the shed and get the tarps and shit. It's gonna take me a while to find ya a spot."

As I was about out the door, Mack stopped me, "Oh, and kid, keep that fucker D outside. I'd like to—"

"Yeah, yeah, and who could blame ya? I'll keep him away."

I went out to the car and got Demented's attention with a rap on the passenger side door. As he rolled it down I told him, "This is gonna take a bit. Just stay in the car, me and Mack got it covered." Demented gave a sarcastic salute, rolled the window up, reclined his car seat, and closed his eyes. Fucking psychopath.

It took over an hour for Mack to sort it out. Fortunately, Demented did just stay in the car the whole time. If he and Mack had gotten into it, I expect I would have had at least one more dead body on my hands. Once Mack got it sorted, he sat me down with a map of a Michigan Green farm field we could use. I do, more or less, remember where it was, but considering how things ended up going, even now, I don't want to say.

It was a typical set-up for crop fields in swampy southern Michigan. The fields were divided into sixty-acre squares by a gridwork of drainage ditches and access roads. These drainage ditches were basically man-made streams, about five feet wide, and with about ten or fifteen feet of brushy, fallow land along each side. This made finding the right field easy; as we drove along the access road on the farm, we just needed to count the drainage ditches on our left until we found the correct field.

It was an ideal place to stash a body. The corn had been cut a week before. All we needed to do was rake aside the debris and dig in the root-free, fairly soft soil. The brush lines created by the drainage ditches made it confession-booth private. Even someone working just one field over wouldn't notice us. The grave went in about as quick and easy as that kind of shit can go.

We carried Avia over and laid her in, on her back, facing up. Before the dirt went back in over her Demented took an occasion to lean on his shovel. He worked his eyes up and down Avia's dead body like it was the centerfold in a *Playboy* magazine, "She *is* a fine-looking woman! Too bad we couldn't have had some fun with her before having to kill her. What a waste!"

I was glad he said that when he did. It made what I had already decided to do all the easier. I never had gotten rid of that little .22 we used on the Jeff Desmond job. I figured keeping it was low-risk, and you never know when a guy like me may suddenly need a tool like that. I had it stashed in the trunk of my car. While waiting that morning at Shillelagh's, it was a simple matter to slip it into the small of my back, under my coat. So, as Demented admired his handiwork, I caressed it out, put the muzzle to the back of his head, and turned his brain to scrambled eggs. Dragging his body over to the grave, I heaved him in, face down, on top of Avia, "There, you sick fucker, you said you wanted to get on top of her, now you are!"

Then I shoveled in the tarp load of sterile soil, then the topsoil, then raked the corn-stalk debris back over, and, *voila*, they were "disappeared."

Gathering up the tarps and tools, I loaded them in the car and drove down the farm lane two drainage ditches to a nearly identical, recently harvested cornfield. I took everything out and arranged it about fifty yards out in that field, laid out just like I was getting set-up to dig another grave. Then I ran over to the drainage ditch along the side of that field, slopped through the mud and water to the adjacent field, then followed the edge of that field back to the access road and my car.

On the drive out I stopped at a marshy area along the farm road and gave the gun a good heave. I spent the next hour taking a leisurely drive around the country before finding a little country store with a pay phone. I made sure to note the name of the store and the names of the crossroads at the intersection it sat at. Then I made the call.

As one can easily imagine, when running an operation like this, the cops know something can go to hell at any moment, and have safety protocols in place. I activated the emergency safety protocol. With incredible speed, the cavalry arrived. Three unmarked cars with plains-clothed state troopers. Several other marked cars prowled the general area. I was whisked off to a safehouse. (I don't know where, wasn't paying any attention to where we were going. Hell, I wasn't even really sure of where I started from.) It took Don a few hours to get to the safehouse to debrief me. As he walked in, "Joey, good to see you're okay. What the hell happened?"

"Oh hell, Don, still trying to figure it out myself."

"Just start from the beginning."

"Okay, so early this morning I go to pick up Demen—Dmetri. Thinking, you know, we were going to do recon work on the—on that job, you know. So he tells me, no, we don't need to do that. Change of plans. Another team had taken out Avia Perdiz that morning, he tells me! What the fuck? So, now, our end of it is taking care of the body—to go dig a grave, you know. So, of course, gotta go see Mack, that takes a while. Gotta drive out to BFE, that takes a while. Whole time, I can tell, I mean I can just tell, something's off with Dmetri. Guy just ain't a very good actor, you know. So, I'm keeping an eye on him. So, anyway, we get out there, get all set up, about to start digging. But I'm watching him outta the corner of my eye, you know. I see him reach for a gun in the small of his back. So, um, so…okay, so as he starts to draw on me, I just—man, I just reacted. Took that shovel and just swung for the fences! Knocked him for a loop. Thank God, there was some cover along a drainage ditch. Ran my ass down there, then hauled ass back to the car. He did manage to crank off one shot, but not even close. Anyway, I drove, so I had the keys. I just hopped in the car and sped the fuck outta there!"

"Okay, but then—"

"Yeah, okay, sorry about the delay. What can I say? I admit it, I was freaked out. I was out in the middle of nowhere. So, yeah, sorry, took me a little time to settle down and find a phone."

Don needed a moment to take it all in, then he started his cop interrogation, "So, basically what you're saying is, Dmetri set you up for a hit?"

"Yes."

"Any chance he did this on his own? I mean, any bad blood between you?"

"No. I mean, I didn't much care for him, but, work-wise we got along fine. Besides, there's no way a guy like Dmetri would do something like this on his own. It had to come from Tony."

"Okay…now what about Avia? Did Dmetri just make that up as part of the story to set you up?"

"Oh, shit, Don…I mean, shit, I hope so. But, I doubt it. Like I said, Dmetri isn't a very good liar. I—I don't think he was lying about that part. I think they got her. I think something got fucked up here. Look, no offense, but at this point I gotta ask, any chance you got a leak here?"

Don thought a few seconds before answering, "Well, with stuff like this, you never know, but I doubt it. We really have kept this operation very small, and very tight."

From there Don grilled me on the details of where all this happened, then dispatched teams to get my car and collect evidence from the farm field. Meanwhile he and the small team he had assembled for the operation were in full-on scramble mode to figure out what to do next. This took all night, during which I just crashed out, as best I could, on a couch at the state police safehouse.

By the next morning, Don and his team were ready to move. He turned me over to two U.S. Marshals who shunted me off to one of their safehouses in, yet another, top-secret, long-forgotten location.

CHAPTER 21

Now, I already know what many of you are thinking at this point. If I was working with the Michigan State Police, why was it federal agents that took me into custody? Well, you see, there's some things I left out of the story until now. From the very beginning of this clusterfuck I knew I could only straddle the fence for so long. At some point I would have to pick a side. That first job I did with Demented pretty well convinced me. Each nasty bit of work thereafter just reaffirmed that I had chosen wisely.

The real *coup d'etat* moment was that day I fixed the mortar around the door of Tony's Bat Cave. Even with his security cameras, it was a simple matter to put a state-of-the-art bug inside one of the wads of newspaper, then seal it in with mortar. The gap on the inside of the doorframe let the sound in just fine. It's said, "don't put all eggs in one basket," but alternately, if you do, "really watch that basket." Tony had an awful lot of eggs in that one basket, convinced it was safe. He really did heavily rely on the safety of his Bat Cave.

That one move alone yielded—no exaggeration—hundreds of hours of incriminating recordings.

But that wasn't all. After I tipped Tony off to the beeper bug I was carrying, he thought he was safe from it. It was a quick fix for the police techs to rewire the switch in the beeper so it activated when turned off instead of on. They left the receiver and tape recorder under my car dashboard, but deactivated the receiver, replacing it with another receiver and tape recorder under the back seat. That way, any time Tony wanted to check, he was free to pull the tape from under the dash, and would find it blank. I mostly used the beeper bug on Demented, Mack, and Big Ed, none of whom seemed to even know about it.

But even that wasn't quite all. So much of successful surveillance work is figuring out the who and where. I passed along to Don dozens of locations to bug. Some bore little fruit, some bushels. About halfway through all this, Don figured out that the type of evidence he was amassing really worked better as a RICO case, and he brought in the feds. While technically a joint task force, it was going to be the United States Department of Justice that would be taking down Tony Mano, his crew, and whatever other fish they could sweep up in the net.

So, that Sunday morning the FBI raided at least a dozen locations throughout the Detroit area. Tony, Big Ed, Mack, and I don't know how many other guys got scooped up. Demented, of course, "remained at large." Since federal prosecutions in cases like this can take anywhere from several months to several years to even get to trial, Tony, Big Ed, and Mack were freed on bail.

The hunt for the fugitive Dmetri Petrovich continued. At one point Don, still acting as a member of the task force, and being the one guy I had a relationship with, came to question me about possible places to look for Demented. Along with him he brought a young agent in a blue suit who was a member of the U.S. Marshals Fugitive Task Force. I don't remember his name. I told them, "To be honest, I would be shocked if you ever find him. After he fucked up that hit on me I expect Tony put him in the ground, right quick."

Agent Blue Suit's eyes narrowed, he tapped his pen on the table, "So, what you're saying is, Mr. Petrovich's failure to kill you was—was so bad his punishment was death? And, that fast? Let's see…" checking his notes, "So less than twenty-four hours between when you escaped and Tony Mano was arrested."

Yeah, nice try, buddy. I had had enough time and enough sense to already concoct the lie, "Well, yes and no. No, just missing a hit isn't a death penalty thing. And, yeah, the timing is tight, but not that tight. So—you guys really aren't getting it are you? Look, this Avia Perdiz thing was a major hit—gonna be major blow-back, ya know. So, two ways to handle that. One, like the Jimmy Hoffa thing. Keep it very tight. A few rock-solid guys. Then anyone even whispers a word about it, whack 'em. The other way to go, you need a scapegoat. That's what it took me a while to figure out. Why would Tony tell Dmetri to take me out? I was the scapegoat! They were gonna pin the Perdiz thing on me! So, I get away, then what? Guess who's next in line? Dmetri. Make him disappear, then pin it on him."

"So, Avia Perdiz did go missing that morning, and is now presumed dead," Agent Blue Suit said. "Who got her?"

I leaned back in my chair and crossed my arms, "Wish I knew. But, yeah, that's the million-dollar question, ain't it? If me and Dmetri were the B Team, expendable, the fall guys," and I threw up my hands, "Then who the fuck are the A Team? Looks like you guys got some work to do."

Meanwhile, I was still being closely guarded and hidden away by the Marshals while meeting regularly with federal prosecutor Walt Beamon. The meetings with Walt were to prepare me to give testimony on the three guys being charged who I had enough direct involvement with to do serious damage to. That was Tony Mano, Ed "Big Ed" Kowalski, and Jim "Mack" Mackelroy. As things turned out, though, I never ended up testifying at all.

Mack was the first to go. The following day he bailed out. On a clear, crisp winter night. After his mechanics had gone home for the day, Mack sat in his car parked outside Shillelagh's, sipping on a bottle of the finest Irish single malt he could find. Once he'd had enough to about pass out, he turned on the ignition. Exhaust fumes went up the hose he had clamped around the tailpipe, into the back window, and filled the car. Mack just closed his eyes and drifted off, all peaceful-like.

It is said suicide is the coward's way out. I suppose, at the societal level, we have to say that. But Mack's suicide was, to me, an act of great valor. With his decades of involvement and the kinds of services he provided, he knew enough to bury the entire Detroit Family. So, as his last act of service and loyalty to them, he made sure they didn't need to worry about it. Of course, one could just as easily point out that Mack was quite old, had already led a full life, and had no desire to spend his remaining days in prison. And, one could point out that, with what he knew, it was likely the Family was going to take him out anyway, so all he really did was save them the trouble. But I genuinely liked the man. He was, at least kind of, my friend. So allow me the kind lie of the delusion that he died a hero.

Tony was the next to go, several weeks later. Don Purdue told me about it. His body was found in an almost finished spec house he was building in Farmington Hills. The cause of death was a single stab wound to the heart, done with some kind of bladed weapon. The cops had no doubt Big Ed had done it. I had to agree, it certainly looked that way. If so, I can only imagine it one way: Tony, as much as Big Ed had always been loyal to him, couldn't take any chances. If Big Ed turned rat, Tony and a bunch of other guys would be up shit's creek. Tony asked Big Ed to meet him in the vacant house so Tony could kill him. But, in typical fashion, Big Ed was half a step quicker, turned the tables, and took out Tony. I just refuse to believe Big Ed would have killed Tony unless Tony betrayed him first.

Regardless, we'll never know. Right after, before Tony's body had even been found, Big Ed jumped bail and went on the run. He didn't make it far. The cops caught up with him in the small north-central Ohio town of Portage. He was holed up in a second-floor room of a Motel 6, and wasn't coming out without a fight. After a six-hour standoff an FBI sniper on the roof of the 7-Eleven across the street saw the chance to slip a .308 round through a narrow slot in the drapes of the room's window. In a style befitting his legacy, the mighty Goliath was slain by one well-placed shot to the head.

So, that was basically it for me. I was never called to testify about anything. I don't know what, if anything, ever ended up happening with whoever else got arrested. What Don told me was, "You have to understand how this works. This is just one little battle in a much bigger war. The true value in the information we passed along has more to do with future investigations, as part of the long game the DOJ is playing against organized crime. It adds to what they already have from other, ongoing investigations, and gives them new avenues to pursue for future investigations. For example, they had no idea until you came along that Michigan Green was a mob front. So now, they have a whole task force just to pick that apart."

What good came from any of this, I don't know. I was like Johnny Appleseed, planting a single seed, then shuffling on down the trail with faith it would one day make Mom's famous apple pie. There was one exception. I asked Don to let me know how things turned out for Barbara. "Why do you ask?" Don said, "I know you two have—have history. You still carrying a torch, Joe?"

"Well…no, not like that. I mean, um…I don't know why. That woman just has a way of making a man obsessed, of getting under his skin."

"Not thinking about doing something stupid? Not looking to reconnect?"

"Oh, no, nothing like that. Just curious."

"Good. Don't. To answer your question, she was charged with some bullshitty accessory-type charges, but worked a deal to just get probation. Which isn't to say she got off easy. Even without a conviction, the DOJ had no trouble getting an asset forfeiture on all of Tony's property."

So, that did, more or less, leave Barbara out on her (gorgeous, perfectly pert) ass once again. But she still had enough of her looks and all of her skills, so I imagine she ended up landing on her feet, or perhaps more accurately for someone like her, on her back. I have little doubt she's somewhere out there right now, cruising along in a shiny, new, little red corvette.

All that was left was to sign my immunity deal and go

through the process with the Marshals to enter the witness relocation program. A new beginning. A third chance to try to get it right. Not that I deserved it.

Chapter 22

Well, shit, you didn't really think it was going to be that easy, did you? I mean, it was, and it wasn't, for almost two decades. They made me change my name. They wanted to change both my first name and my last name. I thought that was just asinine, so insisted on staying Joe, but, of course, had no choice on the last name. I'm not going to even bother mentioning what my last name got changed to. To keep things simple and consistent, let's just stick with my original name.

I got relocated to an undisclosed location in what could be called the South, or perhaps more accurately, an area in the Mid-Atlantic region that had a strong Southern influence. I wouldn't say it was a matter of a culture shock-type of deal, but it did require some getting used to. Everywhere you go people are the same on the grand scale, but different on the small scale.

You have to learn the local language and customs. There was no "pop" available, but plenty of "soda." Those nuts you make pies from are "pah-cons" up North, "pee-cans" in the South, but in the Mid-Atlantic, in order to keep the peace between the two sides, you know, they are "pee-cons." Every man is "sir" and every woman is "ma'am," regardless of age or social rank. If you need to talk to someone about a particular subject, you aren't allowed to just start right in on it. You have to exchange greetings and chat a bit first. Where I grew up that would be considered an absurd, impractical waste of time. The hardest thing was, I needed to be careful about my swearing. Where I grew up, it was just a common element of the language, and no one thought too much about it. Here it can only be done sparingly, and even then only among those you know well enough to know they won't take too much offense.

Of course, anywhere you have to relocate to you worry about how they treat outsiders. As I said before, human beings are naturally xenophobic. You can put whatever "ism," "anti," "hate," or "phobic" label you want on it, but it mostly comes down to that ancient wiring in our brains that "We" don't trust "Them."

The area I moved to was metropolitan enough to not be too bad in this regard. The old-timey genteel Southerners mixed well enough with the blacks, po-whites, rednecks, foreigners, and Yankees. I guess, being from "up nawth" I was a Yankee. But, I came to learn that as a derisive term, it was reserved for people from the urban centers of the Northeast, especially New York and New Jersey. They were considered to universally be loud, obnoxious, and rude, and really just needed to "go back where they come from." I was from the Midwest, which wasn't so bad. When people think of the Midwest, they think of it as farm country, so I got lumped in with "decent country folk" which was more in the middle of the social register.

The reason I got sent where I did, when I did, was because the folks running the Witness Relocation Program are smart people. At the time, the area was experiencing a building boom, so they figured I wouldn't have any trouble finding a job. They figured right. I had no trouble finding full-time employment. Nothing worth talking about. I wasn't following my passion, working in my dream job, or using my God-given talents to do what I was born to do.

Why is it that—especially among men—one of the first things asked is always, "what do you do for a living?" That's about the *least* interesting thing about most people. I worked because I had to. There was nothing particularly fun, glamorous, or fulfilling about it. That's why they had to pay me to do it. Give me a pile of money and I'd disappear so fast you'd think it was a magic trick. I'd move so far up into the hills no one would ever find me. I expect it's that way with most folks, whether they'll admit it or not.

I was determined from the beginning to get it right this time. I knew what was "right" because I had grown up in a community of fine folks who were doing it. Work hard. Advance in your career. Pay taxes. Find a nice girl, settle down, and raise a family. Simple.

So that's what I did. Her name was Laurie. A pretty little thing, smart, sensible, and kind. Just a real sweetheart of a lady. Leaps and bounds beyond being too good for the likes of me. She fell in love with me. And, to the extent I'm capable of it, I guess I fell in love with her. We got married. We had a beautiful little girl together and named her Lily. Life was good. So there it was, all tied up in a bow, with sprinkles and whipped cream on top, and all that shit.

Now, if I had any sense at all, I'd end it there and give the story a happy ending. But, I have to imagine, after reading about all the terrible things I did, a great many of you were hoping I came to some bad end. Well, maybe I did, or maybe I didn't. I suppose it depends upon how you look at it.

Naturally, it only took me a few years to completely fuck up my marriage. Not in any of the traditional ways, mind you. I didn't cheat, or drink away my paycheck, or abuse my wife, or any shit like that. I just wasn't there for her. I mean, I was physically there, just not there mentally and emotionally. It's said that to have a good marriage you have to make your spouse the most important thing in your life, the center of your universe. That isn't exactly right. You have to make the *marriage* the most important thing, the sun that everything else orbits around. The marriage is a living, breathing entity all its own. Sometimes it grows, blooms, and becomes the most spectacular thing this side of heaven. Sometimes it just sits there, survives but doesn't thrive. And sometimes, it just dies. One person cannot make a marriage work. God knows Laurie tried. Her devotion to me was as perfect as anything can be upon this wretched Earth. But one person cannot make a marriage. So it simply died.

Now, I suppose a shrink would point out that to love someone else, and have any hope of making a committed relationship work, you must first love yourself, and I didn't. There may have been some truth to that. But the real problem was that I had made a classic mistake. I defined what was right for me based on what other people thought was the proper path. I tried to live and act outside of my nature. It is trite to the point of being cliched, but it seems true: Success can only be self-defined. Otherwise, there would be one skinny book on the shelf in the self-help section of the bookstore called *How to Be Successful* and anyone who read it would know just what to do. Marriage was a normal thing for normal people to do, but I'm not normal. I was that scorpion in the Aesop fable who hitched a ride on a frog to cross the river, then halfway across stung the frog, killing them both, because the scorpion could not overcome his basic nature. I just wish it hadn't been Laurie who had to play the frog. She damn for sure deserved better. I guess I did love her. And, I suppose, my greatest act of love to her was divorcing her so she would be free to find true happiness with someone actually worthy of her.

This in no way diminished my unquestionable love and commitment to Lily. My baby. My precious little girl. "Princess Gumdrop Lollipop" as I called her when she was so little I doubt she remembered. The animal instinct is ancient. The laws of man go back as far as anyone can remember, in all human societies everywhere: As soon as a child is born, the father signs a contract in heaven to be the protector and provider of that child until they reach adulthood. It may sound old-fashioned, or in modern terms may even be called sexist, but that in no way changes the basic reality. It is what is. It could not be otherwise.

Shortly after Lily was born, I did an odd thing. I went out to this patch of woods, out in the country on some land I had permission to hunt on, and I dug a grave. It took a long time. The ground there was full of tree roots that I had to hack out with a mattock, then dig a little more, and another damn root. It took about all day. It was for the first guy to come along that did anything to hurt my little girl. Any man who dared to fuck with my Princess Gumdrop Lollipop was going in that fucking hole. Not that I actually planned on using it. But for me it was an important symbol of my devotion to my child. Every time I went by that pit for years to come, it gave me comfort.

As Lily grew up we got along fine, but I wouldn't say we were close. We just seemed like we didn't have a whole lot in common. I figured out early on to just let her do her own thing, let her follow her own nature. What emotional support and guidance she needed came from her much more capable mother. I mostly just tried to stay out of the way. Laurie was the star of the show, I was supporting cast and prop man.

Laurie did eventually remarry. Greg was a fine guy who I really can't say one bad thing about. He made a good living, doing computer programming, or some such thing. Laurie, being the kind, sensible lady she was, told me she really didn't need the child support money anymore. I insisted on still paying it, though, and told her if it really wasn't needed to please put it in one of those 529 college savings accounts for Lily. The obligation of the sacred contract is absolute. It could not be otherwise.

And so it was for a long time. I settled into working enough to meet my obligations and…well, nothing more. I was like that soldier who comes back from the war but then never really finds his footing, never really ever finds his place in the world away from the battlefield. I never developed any real relationships of any real meaningfulness. I simply existed. I didn't do anyone any harm, but I didn't do anyone any good either. The Bluebird of Happiness never visited, but the Robin of "eh, good enough" was a constant companion. I was content, and I suppose, that's the best someone like me could hope for. I was either the still waters of a peaceful pond, or just stagnant water, depending upon how you look at it.

The first ripples disturbed the surface of the pond when Lily turned fifteen. Emotionally, she was slower than most to mature, while physically she was faster than most. That's a dangerous position to be in, especially for girls. Laurie was worried about her. She was getting a bit too wild. She was "hanging out with a bad crowd." I tried to calm her. Every teenager goes through this phase. Every teenager is just a fucked-up mess for a while, but they grow out it. I wasn't terribly worried. I will admit, I wasn't thrilled when Laurie told me Lily had a boyfriend who was a senior, while she was only a sophomore, but it still struck me as just dumb kid shit, not anything to get too bent out of shape over.

Maybe it was a premonition. Maybe it was just a whim. That fall after a cold morning of scanning the woods for deer that just weren't there, I visited that grave I had dug so many years before. It had about halfway filled in with many years of leaf fall and erosion. I went to my truck, got a shovel, and spent about an hour digging it back out and sprucing it up. "Just in case," I joked with myself. If it was a premonition, I was a couple of years off. Even now, I can't help but feel guilty. I wonder if by doing that I tempted fate just a little too much.

Chapter 23

David "Davy" Moore was pond scum, but of the gold-plated variety. High-class garbage. The textbook example of a spoiled rich kid. His family was part of the old-money aristocracy. Deeply rooted in the region, they were part of the landed gentry that had ruled the area since Colonial times. Davy grew up in a big house, with the finest of things, among the finest of people, and attending the finest of schools. He was born on top of the heap, with a silver spoon in his mouth, and 250 years of accrued money and power in his back pocket. Membership in the Old Boys Network was his birthright. Every opportunity was laid before him. His success in life was all but guaranteed. What could possibly go wrong?

Mahatma Gandhi, in rewriting the seven deadly sins, replaced greed with "unearned money." Indeed. It would seem that if you were some kind of evil genius, and were trying to devise a scheme to destroy a young person, one almost sure way would be to flood them with wealth. It is a powerful drug, wonderful when used properly, but oh so easy to OD on. For someone not mature enough to handle it, wealth can be a cancer to the soul that only the strongest of the strong can survive. Money can buy pleasure and comfort, but pleasure is not happiness, and comfort is not peace. And thus it is that so often the richest are the poorest. I guess that's kind of what happened to Davy Moore. But I offer that as an explanation, not an excuse.

By the time he was twenty-two Davy had already either failed out of, or been discretely asked to leave, at least three of the finest institutions of higher learning on the East Coast. His only real interest was living a playboy-esque lifestyle of drugs, parties, and general depravity. While trying to help him work through his sowing wild oats phase his family moved him back to the Moore Estate. The "big house" on the property was still owned by his declining grandmother, and the family wanted to keep her there as long as her health would allow. Along the way, they decided to make it into sort of a retirement home for several other elderly members of the clan.

Technically, Davy was in charge of managing this facility. In reality, there was a staff of nurses, cooks, and maids such that, while Davy was the overseer, he really didn't need to do much. Davy had a room in the big house, but seldom used it. It's hard to throw drug-fueled orgies with a bunch of old folks trying to sleep, and generally just getting in the way.

A ways off from the big house was a grandiose four-car garage. While it was being built the family had the second floor finished as a two-bedroom apartment. At one time his grandma did rent it out for a little extra income, but it had sat vacant for years. Davy cleaned it up and converted it into his playboy party palace.

Exactly how, and exactly when, Lily met this scumbag,

I don't know. It was sometime during the summer between her junior and senior years of high school. By then she had physically blossomed as a woman, but mentally and emotionally was still so much a child. He was rich, good-looking, and charismatic. He drew her into his circle of influence. I have little doubt they were having sex, although Lily would never admit it. I have no doubt he introduced her to drugs. At first, just a little pot to mellow out. Then a little Ecstasy to enjoy the party. Then a little cocaine to keep the party going. But living a lifestyle like that creates ragged edges, and to smooth those over, you need heroin. Once Davy got Lily hooked on heroin, he knew he owned her.

By Thanksgiving, it was clear Lily's life was circling the drain. Something had to be done. Laurie, being your basic, honest, law-abiding citizen, went to the police. She was referred to Diane Sullivan, a detective who specialized in cases like this. Detective Sullivan was capable, compassionate, and straightforward. No doubt, giving drugs to a minor and statutory rape were serious crimes, but making a case would be difficult. It would require Lily's complete cooperation, and even then would largely be a matter of "she said, he said."

Diane recommended an alternative route. Step one was for Laurie, as Lily's legal guardian, to get a restraining order against David Moore. The burden of proof was much smaller, and, at least at that time and place, judges were heavily biased toward the parents of minors on such matters, and granted such orders almost at will. Step two was to get Lily into a drug rehab center, preferably one out of the area.

And so the family met for a crisis meeting, what in the modern lingo I guess you would call an "intervention." A plan was agreed on. Lily seemed sincere, at least in the moment, about going along with it. So there was a glimmer of hope.

There was a light at the end of the tunnel. But actually getting there would require a lot of work, and some patience. These things take time. The restraining order was, more or less, about as easy as Detective Diane had said. We started working on looking for the right drug treatment center, far enough away, but also were hoping to find one where Lily could continue with her high school education.

Meanwhile, Laurie and Greg did their best to keep an eye on Lily. But, as all parents know, especially with teenagers, there's only so much you can do. You can't fix people. People can only fix themselves. All you can do is offer to help, but ultimately it is up to them. I guess Lily just wasn't able to help herself.

It wasn't even quite two weeks later. I got the call. That call that every parent lives in dread of getting. My little girl, my Princess Gumdrop Lollipop—Lily was dead. The apparent cause of death was a drug overdose. A bolt of lightning. I will not even try to describe it. Believe me, it is not a road you want me to take you down. On bended knee I pray it is a road you never need to travel. It is that which you would not wish upon your worst enemy.

In an instant, life becomes a tornado, fast and chaotic. A spinning vortex of the most devastating of human emotions mixing and colliding with the rational questions that need to be answered and the practical things that need to be done. It was Laurie who made the call to me, as was her sacred obligation. But she quickly broke down and it was Greg who told me to go, not to the hospital, but rather straight to the police department.

As the story was told, Davy found Lily unresponsive, sitting in her car parked outside of the garage on the Moore estate. He called 911 and an ambulance was dispatched, but it was too late. The young police officer who responded to the call apparently had good instincts. Something seemed off. He requested that a detective be sent to the scene.

Detective Jack Pruitt was exactly what you hope for when you need a professional. Not only did he have a natural, God-given talent for his craft, he also had two decades of experience to hone it. He was very fucking good at what he did. There was no question something seemed fishy. The scene looked staged. Among other things, Lily's car keys were nowhere to be found. Detective Pruitt immediately took Davy into custody, not placing him under arrest, but rather "as a material witness." He wanted to make sure that if there was any incriminating evidence on the property, Davy would not have a chance to dispose of it.

The police had me, Laurie, and Greg tucked away in a small conference room. I was pacing. Greg and Laurie were sitting at a table in the middle of the room. Laurie had her head down, hands over her face, crying. Greg sat next to her, holding her hand. Detective Pruitt came in to speak with us. After the polite introductions and mandatory "sorry for your loss," Detective Pruitt sat down across from Laurie. I stopped pacing and sat next to Greg.

Detective Pruitt began, "Okay, so, we do have David Moore in custody, but he's not been formally arrested, yet." He reached across the table to tap Laurie's hand. When she looked up, "Ma'am, I understand you have a restraining order, taken out against Mr. Moore?"

Laurie could only manage a whimper and a nod.

"It would be helpful to have a copy of that."

Greg reached into his coat and pulled out a folded paper. He handed it to the detective.

"Oh, excellent," Detective Pruitt said, "That's a big

help." Holding the paper up, "With this and—and some, eh, anomalies I noted at the scene, and the fact the victim—Lily, that is—that Lily is a minor, I see no problem getting a search warrant. Now, not to be rude, but I don't know how much longer I can stall Mr. Moore, so I really need to get right on this. Meanwhile, this'll take all night. You folks should go home. Try to get some rest." As Detective Pruitt stood up to leave, he added, "I truly am sorry for your loss."

Laurie cried. Greg held her. I was a statue.

The judge had no problem with signing the search warrant. While Davy sat in a police interview room, no doubt rehearsing his lies in his head, the warrant was executed. What was found in that apartment above the garage was all Detective Pruitt needed to unleash a tornado all his own. He placed Davy under arrest. He read him his rights. Then he did what he was so goddamn good at doing.

Like a professional boxer, Detective Pruitt started the interview with jabs and body blows to wear down his opponent before going in for the knockout. (No, I wasn't there, but for reasons that will eventually become clear, I was later given a transcript of the interview.) Detective Pruitt led with, "Okay, so straight away, there's this cache of drugs found in your apartment, so looking at serious felony charges just for that. But, let's set that aside. Forget about that, we can deal with it later. Let's talk about this other stuff. Lily's purse, containing her car keys, was also found in the apartment."

No reaction from Davy.

Detective Pruitt forged on, "Look, I get it. You get this stupid restraining order taken out by this overprotective mother and it pisses you off. You ask Lily to come over and talk things out."

"Yes."

"Which she does, of her own free will."

"Exactly."

"Okay, so we also found this freshly used condom. Now, I think we both know if I send it for DNA testing what it'll show. I mean, I get it, you had make-up sex."

"Yes."

"Completely consensual, something you had done plenty of times before."

"Right."

"Then afterward you decided to get high, again, no big deal, nothing different than dozens of times before."

"Yes."

"And the heroin came from your stash?" When Davy hesitated Detective Pruitt added,

"I mean, if we need to we can test what's left in the syringe with what we seized from your apartment—"

"Yeah, from my stash."

"Okay, so you prepared the hit and gave it to Lily?"

"Yes."

"Your stuff, you loaded the syringe?"

"Right."

"Now, did she inject it herself, or did you do that for her?"

"She did it."

"Did she know it was a hot shot?"

"No."

"But you did." When Davy didn't answer, Detective Pruitt took the risk to go in for the knockout punch, "I mean, I get it, you were pissed off. Who wouldn't be?"

"Yeah."

"If you couldn't have her, no one could, isn't that it?"

"I guess so."

So, there it was, all wrapped up in a bow, with sprinkles

and whipped cream on top. Physical evidence proving drug possession and use, giving drugs to a minor, violating a restraining order, and statutory rape. Then the cherry on top was the confession Davy had made that he had intentionally overdosed Lily.

The prosecutor assigned to the case was Beth Gunn, another consummate professional with many years of experience. She was charging David Moore with over a dozen felony counts, but at the top of the list was second-degree murder. She did warn us, though, that she may end up using that charge as a bargaining chip to get a plea deal, but wouldn't do that without consulting with us first. No matter what, Davy was going away for a very long time.

I had faith. I "trusted the system." But, as is so often the case, the road to justice is a long, twisting, bumpy path, with no guarantee you will actually get there.

CHAPTER 24

The first indication there was something wrong came just three weeks later. Beth Gunn called me and Laurie in for a meeting about "a major development in the case." That seemed ominous. She had already prepared us for the fact that the Moore family would surely hire a small army of lawyers to put every atom of the case under a microscope. As such, we shouldn't expect to even get a trial date for at least six months.

The second indication something was wrong was when I walked into the meeting and Jack Pruitt was there, along with his partner, Detective Tim Johnson, who I had only briefly met before. There was also another gentleman seated with them who Jack introduced as, "My boss, Captain Brian Taylor." Well, shit, this couldn't be good.

The agonizing duty to deliver the bad news fell to County Prosecutor Gunn, "As expected, Mr. Moore's legal team has been sifting through the evidence with a fine mesh. They found a…well, I'm sorry, they found something. On the night Detective Pruitt got the search warrant, he listed the address of the house on the Moore estate, 906 River Road, along with the phrase 'and all associated outbuildings.' It's standard, boilerplate-type language. This then covered the garage and the apartment above it within the legal parameters of the warrant. Except in this case, it didn't."

Laurie gasped.

I was a stone on the outside, "what the fuck" on the inside.

"Let me explain," Prosecutor Gunn continued, "Here's the issue: All those years back when Ethel Moore—that's the property owner, David Moore's grandmother—when Ethel Moore decided to rent that apartment to non-family members, she went to the county to go through the proper legal procedure. One requirement the county had was that the apartment had to have its own, separate street address. So, while the house and everything associated with it is 906 River Road, the garage and apartment is 906 *and a half* River Road. Unfortunately, this is not a minor discrepancy under the law."

Laurie burst into tears.

I was solid stone outside, molten lava inside.

Prosecutor Gunn continued, voice slower, starting to get a crackle to it, "Mr. Moore's legal team made a motion to exclude all physical evidence seized from the apartment as the product of an illegal search," with a deep sigh. "The judge had no choice but to agree. Defense counsel then made what's called a fruit of the poisoned tree argument—further argued that it was only under the weight of this illegal evidence that Davy made his 'so-called confession.' So, um, therefore, it needed to be thrown out. Naturally, I objected, but really had no legal leg to stand on. Defense counsel started rattling off one precedent after another." She reached across the table to hold Laurie's hand. She looked at me with moist eyes,

"I'm sorry. I'm so sorry. I really had no choice but to drop the charges."

Laurie collapsed into a heap on the table, sobbing.

I really turned to stone—rigid, breathless.

Beth Gunn was a consummate professional. This certainly wasn't the first time she had to give a victim's family bad news. But still, I could tell she was barely holding in her emotions. She took a moment, then sat up straight, shoulders back, "But keep in mind, dropping the charges is simply that, they can be refiled at any time in the future. I assure you my office will continue to vigorously pursue this case. I promise you I will do everything I possibly can to rebuild this case. Have faith. The justice system will prevail."

Laurie was a puddle of goo.

My immediate thought was that I couldn't see any possible way to "rebuild this case," but I sat silent. I saw no point in saying that to Prosecutor Gunn, she seemed about on the verge of tears as it was.

Next up was Jack Pruitt, who said, "I take full and complete responsibility for the mistake. But, as Ms. Gunn has said, this is *not* the end of the road. I am completely committed to starting the investigation over, from square one, with no stone left unturned."

It was at this point that Captain Taylor jumped in, "I appreciate Detective Pruitt falling on his sword, but, ultimately, as head of detectives, I am responsible. I assure you that Detective Pruitt has my full support to take whatever time and department resources are needed to pursue this case. I will personally oversee the investigation."

Laurie continued to weep.

I patted her on the back to comfort her, but continued my stony silence.

The knee-jerk reaction was tempting. No one could blame a grieving parent who lashes out in anger. Emotion is high trump. But there is a basic human obligation to grow-the-fuck-up at some point and become a rational, thinking adult, and over-trump the animal urges. As *The Instruction Book* says, "judge not lest ye be judged," that is, judge others as you want to be judged yourself. What every little kid on the playground knows simply as "play fair."

So when Jack Pruitt apologized a second time, I stopped him, "Don, I appreciate that. You and Captain Taylor taking responsibility is a testament to your character. You both are fine gentlemen. But I don't blame you. I mean, what was the alternative? Even if you had some reason to think of it—and if we're being fair, who would? Even if—the only way to know would have been to go check the land records at the county clerk's office. You couldn't have done that until the next morning. By then you would have had to have let Davy Moore go—given him a chance to get rid of the evidence. So it's six of one, half a dozen of another, isn't it? At least this way we know for certain what happened. That's at least something. No one here did anything wrong. It's just one of those god-damned things about life: Sometimes you do everything right and still don't get the result you want. It sucks, but it's just—" Shrug.

The meeting ended. I walked Laurie to her car, "You okay to drive? I can drive you home."

She managed a half smile. "No, thanks, Joe, I'll manage."

I lit a cigarette as I walked to my car. I had finally managed to quit two years before, but this shit—well, you know. Jack Pruitt jogged over to me. He was a damn good cop. He had read something in my demeanor. I had set off his cop radar. Taking my arm, "Really, Joe, let me handle this. Promise me you won't…you know, do anything stupid."

"Of course not, Jack," I told him, but a little too calm, a little too cold. I think Jack knew. I had signed the contract the day Lily was born. It had to be honored. It could not be otherwise.

And, just like that, the tornado stopped spinning. Complete calm. The utter peace that comes when you know with perfect clarity what needs to be done along with a resolute acceptance of what the consequences will be. The near nirvana of knowing the right path, knowing how to follow it, knowing where it must lead.

It wasn't that I didn't have faith in the abilities of the police department and prosecutor's office. I, in no way, doubted their sincerity and commitment. I, in no way, doubted their skills. I just didn't see any hope they could possibly succeed. The window of opportunity had closed. The money and power of the Moore family then nailed it shut. An army of lawyers then piled antique oak furniture against it. Justice was not getting in. But vengeance could. Normally, I would say justice is good, it is human beings acting as the children of God we are supposed to try to be. And, normally, I would say vengeance is bad, it is the animal side of human nature we are supposed to fight against. But, every once in a while, justice and vengeance merge into one, and become the same thing. The path was clear.

I already had the skill set needed. Yes, the skills to do the surveillance and plan the job, but that really isn't the key. I had the *ability* to actually do it, without hesitation, without fear, without remorse. For the first time I understood why, all those years back, after I did my first contract killing for the mob (under the toenail moon, you recall), it gave me a feeling of *comfort*. Comfort in knowing I was capable of doing it. Comfort in knowing I could do it again.

But that was the easy part. The hard part is always the same: You can do it, yes, but how do you get away with it? This is where the real power of a criminal organization lies. Murders can be done by someone who has no association with the victim. The police don't know where to look. Even if they have physical evidence, they don't know who to try to match it to. It's like if you're lost and someone hands you a map, but doesn't tell you where on the map you're currently standing. You now have a bunch more information, but it does you no good, you are still equally lost. But, I no longer had the luxury of the support and cover of fellow thugs. If I went after Davy Moore, I would be the prime suspect, and no amount of planning or cunning was going to keep a cop like Jack Pruitt from finding the evidence.

But that, as it turned out, was the simplest part of all. It didn't matter. I had no intention of trying to get away with it. Twenty years before I had made a bad decision to choose to do a lot of bad things—to fuck up a lot of peoples' lives—to avoid going to prison. And to what end? I had turned my life into a sin of omission. I was drifting through life, doing no good to anyone, in essence, in a prison of my own making. Certainly that could be done as well on the inside as on the outside.

But the real epiphany was a step beyond that. It came down to a simple question: Which would be worse, to be locked up forever but at peace, or to be free and die a little more every day from the guilt of knowing I let some sick son of a bitch get away with murdering my baby? That was an easy question for me to answer.

As it was, the recon work was already done. I had been keeping tabs on Davy Moore since he bonded out after his arrest. There were two neighborhood streets across from the Moore estate, both of which had a clear view of the apartment. Being the middle of winter, it got dark by five, so it was easy to just park and watch. I knew what his car looked like, and he always parked it outside the garage in plain view. The apartment had enough windows to easily see if anyone was home by what lights were on and what shadows danced between them.

It wasn't that I had any plans or intentions at the time, it was just a coping mechanism. I have never been good at waiting. "Doing recon" was just a way to make me feel like I was doing *something*. So I already knew the mark's schedule. I already knew when he would be in the apartment. I already knew when he would be alone.

The tool for the job was chosen from equal parts nostalgia and sheer malice. I recreated that mace-club-thingy Little Louie Lafata had given me all those years back. Two weight clamps attached to the end of an eighteen-inch steel tube. A bone-breaker. A meat mallet. Blunt-force trauma and pain with speed and precision.

Davy Moore came home that night a little before six. He parked in front of the garage, as usual, and went inside, alone. I knew no one was already in the apartment because the whole place was dark. As soon as I saw the first light flick on in the apartment, I left my parked car and crossed the street. I wanted to get to him right away, before he could take a drink, or down a pill, or shoot up, or take any substance that could possibly dull the pain.

Into the garage and up the steps to the apartment door, fast and quiet, like stalking a squirrel cutting nuts up in a hickory tree. The apartment door was unlocked, and I slipped in like a phantom.

I caught him as he was coming out of the kitchen with a sandwich in his right hand. He had no time to react. The first blow shattered his left collarbone. As he clutched it in pain, I swept the weapon low to blow out his left kneecap. With Davy on the floor then, I jockeyed for position to smash his right knee, then right collarbone. This left him incapacitated, unable to escape or fight back.

It was only then that I put my foot on his chest, and leaned down close so he could stare into my face, "You know who I am?"

His answer was a groan and a nod.

"Good, then you know what has to happen."

I couldn't help but grin while I beat his legs to a bloody pulp. By the time I moved up to his arms, I was giggling. By the time I started on his midsection, I was laughing so loud it almost drowned out his screams of agony. It was only after he passed out, only after he could feel no more pain, that I finished the job. I rained blow after skull-crushing blow down on his head and face. The best special effects wizard on the set of a Hollywood slasher film could not have created a more gruesome scene.

I left the bloody weapon next to the body and calmly made my way out of the apartment, down the steps, and out the garage door. I was only three steps down the driveway when the car pulled in, blinding me in its headlights and lighting up the crimson blood covering my clothing.

Out hopped Detective Jack Pruitt and his partner. It was both a shock and a relief. Jack put up his hand toward me in the "halt" position and gestured to Detective Johnson to go inside to see what had happened. Only after his partner was inside did Jack finally speak, cold-steel, "Don't say a single word."

It seemed mere moments for Detective Johnson to come clunking at a trot back down the steps. As he exited the garage he could be heard on his phone calling for a medical examiner and crime scene technicians. Jack gave him a querying look and was answered with, "Bad, very bad." Then back talking on the phone he extended his left index finger and made a helicopter motion, cop-hand signal for "hook him up." Jack put me in handcuffs and read me my rights. As he finished he leaned into my left ear and whispered in a plaintive hiss, "Do *not* say anything without a lawyer."

So, there I was, caught red-handed, literally. It did strike me as mighty odd, though, that Jack Pruitt showed up when he did. Officially, he would report that he was making a routine check of the area, just in case anything crazy might happen after it was announced earlier that day that charges had been dropped against David Moore. After spotting my parked car across the street from the Moore estate, he decided he had better investigate. He just happened to get there a little too late.

Maybe, but, that would be one hell of a coincidence. I have a strong suspicion he was staked out on Davy the same as I was, on the next street over. When he saw me go into the garage, he decided to let me have a few minutes alone, man-to-man, so to speak, with Davy. Which isn't to accuse him of any kind of negligence, or possible complacency in the crime, mind you. Jack Pruitt was a good man. I'm just saying it's maybe, only maybe now, a case where a good man did the wrong thing for the right reason. Sometimes the line between justice and vengeance is as thin as a cat whisker, even for a good cop.

The next few hours went by in a blur. I was processed and booked into the county jail. All my clothes were taken as evidence and replaced with an orange jail jumpsuit. I was asked if I wanted to make a call, but declined; I had no one to call. As soon as I lay down on the hard cot in the stark jail cell, I fell asleep. It was the most peaceful sleep I had had in a long time.

In the morning the guard came to get me, I expected, to be taken to an interrogation room for questioning. Instead he mumbled something about, "Your lawyer is here to see you." That seemed odd. I didn't have a lawyer. I hadn't requested one yet, so couldn't imagine that the public defender's office would send one over automatically. Hell, I hadn't even made a phone call, who even knew I needed a lawyer? Well, unless it was—

I was escorted to the little windowless cinder block room used for attorneys and their clients to have private meetings. It reminded me, quite a bit, of Tony Mano's Bat Cave. I was greeted by a fine-looking older gentleman in a fine-looking suit, rather rotund, with thick, wavy white hair and a jolly face. He looked like Santa Claus, without the beard and red suit. He introduced himself as "Craig Patrick, attorney-at-law," shook my hand, and asked me to sit down at the small wooden table in the center of the room.

I recognized the name from various newspaper articles and TV news reports I had seen over the years. He was one of the best-known criminal defense lawyers in the area, specializing in high-profile cases. Which, clearly, begged the question, "Why are you here? I haven't asked for an attorney yet. Hell's bells I haven't even been questioned yet, or made a phone call, or anything!"

"Yes, but you do agree, you do *need* an attorney?"

"I suppose so, but how did you know I was even here? I mean, I just—"

"A little bird told me."

"Was that bird named Jack Pruitt?"

He got a smile on his face that was charming, but also a bit too sly, "Oh, no, that would be a violation of police department policy."

"It's just us here."

"Maybe so, but attorney-client privilege only works in one direction. I can't reveal anything you say to me, but you can talk about it all you want."

I let that drop, feeling I knew the answer and moved on to the elephant in the room issue, "I couldn't possibly afford you."

"I am offering my services *pro bono*."

"Why would you do that?"

"Two reasons. First, I'm going to be honest with you. I'm a master at working the media and a high-profile case like this is good advertisement, so that covers the practical side of it. But the older I get the less I care about the money. What happened to your daughter…" he took out a handkerchief and wiped his face, "It just… It just sickens me. I have two daughters of my own…" he cleared his throat, "So let's just call it one father helping another father."

"Um.. Okay…I mean, thank you, sir."

Chapter 25

From there Mr. Patrick moved on to the nitty-gritty of the matter at hand, "Going forward there is an incredible amount of details we need to attend to, but for right now, today, baby steps. All we need to worry about right now is a few little things. Your preliminary hearing will be later today. The judge will ask you how you plead, you will answer, 'not guilty *your honor*,' that's it."

"But I am guilty. I was caught red-handed. And I have no regrets—no remorse at all. I planned on just pleading guilty and being done with it."

Mr. Patrick leaned back in his chair and stroked his chin like he was really contemplating it, then in a gentle, wise tone, "That's fine, if it's really what you want to do. But, not today. That's something we really should discuss at length. There's different ways to get that done. You can change your plea at any time in the future you want to, but for today, plead not guilty. That will give us a chance to sort things out, buy us time, so to speak. Okay?"

"Okay."

"Good, then up next will be the issue of bail. The prosecutor, citing 'the brutality of the crime' or some such thing, will have no choice but to ask that you be remanded, that means no bail, you stay in jail until the trial. I, as your defense attorney, have no choice but to ask that you be released on your own recognizance, arguing that you have no criminal record, the extreme circumstances leading up to the alleged incident, and that whatever malice you bore was directed at just one person, so you are not a danger to the community, and that kind of lawyerly talk. The judge will act annoyed, and ask both sides to throw out a reasonable figure. That will bounce around a little and I expect it to land at somewhere between a half million and a million dollars. Now, keep in mind, you only need to come up with 10 percent of that. I know several good bail bondsmen who can help us with the rest. Does that sound doable?"

"Not even remotely."

"Really? You can't think of anyone who could help out?"

"Well, it's not just that. I don't *want* anyone to help out. I see no chance of it being anything other than a wasted effort. I really don't mind just staying in jail. It's what I expected."

"Hmm…you sure about that?"

"Yes."

"That being the case, I may pull a bit of a stunt in court, something I want you to trust me on."

"I trust you know what you're doing."

"Okay, last thing. As soon as we're done talking, the lead detective needs to formally question you. This is just a formality. You will invoke your right to remain silent, and tell him I am your legal counsel. That means the police cannot question you at any point in the future unless either I am present, or you formally waive your right to have counsel present. Understand that?"

"Yes."

"Good, and one more very important point: Anything you say voluntarily, to anyone, can be used against you. Don't talk to anyone about this! Be especially careful of chatting with other guys in jail—"

But I cut him off there with a wave of my hand and a light chuckle, "Trust me, I already have that part down pat."

My formal questioning was done by Jack Pruitt, and it was the brief formality Mr. Patrick had said it would be. I then had several hours alone in my jail cell to reflect on the morning's events. I didn't doubt Craig Patrick's abilities, and his intentions did seem sincere, it's just that it's hard to trust a lawyer. It just seems to be one of those professions where, to have any level of success in the field, you need to sort of sell your soul to the devil.

Of course, anyone faced with any legal issue that is even slightly complex needs a lawyer, but that's only because the goddamn lawyers have made the law so complex to begin with. It would be like a doctor that goes around spreading the plague, then acts the hero as he treats the afflicted. It's a racket way beyond what even the craftiest Mafia boss could concoct. Then, in any legal matter, you get these lawyers, on both sides, that pull every dirty trick they can to win. Somehow, from all that mess, we get justice? Law is the only profession that seems convinced, absolutely, that two wrongs are the only way to get a right. It isn't my place to say, but I would be willing to bet that, at least on a percentage basis, there are as many lawyers in hell as there are thugs. I expect I'll get to find out for myself soon enough.

So, at the hearing that afternoon I pleaded "not guilty

your honor," as instructed. And, when the issue of bail came up, as expected the prosecutor asked for remand while defense counsel asked for ROR. The judge bristled. And so the ping-pong match was to commence.

The prosecutor got to go first, asking for, "no less than one million dollars." Craig Patrick stood up, and with wringing hands, knitted brow, and a sad sigh in his voice, addressed the court, "Your honor, I discussed this subject in great detail with my client before coming here this afternoon. He is a man of very modest means. He does not wish to trouble his family, friends, or any well-intentioned members of the general public. He would rather stay in jail than have anyone spend money on him that he will never be able to repay. So, your honor, I have no choice but to renew my request that my client be released on his own recognizance."

No doubt the wizened old judge had seen this kind of grandiose theater before. But, no doubt, Craig Patrick was especially good at it. For about half a second I thought I saw a crack in the judge's stony facade. Then he barked out, "Five hundred thousand dollars." And rapped his gavel.

Of course, Mr. Patrick's "little stunt" wasn't intended to sway the judge, although the bail he set was considered low for such a serious charge. Its true intent was as the opening line of the narrative Craig Patrick was starting to write. First, he needed to paint me as a sympathetic defendant. Then, nudge it along until I was as much a victim in this case as the man I killed. Ultimately, he wanted the general public, and by proxy then, the jury, to boil the case down to just one question: What was worse, what Davy Moore did, or what I did?

He discussed this with me in detail over the course of the next week, "You have to understand, Joe, I'm not allowed to outright argue for jury nullification. I would get in big trouble there. But there is a vast gray area and I know the nuances of every subtle shade. I have gotten very good at walking right up to that line, having my toes almost touch it, but not actually crossing it. All we need is *one* person on that jury—*one* father, most likely—willing to dig in his heels and think, 'I don't care if this guy *is* guilty. I'm glad he did it. Good for him. I refuse to send him to prison.' Now, all that gets us is a mistrial, but we gain a lot of yardage. The more public support you get, the more likely the DA is to offer you a deal. If we go ahead with it and get a mistrial, we have that much more bargaining power. If you still want to roll the dice, we go again. A second mistrial and I can almost promise you a deal for less than ten years. If we push it and get a third mistrial, I would be shocked if the DA doesn't drop the case."

Wait, what? I had to ask, "This makes it sound like you intended to simply ignore the rather overwhelming evidence the prosecution had against me."

"Of course I need to do my due diligence and poke what holes I can in the evidence. You would be surprised how a good lawyer can nitpick! But, that alone isn't going to get us past the reasonable doubt threshold. What it will do, I hope, is create just enough of a question to allow that *one* juror to justify in his mind doing what he already *wants* to do. I mean, think about it. Imagine it's you on the jury in a case like this. You go into it thinking what the guy did was right, maybe even admire him for doing it. But you also have a civic duty to uphold the law. All you need is one little doubt to snowball in your mind, and, *voila*, you are going to deadlock that jury. So, tell me, if it was you on the jury, would you vote to convict?"

"No."

"And when it went into days of deliberation and all the other jurors are complaining about how unreasonable you are being, how they have jobs, and families, and lives to get back to, would you hold your ground?"

"Yes I would."

"See, there you go. All we need is one guy like you!"

I let the subject drop at that point, but couldn't help but think, ah, 'one guy *like me.*' If Craig Patrick only knew…

I probably let things go on longer than I should have. From the beginning I knew the clear and straight path I was embarking upon. I had let the zeal and hope of Mr. Patrick temporarily divert me. But there could only be one destination, and what happened at our next meeting told me it was time to finish the journey. Mr. Patrick was more pepped up and animated than usual, "Good news, Joe, you won't be in jail much longer!"

"How's that?"

"You have a lot of public support out there. Ever heard of one of those 'GoFundMe' pages on the internet?"

"Umm…yes…"

"Well, someone set one up for you. Don't even ask, it wasn't me, and I don't know who it was. Doesn't matter. Anyway, this morning it went over forty grand. I expect in a few more days, it will hit the fifty needed to pay the bail bond company."

"But, I already told you, that's not what I want."

"Look, Joe, this is really good for us. Besides, it isn't actually up to you. The court doesn't care where the money comes from. Any random person can show up to post your bail, and that's it, you're out."

This had already gone on too long. It was already a complete circus. Poor Laurie had been so hounded by the press she had to leave town and hide out with relatives. Now a bunch of decent, well-intentioned folks were about to throw away their money to try to help…well, if they had any idea who it really was they were helping. I needed to stop this. Once the money was spent on bail, it was gone. If I acted right away, the donations could be refunded. Mr. Patrick was on his feet, pacing around and gesturing with his arms, as he always did when he was passionate about the discussion. I asked him to sit down. Then, deep sigh, I began, "I'm sorry, Mr. Patrick. I feel like I've wasted your time. It's like I told you at our first meeting. I *am* going to plead guilty to first-degree murder, and I *am* going to go to prison for the rest of my life. I made my peace with it from the beginning. That's just how it has to be."

"Maybe so, but we certainly aren't there yet—"

But I cut him off, "I understand, you view a guilty plea as a bargaining chip, as a possible way to get a reduced sentence, or whatever. You're focused on doing your job as my attorney to get me the best result possible. But what I'm telling you is, that isn't what I want."

"Is it because you see no hope of winning?"

"That's part of it, but a minor part."

"Is it because you feel remorse over killing Davy Moore?"

I smiled, and looked him square in the eye, "Oh, no! That's one of the few people I've killed that I have absolutely no regrets over."

I could see in his eyes that Mr. Patrick had picked up on the hint there, "Clearly there's more to this than you're telling me. What exactly is going on here?"

"I'm not sure how deep into it to go…"

"Joe." He reached across the table to put both his hands on mine, "Let me give you some of the best advice you will ever get: There are two people—heck, *only* two people—you should always be completely honest with, your doctor and your lawyer. Both deal with issues that are so complex that even the smallest detail is often critical, and both are bound by ironclad confidentiality. Anything you tell me will always stay just between us."

So, I told him. I confessed my past sins. I went into enough detail for him to understand. I don't know how long it took. Time stood still. He absorbed every word, asked no questions. At the end of it, I gave my own lawyerly summation that I had already rehearsed a hundred times in my head, "I understand that your job is to narrowly focus on one side of one case, but in the bigger picture, someone has to ask, 'what does justice look like here?' Even if we just focus on what I did to Davy Moore, as tempting as it is to say I was justified under the extremes of those specific circumstances, isn't it the textbook example of the slippery slope? Then, add in all the rest. By my count I should already be doing at least a dozen life sentences. If I go to prison right now, today, and live to a ripe old age inside, what does that come to? Three or four years for each murder I did, or was directly involved in? In a good and right world, how is that justice?" I had more than that in my head, but ran out of steam.

Mr. Patrick allowed me the courtesy to think a bit without saying anything.

I decided to just move on to the next issue that had been weighing heavily on the conscience I was so late in life at acquiring, "I get it that this isn't what you signed on for. I'm sorry if I led you on. I already owe a debt to you I can never repay. I understand that at this point you need to just dump this mess and—"

But now Mr. Patrick did interject, calm and resolute,

"No. I told you I would represent you in this matter. In for a penny, in for a pound. You owe me nothing. I am not going to quit, and I'm asking you not to fire me. There are still things that need to be done. Allow me to walk you through the rest of the process."

"Thank you, sir."

"Just to make sure I understand, you want me to take a guilty plea to the DA, with no strings attached? Don't even see if there's any wiggle room on a deal?"

"That is correct."

"And, again, just to be sure, you've had enough time to think all this through, you want to go straight ahead with it?"

"I am certain. The sooner the better, please."

Craig Patrick started right after our meeting to do all the behind-the-scene things needed with the district attorney's office. My hearing before the judge the next day was a mere formality. I had to stand up in court and formally change my plea. The judge had to do his due diligence and question me to make sure I understood what I was doing. As had already been agreed upon by both the prosecution and the defense, the judge immediately passed sentence. He really had no wiggle room on the matter. I was sentenced to life in prison.

I had a brief moment before the deputies took me into custody to lean over and thank Mr. Patrick again, adding, "And tell Jack Pruitt I said thanks too."

He nodded and sent me off with, "Take care of yourself." Mr. Patrick made a lovely statement to the press about how I had decided to "take responsibility for my actions and didn't wish to burden the families involved, the court, or my fellow citizens in general with a long, drawn-out trial."

There was a brief media storm, then the public found something new and sparkly to entertain them. Laurie came home. I went home to the state pen.

So, that's it. I'm inside now, have been for quite some time. (No point in keeping track of exactly how long.) Prison damn for sure isn't a good place, but isn't terrible. For the most part, everyone just leaves me alone. Part of this is because I'm a lifer. Guys are less prone to fuck with a lifer. A lifer has nothing left to lose. If you mess with one, he might as well try to just rip your goddamn throat out. I mean, what more can the legal system really do to him?

Part of it is because a prison is like a small town, where everyone knows everyone else's business. It's well known that I am a killer. Well, more than that, a guy who didn't just kill someone, I tortured a guy to death by turning his body into hamburger, then beat his brains out. So, there's a fear factor. I mean, would you take a chance with a guy like that?

But mostly it's because of—well, I'm reluctant to put it in these terms, because it makes it sound like a positive thing, but—a respect factor. Prison is very much a law of the jungle-type society. One of the most basic laws of the jungle is that you protect the ones you love. Every animal in here has someone they care about, and has some level of admiration for a father who goes after the guy responsible for his daughter's death.

I've done a lot of reading. It's given me a chance to read all kinds of classic literature I missed out on earlier in life. You know, *To Kill a Mockingbird, 1984, The Catcher in the Rye, A Farewell to Arms*, that kind of shit. I've read the Bible in its entirety, and the Gospels several times. There is some seriously good stuff in that book! I read the Koran all the way through, but didn't get much out of it. Then, a few years later, I found a more recent translation and reread it. That second time through was much better. I tried to read *The Book of*

Mormon, but lost interest about a quarter of the way in. I don't mean any offense by that; I expect I'll try again at some point. I read several books on Buddhism, but couldn't make any sense of it no matter how hard I tried. I spend a lot of time just thinking about stuff. I said before I thought maybe I would have been a good contemplative monk. I guess, in a sense, now I am.

One thing I've thought about is that I'm never getting out. I don't just mean I've made peace with the fact I'm never getting out, I mean I've made the resolute decision I'm never getting out. Keep in mind a life sentence doesn't necessarily mean never getting out, not unless they tag it with "no possibility of parole," which wasn't done in my case. So technically, it's possible. Except it isn't, because I'll never let it happen. I can't leave prison because I have nothing left to go back to. No job, and I did manual labor, so not good work for an old man. No house. No bank account. No friends. No family. So, as you can see, I really do just need to stay inside. If the day ever comes when some do-gooder tries to parole me, I'll just confess to one or several of my past crimes. Now, technically, they are probably covered under my immunity deal, but I think just telling them to the parole board would be enough.

I think maybe the one I would confess to first would be the Little Napoleon hit. I fibbed a little earlier when I said I didn't remember his name. It was Jim Smith, but with such a common, boring name, you can see why I gave him a nickname. I didn't exaggerate too much about what a cocky guy he was, but then again, he had accomplished a lot, and had at least some right to it. And while it may be so that his philanthropy was somewhat self-serving, he did give real money, to real charities, that had real needs, and did real good in the world. And, Jim Smith was a real person, with real friends and family that loved him.

I mentioned earlier that I went into a "media blackout" after his death and didn't know what was reported about the case. That's true, but not entirely so; there was no way to completely block the information out. The day after I murdered Jim Smith, his twenty-seven-year-old daughter, Anna, went to visit him. When he didn't answer the door, she went around back to see if he was down by the lake. She was the one to find him—her daddy—dead on the back patio—damn near decapitated.

That's how it was with all of them. I mean, unless you truly are a psychopath completely devoid of human empathy, you need to find a way to dehumanize your victims. To focus on their worst traits. To blame them for their bad decisions. To make yourself believe they actually deserved what happened to them. You have to ignore the emotional tornadoes you will send spinning out in every direction through the lives of the people who love them. You have to be an animal, not a human being. You have to lie to yourself. You have to be the worst type of hypocrite it is possible to be. You have to judge as you would not want to be judged.

The laws of the universe demand balance. All forces seek equilibrium. This is why it was established from the being that as one judges, one will be judged. On judgment day the weight of all one's good is placed on the scale opposite the weight of all one's bad. What is not paid for here must be paid for there. The scales must balance.

And that is the real reason I decided to plead guilty and go to prison. And that is the real reason I can never allow myself to leave. It gives me at least some chance to pay down my debt. Enough? No, not if I lived to be a thousand! But maybe enough to get sentenced to a slightly higher level in hell. Maybe just barely enough to buy me one second in heaven to give Lily a hug. That alone would make it all worthwhile.

So, yes I have regrets. And, I suppose, I could prattle on with them, but who the hell really wants to hear that? Maybe I'm going through my own mid-life crisis. I can't help but wonder…I mean, I know better than to play woulda-coulda-shoulda; it's a game no one can win. But still, I can't help but wonder…how things would have…maybe could have… certainly should have, been different, if I had just made a different choice, all those years ago, under that pretty little toenail moon.

A Note from the Author

If you enjoyed this book, I would be very grateful if you could write a review and publish it at your point of purchase. Your review, even a brief one, will help other readers to decide whether they'll enjoy my work.

If you want to be notified of new releases from myself and other Alkira Publishing authors, please sign up to the Alkira Publishing email list. In return you'll get a free ebook of short stories and book excerpts by AP authors. You'll find the sign-up button on the right-hand side under the photo at www.alkirapublishing.com. Of course, your information will never be shared, and the publisher won't inundate you with emails, just let you know of new releases.

About the Author

J.G. Cope is either odd or eccentric, depending upon how you look at it. Growing up in the Detroit area, he was odd. As an adult he moved to Richmond, Virginia, where the genteel nature of the Upper South labels him merely as eccentric. He spends too much time in deep contemplation overthinking things, but also enjoys the company of his wife, three children, cat, and a flock of semi-feral chickens. He has an intense curiosity about what makes people tick—at both the personal and societal levels. At their cores, his books try to dig into these kinds of questions.